Hope for the Holidays

Daryl Wood Gerber

Published by Daryl Wood Gerber, 2023.

This is a work of fiction. Similarities to real people, places, or events are entirely coincidental.

HOPE FOR THE HOLIDAYS

First edition. November 14, 2023.

Copyright © 2023 Daryl Wood Gerber.

ISBN: 979-8215261927

Written by Daryl Wood Gerber.

Chapter 1

"Oh, oh, oh, who wouldn't go?" Hope Lyons crooned to "Up on the House Top," humming the rest as she rolled out a pie crust.

She adored Portland, Oregon. She loved owning Pie in the Sky. Most of all, she relished the way her children's eyes lit up whenever they entered the shop and inhaled the aromas of freshly baked pastries.

Starting on the first of December, all of the excitement of the holiday made Hope's life brim with joy. Yes, Pie in the Sky specialized in pie, but in December, she made yule logs and gingerbread houses and sugar cookies—with sugar-free variations for her daughter, of course. She decorated the shop top to bottom with Christmas cheer. And she played joyful music non-stop while singing out loud.

The door to the shop swung open, and cool air from the fresh snowfall wafted in.

"Hi, Hope, ho-ho-ho," a woman chimed in time to the music. She brushed off her snow-dusted coat and headed to the display of pre-boxed pies. A public relations wizard, she purchased over a dozen pies every week for her workplace. "Merry Christmas."

"Merry Christmas to you, Mrs. Smith." Hope swiped a strand of loose hair off her face, hair that should've been constrained by her hairnet. She sighed. Her hair had a will of its own, like her mother's. She remembered how her father would swoop her mother's hair off her face and then plant a steamy kiss on her lips. When Hope was in high school, she'd been grossed out. Now, she cherished the memory. They had been so in love.

"Busy afternoon?" Mrs. Smith asked as she set a stack of boxes by the register.

"Busy enough."

"Do you need more customers? I can spread the word."

"It's okay. I'm doing fine," Hope said. "Although I think people are being a bit more frugal this year. You know, watching their pennies."

"Or their waistlines," Mrs. Smith joked, patting her thick frame. "Not all of us have your svelte figure. How do you manage it? Don't you eat your own wares?"

"Oh, I down plenty of pie, but I'm on my feet all day, and at night, the kids want to run and tumble."

"How old are they now?"

"Melanie is nine, Todd is six. She loves to throw hoops. He likes to climb anything and everything." Hope snorted. "I wish I had their energy."

An elderly woman with a brood of six children under the age of seven trooped into the shop. "Don't touch," she cautioned them. "Hi, Hope. Six sugar cookies, please, for my very well behaved grandchildren."

"Coming right up, Mrs. Lundstrom." Hope used tongs to grip the cookies and insert them into individual parchment paper sleeves. She slotted the sleeves into a Pie in the Sky to-go bag and tossed in a handful of napkins. "Anything else?"

"Not today, but I'll be ordering all my holiday pies from you next week." Mrs. Lundstrom paid in cash. "You do make the most delicious crust."

Hope warmed to the compliment. It was her grandmother's recipe, handed down to her mother, and then to Hope. The secret ingredients were rice wine vinegar and sour cream.

As Mrs. Lundstrom and the children exited, a pair of handsome, dark-haired men entered the shop. Hope recognized them. Steve Waldren was a well-known sports announcer on KPRL. They'd met briefly in high school when she was a freshman and he a senior, though he didn't seem to remember. From what Hope could tell, he'd turned out to be a decent guy. If asked for autographs by customers when he was in the shop, he happily complied. His buddy Harker, on the other hand, a sports reporter who was edgy and decidedly shallow, couldn't be bothered. Most often, he was too busy talking about his latest date.

Today, they waved to her. She waved back. Steve smiled, but his gaze didn't meet hers. He was focused on the contents of the glass display case. Hope didn't take the snub personally. In high school, she'd faded into the background, too. Not because she wasn't attractive but because she'd been a nose-to-the-grindstone, super studious sort. Her parents had instilled in her at a young age that nothing came easy, and in order to succeed, she'd have to work harder than everyone else. *No one is guaranteed a livelihood,* her father told her. *One forges one's own destiny.*

Per usual, Steve ordered a caffè Americano and a slice of the pie of the day. Hope heard him once say to Harker that he loved to take chances. Harker, on the other hand, always went for pecan pie and black coffee.

"She's the devil," Harker said to Steve as he handed Hope twenty-five dollars, continuing the conversation that he and his pal must have been having upon entering.

"She's not," Steve countered.

Hope wondered if they were talking Portland's mayor or Oregon's governor or Harker's latest conquest.

"Does she tell you how good you are?" Harker asked. "How brilliant you are? What a kickass dude you are?"

"She says I need to expand my horizons."

Aha. Steve's wife, Hope guessed, although she didn't see a wedding ring on his hand. Maybe he, like his friend, had a flavor-of-the-month girlfriend. She didn't pay much attention to celebrity gossip columns. She made change and then prepared the coffees and set slices of pie in biodegradable clamshell containers. She slotted the containers into a to-go bag and added utensils and napkins.

"Why do you need to expand your horizons? You're a star here"—Harker spread his arms and turned in a circle—"and Portland is a fabulous city. Who needs more than this? I mean, honestly, what does she want?"

"Los Angeles," Steve said.

Harker coughed out, "Smog City."

"Or Chicago or New York."

"Craven."

Steve laughed.

Hope set their coffees on the counter and slid the to-go bag toward them. Harker thanked her. By then, Steve was too engrossed with something on his cell phone to acknowledge her.

A few new customers entered as the men moved to one of the four bistro tables by the window. Hope intended to add more tables next year. Building a business took time.

"Good afternoon," Hope said to the customer dressed like Santa Claus and the elf that trailed him. "Welcome," she said to a starry-eyed young woman who was hanging on an equally head-in-the-clouds man. "Happy Holidays," she said as two regulars traipsed in.

And then the door swung open, and Hope's husband, Zach, stomped inside. Once upon a time, he'd been a loving, caring soul. Now, his eyes were smoldering with something close to disgust, erasing all the momentary joy Hope had been experiencing.

"Hope!" he called.

Hope released the breath she was holding. When was the last time he'd looked at her with love? When was the last time she'd wanted him to? Even so, she quickly checked herself in the mirror behind the cash register. Flour dusted her cheeks. Her eyes were glassy with fatigue. She brushed the flour away and spun back.

Zach pushed past two customers, grunting, "Let me through." A lock of dark hair dangled on his forehead. His denim jacket hung open, a T-shirt with the words *Card Shark* visible beneath. "Hope, I'm talking to you."

"I heard you," she said weakly, forcing a smile.

"Hey, pal." To Hope's surprise, Steve Waldren cut off Zach before he could skirt around the elf. "Take it easy and wait your turn."

"Back off, man," Zach hissed, pushing Steve with his palm.

Hope saw Steve's hands ball into fists. "It's okay, Steve," she said, not realizing until the words came out that calling him by his first name might sound too familiar. "He's my husband."

Steve held his ground for a long moment before throwing up his hands in surrender and shuffling back to his table.

"Hi, sweetheart," Hope said, knowing her tone lacked sincerity. "What brings you in?"

"Where are they?" Zach demanded.

"At school. They don't get out—"

"Not the kids. The keys."

"To what?" Hope squinted, not understanding. They each had sets of keys to their apartment.

"To the Explorer."

"Why?" It was her car. Bequeathed to her by her parents.

"Because I want them. Now." He snapped his fingers.

A shiver ran through her, but she said, "By the register."

Without invitation, Zach rounded the counter, swiped the keys, raised them in his fist like a trophy, and blew her a dry kiss. "Bye, babe. We're through."

"Wait. What? What do you mean we're through?"

"Through. Finito. I tried."

"You tried? You did not. You—"

But Zach didn't break stride. He stomped to the exit and threw Steve Waldren a nasty look before pressing through the door.

Hope slumped against the counter. What the heck? She couldn't believe it. They'd had *the talk*. He was going to change. He was going to seek help. She'd thought that he . . .

No, if she was honest, she hadn't thought. She kept burying her head in the sand while wishing and praying. But none of that was enough. Zach had emptied their savings and gone through the inheritance from her parents. He'd expected Hope to pay every bill for the last year, and now he was taking the car.

She growled and cursed inwardly. Then a soft moan of inevitability escaped her lips. If only she'd been smarter. If only she'd foreseen the future. She glanced at the Christmas photo of her parents and children that she kept pinned to the wall near the mirror, taken four years ago before her parents died in the crash. Before Zach started tumbling down a rabbit hole of debt. They were posing in front of the Christmas tree in her home town, Hope Valley. All grins. Sweeter times.

Hope fought tears, but she lost the battle. This was it. Her dream, her future, was over. Zach—Mr. Right once upon a time—was gone, and she was a failure. She would have to give up the shop.

Chapter 2

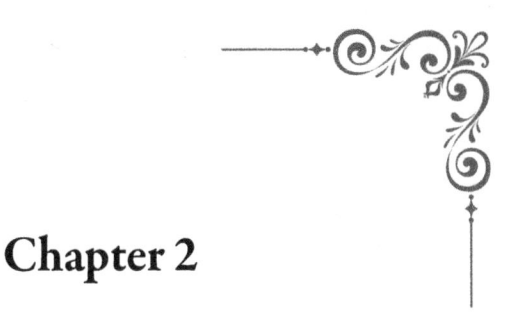

Steve Waldren hated airports. He always had. It wasn't because he hated traveling. He actually liked being on an airplane. He enjoyed the private time it afforded him. But airports, with the crush of people and everyone in a hurry to get somewhere for the holidays, drove him nuts. Luckily, he didn't have to go inside the terminal this time. He was simply dropping off Gloria. She had an important interview in Minneapolis. He bit back a grin betting, dimes to donuts, Gloria couldn't spell the city's name.

Bad, Steve. Not nice.

"What's wrong?" Gloria asked as she stepped up to the trunk of his Lexus SUV and waited for him to lug out her gigantic suitcase.

Steve ran his hand along the side of his neck. Why did she need so many clothes for a two-day visit?

"Stevie?"

He glanced at her sideways and studied her. Ash-white hair, windblown and teased on purpose, narrow nose, wide-set expressive eyes that the camera loved, perfect body that rocked a tight sweater dress belted at the waist. She was the epitome of a weather girl. Even her last name, Storm, fit the bill. Gloria Storm. Stubborn and imbued with the attitude that the world owed her. Proud owner of a million-dollar smile.

"Nothing's wrong," he said, pecking her on the cheek and slamming the trunk while righting the silly Santa hat he'd worn to add a little humor to their parting.

She held up her left hand and admired the magnificent diamond ring Steve had given her last night when he'd proposed. "It's so pretty."

"I'm glad you like it."

She lowered her hand and her expression turned serious. "You're going to do what I said while I'm gone, right?"

"Yes. No sugar cookies. No eggnog. Gotta watch my weight." He patted his firm midriff.

"Apply to Los Angeles."

"Right, Los Angeles." He snapped his fingers.

"And Chicago and New York."

"Yes and yes."

"You need to get a gig in a bigger market."

Steve wanted to. He'd applied before. But the big guns weren't calling. And what was wrong with being a top dog in Portland sports, anyway? He knew everyone on the Trail Blazers as well as on the Timbers and the Winterhawks. He knew their stats. He knew the names of their spouses or significant others, and he knew the names and ages of their children. Plus, he lived close enough to his family to visit. Why move? Because Gloria thought he deserved to be a star in a bigger market, that's why. And she was right, except—

The sleigh bell ringtone chimed on his cell phone. He read the text his brother had sent: *See you soon?* He responded: *Sure thing, buddy. Real soon.*

"Lincoln?" Gloria asked, rolling her eyes as she always did whenever he responded quickly to a text.

"Yep."

"Again?"

"Yep."

"Tell him hi."

She didn't mean it. She didn't *get* Lincoln. To her credit, she'd tried, but being an only child in a doting family, she didn't understand sharing. She didn't appreciate listening. She didn't have a clue how to accept someone exactly where they were, no strings attached. Steve's parents had coached Steve from the moment Lincoln was born about how to be the best big brother he could possibly be. Steve failed at times, but he did try.

"Steve!" a man in a parka shouted, raising a hand. "Yo, Steve Waldren! Great show last night!"

"Thanks, buddy," Steve replied.

"Love the Santa hat."

Steve grinned. "Thanks. Ho, ho, ho!"

"Stevie, focus." Gloria gripped his shoulders. "Promise me you'll be good while I'm gone."

"I'll be so good, I'll make Santa's nice list this year."

She let loose with a burbling, somewhat annoying laugh and slung both arms around his neck. She kissed him on his cheek, leaving what he presumed was a big red impression of her beautiful mouth, and whispered, "Love you."

"Love you, too," he echoed. But did he?

Chapter 3

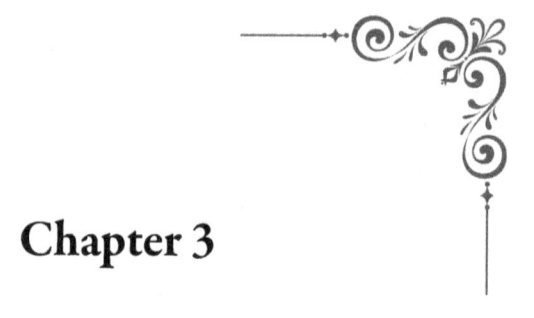

"Eyes left," Hope crooned. She pulled onto Poinsettia Drive and stopped the VW camper in front of a two-story colonial. The eaves and ionic columns twinkled with running Christmas lights. Against the starlit night sky, it was magical, as always. "Look at my childhood home, kids. Just look at it! Isn't it a beauty?"

"Mo-om, we know," Melody droned like a typically bored nine-year-old.

"You showed us when we moved here ten days ago," Todd said, his young voice squeaky.

Had it only been ten days? It had felt like a lifetime. Selling the pie shop to pay off Zach's debts. Purchasing the VW. Finding a job that could cover the bills.

"Yes, but it wasn't dressed up for Christmas then." Hope glanced over her shoulder at her children and her heart melted. How she adored them, whining and all.

She eyed the house again and felt a bittersweet tug on her heart. Her parents had always decorated it to the nines. When Hope had been forced to sell it in order to bail Zach out of one of his *investments*, she'd thrown in every stitch of décor, and the new owners had been ecstatic, even if not as gung-ho as her parents who'd put up the lights the day after Thanksgiving.

"It's very pretty." Melody toyed with her long blond braids. She'd insisted that Hope plait her hair today, claiming she was too old to wear a ponytail.

"It is, isn't it?" Despite the past two week's disappointments, Hope still wanted to enjoy Christmas. She loved the memories. And the aromas of peppermint, pine, and cinnamon. And the smiling faces. And the overwhelming feeling of goodwill to all. She wished these new memories would magically erase the horrible ones created by Zach. If Steve Waldren had punched him, how might that have changed the course of her and her children's history? She pushed thoughts of Steve aside. Last week, she'd read that he'd gotten engaged, not that it mattered. Any fantasies of him and her crossing paths again now that she had moved out of Portland were slim and nil. "See the tree in the plate glass window?" Hope asked. "That's where we put ours when we lived here."

"Yes, Mom, we know," Melody said, exasperated. "We visited Gran and Pop-Pop five years ago. Don't you remember? Gran made me sugar-free sugar cookies and sugar-free pumpkin pie. We had turkey dinner with all the trimmings."

"I ate cranberry sauce!" Todd cried.

That was all you ate, Hope mused. Fortunately, he didn't have a problem with sugar like his sister.

"And Gran let us open one present on Christmas Eve." Melody held up a single finger.

Hope could still hear her mother saying *One, only one*, and her eyes grew moist. It had been her mother's litany throughout Hope's life.

"Don't you remember?" Todd's voice cracked. He'd just gotten over a cold.

Hope recalled all too well. Every minute of that last Christmas together. Her parents' loving faces. Their warm hugs. "Let's sing Gran's favorite song," she chimed. "Okay, here we go. 'Hark the Herald Angels Sing.'"

As she launched into the song, her last memory of her parents was so powerful she could barely breathe. She missed them so much and wished—

Stop, she chided, knowing what her father would say. *We can't turn back the hands of time.*

"C'mon. Hark the herald angels sing, glory to—" Hope paused, waiting for her children to join in.

Begrudgingly, they complied. "The newborn king."

Hope continued on, heading toward the center of town. Hope Valley had done it up right. Twinkling white lights lined all the buildings. Even the gazebo in the roundabout at the intersection of Pine Lane and Main was resplendent. The nativity scene in the gazebo brought a smile to Hope's face as she recalled the first time she'd ever seen it. On that night, like tonight, there had been a fresh dusting of snow. Hope Valley was low enough in elevation that it didn't snow heavily, and sometimes the town needed to enhance the holiday scenery with fake snow, but not this year.

"Mom," Todd said. "I like the holiday flags on the lampposts."

"Me, too," she murmured.

"Hey, can we watch Steve Waldren on TV tonight?" he asked out the blue.

They were huge fans of his show. It was one of the reasons Hope had continued to think about him over the past few weeks. She saw him almost nightly. "We'll see," she said.

Melody said, "Mom, can we write Christmas cards to Daddy, too?"

Hope deflated. *Daddy*. The reason Todd had russet hair and Melody had adorable freckles. The reason both had an affinity for numbers. The reason Hope had been forced to sell her beloved bakery and was underwater, struggling to make ends meet.

"Yes," she said finally, unsure of Zach's address. He hadn't touched base with her since he'd grabbed the keys to the Explorer and stormed out. She doubted one of Santa's post office elves would be able to locate him.

THE NEXT DAY AFTER dropping the children at Hope Valley Elementary, Hope headed to Aroma Café, where she had been lucky enough to land a job the day she'd pulled into town. Her boss had known her parents, and even though Hope didn't have a lick of experience as a waitress, he'd said he knew she was trustworthy and talented. Luckily, having owned and operated her pie shop, Hope wasn't without skills. She could easily carry three plates on an arm and skirt oncoming traffic in the kitchen.

Driving along Main Street, Hope checked out the window displays. Hope Valley was known for its charming art galleries, but the quaint shops lured tourists, too. Each had adorned their windows for the holidays. The display at Good Sports featured a Santa shooting hoops. Dreamery Creamery had frosted its windows with fake snow. The Christmas tree in the Curious Reader, the bookstore once owned and operated by her parents, was aglow with white lights that reflected off the silver and gold ornaments. Fondly, she recalled drinking in the scent of new books as her mother pulled them from cardboard boxes and arranged them on shelves.

Hope noted the line forming outside Sweet Place and murmured, "What delicious samples are you offering today? Gingersnaps? Peppermint pinwheels?" There hadn't been a position open at the bakery when she'd arrived in town; otherwise, she would have tried for a job there before landing the one at the café.

She slowed as she passed the Toy Palace so she could take in the adorable ballerina marionettes dancing in its display window. The banner over the front door boasted that the Palace was sponsoring a make-your-own-teddy bear session on Saturday. Yesterday, as she'd tootled around town with the children, Hope had diverted Todd's attention from the store. His well-loved teddy bear would have to be his companion for another year. By then, maybe she would have a larger savings account. If she was ever going to own a pie shop again, she had to scrimp. All she could set aside with her current paycheck was ten dollars a week. At that rate it would take her years to build up a buy-in for another bakery, but she was determined to succeed, Zach be damned. He would not destroy her dream.

Minutes later, Hope pulled into the parking lot at the café and headed inside. Thanks to its green-and-red décor, the café seemed decorated for Christmas year-round. Even the uniforms of red slacks, white blouses, and green aprons were jolly. During the holidays, the addition of wreaths hanging in each window added to the cheery look.

"Hope, can you reboot the music?" Gabe asked after she clocked in.

"You bet."

With cherub cheeks and white hair, Gabe Greeley had the soul of a saint and the full-bellied laughter of a happy man. The day she'd walked in, Gabe had put a hand on her arm and asked what had sent her back to Hope Valley. She couldn't give voice to her pain. To what Zach had done to her. To what he'd done to their kids, leaving them without a father. She'd answered, *Family*.

She pushed thoughts of the past from her mind, tied on her apron, and tended to the music.

Hope enjoyed working at Aroma Café. The clientele were polite, and the cozy atmosphere was warm and inviting. The only thing she didn't appreciate was Gabe's preference for cheesy Christmas classics, the songs Hope used to sing at the top of her lungs. She particularly despised "Frosty the Snowman" and "You're a Mean One, Mr. Grinch." After three days on the job, she'd tried to talk Gabe into playing instrumental Christmas music, like the strains of Kenny G, Winton Marsalis, or Yoyo Ma, or classics like "O, Little Town of

Bethlehem," but he wouldn't go for it. People wanted to hear the silly ones, he'd told her.

She cued up "Santa Claus is Coming to Town" and returned to her spot at the counter.

Gabe said, "Next, can you do something with those ornaments?"

"On it, boss."

In a mad dash last Friday, Hope and Gabe had decorated the tree next to the entrance. Well, Hope had. Gabe had brought out the boxes of ornaments and lights and had put her in charge of them while he'd attended a daytime holiday party at the mayor's house. Hope, who had been too busy for words—a busload of tourists had come to town for the holiday art festival—had hung the ornaments willy-nilly. She'd intended to do a better job when there was a lull, but there hadn't been one. When Gabe returned that afternoon, he'd added the angel topper and had jokingly critiqued her ragtag assembly. Hope had promised to fix it when she found the time. Now, apparently, was it. Traffic at the café hadn't picked up yet.

"When you're done with that," Gabe said, "help Zerena fill the sugar dispensers."

"But first, girlfriend"—Zerena bounded into view, her raven hair bouncing in its snood— "you have to try my new concoction."

Hope and Zerena Saunders, a beautiful Latina woman with the most gorgeous amber eyes and flawless skin, had played on the high school basketball team together. Hope was tall, but nothing like Zerena, who towered over her.

Zerena handed Hope a mug brimming with pink whipped cream. A candy cane jutted from the foamy splendor. "It's my new specialty. Hot chocolate with peppermint whipped cream. Taste."

Hope took a sip and hummed her approval. "Wow. Double-wow."

"I'm trying to convince Gabe to let me spruce up some of our standards."

"This rocks," Hope chimed, thinking of Melody, who used the phrase a lot. She high-fived Zerena. "I vote yes!"

"Glad you approve."

Hope and Zerena had lost touch after Zerena moved to New York to pursue her dream of becoming a supermodel. Over the years, she'd landed a few jobs, but her career never took off. Disheartened, she'd returned home to help her mother tend to her aging grandmother and scored the waitressing position at the café. To Hope's delight, they'd instantly re-bonded.

"Drink more." Zerena flicked a finger. "Be sure."

Hope did as asked and deliberated. "*Hmm*. Maybe it needs a little more whipped cream?"

"I knew it. You hate it." Zerena reached for the mug.

"Don't. Touch." Hope protected her drink as if it was her bear cub. "Mine! Mine, mine, mine."

"You sound like Todd," Zerena teased, and knuckled Hope. She hadn't married and didn't have children. She wanted to, but she wasn't sure she'd have the patience for a husband, let alone kids. She often said she was fascinated by how Hope made it all work.

Except Hope didn't, did she? Not with all the bills and no family support. She was hanging on by a thread. At least she had the VW camper.

"Hi, Hope," a man called. "Hi, hi, hi!"

She turned and saw Lincoln Waldren waving to her from his favorite spot, table four. He was seated with his mother and father and . . . was that Steve?

Hope tucked an errant hair behind her ear, smoothed her apron, and approached the table. "Good morning, Waldrens," she said.

"This is my brother Steve," Lincoln said, enthusiastically.

"Hi," Hope said, surprised to see Steve with his family.

According to his parents, his demanding schedule made it impossible for him to visit. Handsome in high school, he was even more good-looking now, with attentive warm eyes and an engaging smile. His father, Frank, who owned Good Sports, was an older version of Steve, with salt-and-pepper wavy hair. At thirty-three, Hope's age, Lincoln was a younger, lankier version of his brother, though he didn't and never would have Steve's presence.

"He's in town for a few days," Lincoln said. "No, not a few," he revised quickly. "That's three. He's here for two days." He held up two fingers. "Just two. Two. Two. Two—"

"Okay, Son." Ellery patted Lincoln's arm. "Look at the menu." Lincoln was on the spectrum. He had a tendency to talk at a fast clip. One of his parents always accompanied him to the café.

"Say hi, Steve." Lincoln nudged his brother.

"Don't I know you?" Steve asked, squinting as if drumming up a memory. "Holly, right?"

"Hope," she replied. "We've actually met. I'm from here, but I lived in—"

"I want banana nutmeg pancakes," Lincoln announced, cutting her off.

"Lincoln, dear," his mother said. "Be patient." Ellery, who owned the year-round Christmas Attic, reminded Hope of Mrs. Claus, without the costume. She was a charming woman with wide eyes and apple cheeks and so few wrinkles that Hope wasn't sure she'd ever frowned. "I like how you've braided your hair, dear." Ellery pointed at Hope. "It really shows off the blond highlights."

"My daughter did it for me," Hope said. Melody had insisted on making multiple skinny braids for her mother. The moment Hope had arrived at the café, like always, she had snared them into a ponytail and had tucked them into her snood, but a few hairs always escaped.

"Hope is our favorite new waitress, Steve," Lincoln said.

"New?"

"She just moved here," Ellery explained.

"Isn't she pretty?" Lincoln asked.

"Very." Steve's eyes twinkled with amusement.

Ellery bit back a smile and redirected the conversation. "How are the sugar cookies coming, Hope?"

Gabe had put Hope in charge of Aroma's annual cookie decorating contest. For the past three days, she'd been making oversized Christmas tree-shaped sugar cookies. The freezer in the rear of the café was almost full.

"Only a few dozen to go," Hope said.

"How many have you made so far?" Steve asked, sounding as friendly as he did when he was on TV, a quality that had earned him the moniker, *the Voice*.

"Ten dozen."

He whistled. "That had to be a daunting task."

"Not really. I used to be a baker."

"Used to be?"

Clearly, he didn't remember having seen her at Pie in the Sky and didn't recall coming to her rescue when her miserable cur of a husband had landed the final blow. Oh, sure, he'd asked *Don't I know you?* a second ago, and the name Holly was pretty close to Hope, but that could've been a good guess. Maybe he'd thought that was her name in high school. Whatever.

"Long story," she murmured.

"I'd love to hear it sometime."

Hope felt her cheeks warm.

"She makes all the pies here, now," Lincoln said. "Tell him the list. Tell him."

Hope didn't know where to begin. Cheesecake pie with a hint of nutmeg and cloves had been the first one she'd suggested to Gabe. Cranberry apple made with tart Granny Smiths was the current hit. "They're listed on the specials."

"I had cardamom pumpkin pie here last night," Steve said. "Best crust I've ever eaten. I'm impressed."

Because of the kids, Hope didn't work night shifts so she hadn't seen the Waldrens.

"Steve's fiancée doesn't bake," Lincoln said. "Steve does."

Hope glanced at Steve. "Really? You're a man of many talents." His cheeks reddened, which made him look vulnerable and that much more attractive. "I love making snickerdoodles. It calms my mind."

"His fiancée doesn't even like to eat," Lincoln went on. "She's really, really skinny. Bro"—Lincoln punched Steve's arm—"you should leave her and marry Hope."

Steve chuckled. "Okay, buddy, TMI."

"TMI," Lincoln said. "Too much information. FYI, for your information. BTW, by the way." He ticked the phrases off on his fingertips. "Steve says *by the way* all the time on TV."

"No, I don't."

"Yes, you do." Lincoln altered his voice to match Steve's. "By the way, folks, did you know—" He chortled. "Steve is a sports announcer, Hope. He's memorized all the statistics of all the players. Every one of them. Give her your business card, Steve. Go on."

"Linc, c'mon, man," Steve protested.

"On the way here, he showed me his new card." Lincoln flapped a hand. "Give her one."

Apparently unable to say no to his brother, Steve pulled a card from his pocket. "Here you go."

Hope accepted it. "I know what Steve does, Lincoln. My children watch your brother every night." Hope wouldn't admit that she viewed the show along with them.

"He's not on every night," Lincoln said. "Only five nights a week. Five—"

Steve knuckled Lincoln. "I'm sure that's what she meant."

Hope tucked the card into her apron pocket and raised her order pad, pencil poised. "What would you like for breakfast, Steve?"

A cell phone lying faceup on the table buzzed. Steve glanced at the readout and apologized to his parents. "I have to answer this. Work."

He scooted out of the booth, accidentally bumping into Hope. She sidled left; so did he. She moved back to the right, losing her pencil. She bent to retrieve it, as did Steve. When they knocked heads reaching for it, both of them laughed.

"What a klutz I am," Steve said, picking up the pencil.

"No, I'm the klutz," Hope replied.

He inhaled. "You smell nice. What's the perfume you're wearing?"

"Eau de café," she joked.

Chuckling, he got to his feet. She rose, too, teetering a tad. He steadied her by the shoulder, and the warmth of his touch zinged through her. Hope shimmied away, refusing to let on how he'd affected her.

Steve handed her the pencil. "Here you go."

"Um, your order before you go outside?" Once again, Hope held the pencil over her pad.

"Two scrambled eggs, crisp bacon, and coffee . . . *hmm*, how do I want it?"

"How about an Americano?"

"My favorite. And a piece of pie. You choose the flavor." He winked. "I trust your judgment."

As Hope was putting up the order at the counter, Zerena sashayed to her. "My, my, you and the Voice seemed to have hit it off."

"Get out of here. He has a fiancée. In Portland."

"The weather girl? That won't last. *Brr.*" Zerena shivered and melodramatically clutched her arms. "I feel a cold freeze coming on."

Chapter 4

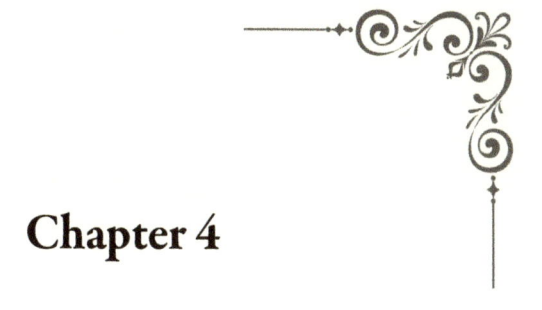

Six months later

Steve was sitting in the wood-and-leather booth at Piccolo's Restaurant staring at a single sheet of floral stationary, his eyes glazed over by the words written on the paper. When he'd first found the letter, he'd felt maudlin, but now he was numb. No, to be honest, he was angry. His cell phone jangled, jolting him from his funk. His mother was on the line.

He stabbed Send. "Hey, Mom, what's up? Everything okay?"

"It's Lincoln."

Steve scratched the back of his neck. Lincoln. Salt of the earth. He deserved better than what life had dished out to him in the gene-pool department.

"He misses you," his mother said.

"And I miss him." Steve wasn't lying. Seeing Lincoln always brought a smile. Years ago, before Steve was old enough to know something was wrong with his brother, he'd enjoyed climbing on Lincoln's bed and reading stories to him by flashlight. Lincoln, always Steve's greatest fan, had loved the way Steve had acted out every role.

"You haven't been here since last December," his mother said.

"I know, Mom. I've been meaning to come, but work has been crazy."

"Even for a night, Son. It's only a two-hour drive."

"Yeah, okay, I'll see what I can arrange."

His mother sighed. "Are you all right? You sound tired."

"It's been a rough week." He eyed the stationary again. His heart felt heavy. Drained.

"Want me to send you some cookies?"

"No, Mom. I'm good to go. You don't need to spoil me." He really did want to visit Hope Valley. His parents were good people. He missed his little brother. He'd make it happen. "Love you."

"Love you, Son."

Steve ended the call, sighed, and then read the letter from his fiancée for the tenth time.

> *Steve, we're not going to work out. We're on different career paths, and you will never rise to your potential. You've settled for less. You've let your love of family hold you back; you're too scared to move to another state; too afraid to get a job in a bigger market. Too frightened to . . .*

He paused, wondering what else she'd intended to write after the ellipsis. Probably nothing. Gloria wasn't the brightest bulb in the chandelier. She had a tendency to overuse ellipses and commas and semicolons. He kept reading.

> *Well, I'm not scared. I have to spread my wings and fly.*
> *It was good while it lasted, babe.*
> *~ Gloria*

Had it been good? Steve wondered. Had it really? No, not always.

"What's that you're reading?" Harker set two pale ales on the table and slid into the booth opposite Steve.

"Nothing." Steve started to fold the note.

"Crap-ola. Let me see it."

"Not a chance."

Steve had met Harker in his sophomore year of college—Harker, born Harkington Thomason the third, what a ridiculous mouthful. They had become kindred spirits because of their love of statistics and history of sports. Harker had never had a craving for the limelight, like Steve. A sports reporter for the *Portland Oregonian*, he preferred the quasi-anonymity of writing for a newspaper.

"Gimme." Harker held out his hand.

"It's nothing. Just a *Dear John* letter."

"What the—" Harker snatched it out of Steve's hands and quickly perused it. "Oh, man! She was such a . . ." He handed the letter back. "She was never good enough for you."

"We were engaged. We were supposed to get married next year. We—"

"Did she leave the ring?"

"Nope."

"That sucks. *She* sucks. When did you get that?"

"Last night."

"Any warning?"

"None." In fact, not a hint. Not a frigging clue. Steve had been totally blindsided. "When I got home from work, her side of the closet was empty. This was lying on my pillow."

"Did she at least leave a goodnight chocolate?"

Steve grimaced. "No chocolate."

"She totally sucks." Harker took a long pull on his beer and slammed the bottle on the table. Hands on the bottle's neck, he leaned forward on his elbows. "So here's the plan, bro. Time to get back in the saddle. Right now. Ready? Take a gander. There are a lot of women here who would be over the moon to be your plus one." He brandished a hand.

"Are you nuts?" Steve whistled soft and low. "I have no interest."

"Many of the females present are hot, my friend. Hot with a capital H." Harker, muscular in a running-back kind of way, his head shaven within a quarter-inch of its life, had a thing for the ladies, and they for him. He hitched his chin. "How about that one at the bar? With the long blond braid."

From behind, the woman reminded Steve of the waitress he'd met at Aroma Café. Same breadth of shoulders, same curve of her hips. For some reason, he'd been thinking about Hope a lot lately. Every time he went into Pie in the Sky, the bakery near KPRL, he inhaled the aromas and thought of her and the cute way her nose twitched. Each time he ate a slice of the shop's pie, he'd wanted to see if the crust would compare to hers. It hadn't. Hers had been something special.

"Earth to Steve," Harker said.

"Yeah?" Steve refocused on his friend.

"Not into blondes?" Harker smirked. "Okay, I'm sure brunettes—thanks to she who shall remain nameless—won't interest you at the moment, so how about the beauty to the right of the blonde? The redhead?"

"No."

"Did you love her?"

"Who?" Steve asked.

"G-l-o-r-i-a, Gloria," Harker crooned, using his beer bottle as a microphone.

"Yes. Of course."

"And now?"

"No. It's over. She's gone. She's—" Steve shook his head and pocketed the letter. Had he loved Gloria? Had he adored her with his whole heart the way his father loved his mother? The answer was a hard no. They'd been a couple. That was all.

Harker snapped his fingers in front of Steve's face. "Concentrate."

Steve sighed. "I've been finding it hard to concentrate all day."

Harker aimed the tip of his bottle at Steve. "And therein lies the problem with relationships, dude, which is why I will remain unattached for eternity. I like to keep my wits about me. Having a steady woman demanding my undivided attention? Meh. Too much work." Harker held up his bottle as a toast. "Here's to keeping your head in the game, Stevie."

"True that." Steve clinked his bottle against Harker's and took a long swig.

"Shall we order?" Harker asked.

"Huh?"

"Food?" Harker mimed stuffing his face. "Me hungry." He thumped his chest. "Triple cheese burgers are the special tonight."

"Burgers? No, thanks." Steve didn't want anything remotely like a burger. All he wanted was a piece of pie.

Chapter 5

December, present

"I can't believe it's already Christmastime again, can you?" Hope called over her shoulder.

Todd and Melody were nestled in the backseat of their VW camper. Despite the fact that their school clothes were slightly rumpled—the iron had been on the fritz—their faces were eager. The two were stringing popcorn with a needle and thread. They couldn't wait to decorate the tree after dinner. Last night, they'd each made a new flour-and-water ornament. Hope had baked them in the toaster oven, and the kids had painted them and added the year. *Traditions were to be maintained no matter what,* her mother used to say. *No matter what.*

Tears pressed at the corners of Hope's eyes as she thought of her parents. *No, no, no. No tears.* She'd seen a therapist a couple of times after her parents died, and tears had flowed freely then, but when Zach left, she didn't shed one. Not one. She'd screamed. She'd cursed. But she hadn't cried. Tears were to be shed sparingly. They were for true sorrow only, not anger, and definitely not self-pity. *Find your sense of humor, Kitten,* her father would say whenever she faced a disappointment like not making the cast of *Jesus Christ, Superstar,* not making the drill team, not being voted class secretary. *You'll have plenty of successes in your lifetime.*

Would she? She wasn't so sure. But two of them were sitting in the backseat.

Shaking off her sadness, she sat taller in the driver's seat and said, "Okay, it's singing carols time, you two. 'It's the most wonderful time of the year.'"

Neither child joined in.

"*Ahem.* I am not a soloist."

"No kidding," Melody wisecracked.

"'It's the most wonderful time of the year,'" Hope started again. "C'mon. Don't hold back."

The children bellowed out the words.

"Melody's singing off key," Todd said.

"Am not."

"Are, too."

Melody stuck out her tongue.

"Stop it, Melody." Hope sighed. Ten-year-old girls, she decided, weren't much more mature than seven-year-old boys.

"Hey, look!" Todd reached over his sister's shoulder and pointed out the VW's window. "There's the nativity scene."

"Mom," Melody cried, "isn't the tree by the gazebo beautiful?"

"It sure is."

A towering thirty-foot Christmas tree, decorated in gold and red but unlit until the upcoming tree-lighting ceremony, stood to the right of the nativity scene.

"Roll down the window, Melody," Todd pleaded. "I want to smell the fresh snow."

"You can't smell snow, dodo," Melody taunted.

"Roll it down."

"Fine." Melody whisked her hair over her shoulder before complying.

Cool air rushed in. So did the strains of "It's the Most Wonderful Time of the Year," which were being piped through speakers attached to each of the lampposts. Hope wondered if it was Kismet that they'd been singing it first. Maybe the fates would align this Christmas and make it a happier one than last year's. Maybe.

Tenderly, she remembered the time when she, Miss Hope Valley, had been invited to trigger the tree's lights at the lighting ceremony. Twenty-eight years ago, to be exact, at the sassy age of six. Looking back, her father must have begged someone like the mayor to give her the title. He and the mayor had played golf together. Hope remembered the lacy white dress she wore, the white coat, the winter stockings. Her mother had spent an hour styling her long hair into a ponytail with curls. A five-piece band had been playing the same song as now. She could still feel the warmth of her mother's and father's hands clasping hers as they flanked her. She'd looked up once. Their smiles had been radiant.

Time gone by, she thought sadly.

"See the baby Jesus in the manger?" Todd asked, bringing Hope back to the present. "See his halo?"

"It's a doll," Melody said.

"I know it's a doll. Duh." He knuckled her.

"Ow! Mom!" Melody whined.

"Todd, stop," Hope chided.

She knew Todd hadn't hurt his sister. He never would. The two had bonded when Zach left town. *Zach*. How she wished she'd known his true, weak character before she'd fallen in love with him. If she had, would she have done things differently? Yes. But if she had, she wouldn't have born two beautiful children, and she loved them more than life itself.

"Mom, doesn't the school look pretty?" Melody exclaimed, yanking Hope from her reverie.

Hope pulled to a stop in front of Hope Valley Elementary and clambered out of the VW. "It sure does."

Evergreen boughs adorned each of the school's windows. A huge sign reading *Merry Merry* hung between the columns leading to the school's entrance.

"Hop to it, kiddos." Hope opened the van's side door. "School's a-waiting. Is the popcorn strung?"

"Yes," Todd said.

"Good. We'll hang it tonight. Get a move on. I'm late. Walk yourselves in. See you after school. And Melody..."

"Yes?" Her daughter was still perched on the car seat, checking the buttons on her plaid blouse and raising the collar of her pink parka. Her basketball and backpack rested at her feet.

"Remember, no sugar. I don't care what parent is offering holiday treats at rehearsal."

"I know. I'm a diabetic. I have a strict diet." She pulled a long face. "You don't have to remind me *every* minute of *every* day."

"Lose the tone, young lady," Hope warned.

"Sorry."

"And Todd," Hope continued, "take *The Hero Two Doors Down* back to the library."

"I will." *The Hero* was a story about Jackie Robinson and his friendship with a young boy. Todd enjoyed reading about sports. "Can I check out a new book, Mom?"

"May I," Hope said reflexively, and chuckled. How many times had her mother, a teacher before a shop owner, called her out on improperly using pronouns?

"May I?" Todd repeated. "The other day I saw one about sports statistics. Dad was a whiz with statistics."

Hope grunted. Zach had been a whiz, but statistics hadn't helped him win at poker. "Yes, of course," she said. "Why don't you check out *The Gift of the Magi*, too?" It was one of Hope's favorite stories.

"Ugh. Sounds boring."

"It's for me. Please?"

"K," he said in verbal shorthand.

Melody scrambled out of the VW, shrugged into her backpack, waved good-bye to Hope, and then immediately started dribbling her basketball. Todd shuffled out and waited for his mother to close the van door. Hope winced at the resulting *creak* and made a mental note to spray WD-40 on it later.

"Bye, Mom!" Todd shouted.

"Bye, sweetheart."

Trotting away, Todd dropped his backpack on the wet sidewalk. He collected it quickly and glanced back at his mother. Shyly, he blew her a kiss.

Kisses. Hope pulled her parka tightly around her uniform. *If only kisses solved the world's problems.*

Chapter 6

Hope drove down Main Street and spied a quartet of carolers in Dickensian garb singing outside Always in Bloom. At the stoplight, she rolled down the window to listen to "What Child is This?" ringing out in four-part harmony. A rush of joy stirred within her.

"Hey, Hope," a man yelled.

Denny Benton, a hunky thirty-something and one of the town's most dedicated city employees, was testing the lights that were strung on the lampposts. "Looking good," he said.

"Your lights are looking good, too."

He chuckled. "How about dinner sometime?"

"Can't right now. Too much on my plate." Hope never wanted to date again if she could avoid it, although for some odd reason she had to admit she'd been avidly watching sports recaps on KPRL with the kids, of late. She told herself she was paying attention so she and her kids could bond—not so she could see Steve Waldren.

"But sometime?" Denny asked.

"Sometime."

"Cool." He shot her a thumbs up. "Be thankful and be of good cheer! Tis the season."

"Tis, indeed," she responded.

Be thankful, Hope coached herself. Yes, that would be her mantra for the day. Even though broken promises had hit her hard and life had left her wanting, she dug deep to find something to be thankful for. Her health. Her job. Her children. So what if the VW was on its last legs? So what if she hadn't been able to save more than five hundred dollars in twelve months? So what if they'd had to eat mac-and-cheese every day last week to stay within their budget? Hope would not allow herself a pity party. No one would guess that she was struggling, and she'd never tell. She would put on a good face, be strong like her parents had taught her to be, and save, save, save.

An hour later, while rolling out dough for a pecan pie at the café, Hope was surprised by how upbeat she felt. Maybe her personal pep talk in the camper had helped.

"Order!" the chef, Roman Capellini, shouted. A forty-something man and easy on the eyes, he wasn't easy on the waitresses. He expected them to jump and to ask *how high?*

Hope abandoned the dough, smoothed her apron, rushed to the warming area, and fetched two plates of cinnamon apple pancakes. Expertly, she skirted the counter and its bay of red stools and made a beeline for the elderly couple sitting at table two.

"Here you go." She freshened their coffees. They were newcomers to town. "Anything else?"

"No, thank you, ma'am," the husband said. "By the by, what's a pretty thing like you doing working so hard?"

"You!" His wife spanked his arm playfully.

"Just asking a question." He chuckled.

"If you must know," Hope said, "I make the best pot of coffee this side of the Rockies. Where else am I going to find this kind of appreciative crowd?" She motioned to the café.

"And mighty good coffee it is," the wife said.

Hope smiled. "Thanks for the compliment."

There were always visitors during the holiday season in Hope Valley—young, old, and in-between. Shopping for gifts was a huge draw. The Christmas Attic always sponsored a gingerbread house-making contest, and the annual Holiday Bazaar, a huge burgundy-and-twinkling lights extravaganza, filled with handmade crafts and baked goods and a Santa's Village to entice the children, was a sight to behold.

Hope returned to the kitchen and her chore of rolling out the dough. As she was preparing to drape it in the pie plate, Zerena swooped to her side.

"Girlfriend, did you hear?" Zerena asked. "Gabe wants to retire."

"No way."

"Way. I heard him talking to Roman. He wants to travel the US of A. Top to bottom. Roman said Gabe has been saving for years and can afford to hotfoot it out of here."

"Who's he going to travel with?" Hope asked. Gabe was a widower. His daughter, a powerhouse in politics, lived on the East Coast.

"Beats me."

"Is he dating anyone?"

"Not to my knowledge."

To hear the other staff talk, Gabe still carried a torch for his beloved wife. She'd been gone eight years now. He had pictures of her everywhere in the café's office.

Hope tensed as a thought occurred to her. "Will he sell the café? Will we have to look for new jobs?"

"He'd better not. I like it here."

"*Ahem.*" Hope cleared her throat. "You like Roman."

"*Pfft.*" Zerena made a face in protest.

Hope didn't press, but she knew her friend did. Zerena simply hadn't let Roman know. Sure, she had flirted with him a time or two, but she would always pretend that it was in jest. Zerena had been rejected by the love of her life in New York—one of the reasons she didn't think she could make a go of marriage—and she didn't want to be rejected again. Not in Hope Valley, of all places.

Hope held a hand over Zerena's head like an emcee on a game show. "Audience members, I ask you, is this woman lying or telling the truth?"

"Stop, you goofball."

"Buzz! Wrong answer."

Zerena batted Hope's hand away. "I like the schedule here. That's all. Besides, where would I find a boss as understanding as Gabe?" She shot a finger at Hope. "Say, maybe he'll sell it to you."

"Of course he will." Hope grinned. "Right after I win the lottery."

Chapter 7

The school bell rang, and a minute later children spilled through the doors of Hope Valley Elementary. Hope stood on the sidewalk waiting for Melody and Todd to appear. The rule was Melody always went to Todd's classroom, and the two came out together. Hope wasn't typically a worrywart, but like any mother, a flurry of *what ifs* cycled through her mind at a rapid rate.

"Mom!" Todd skipped across the snowy grass, kicking up clumps as he ran. He waved a book at her. "Look what I got at the lib-ary."

"Library," she corrected, adding in the extra *R*.

He repeated the word correctly. "It's called *The Breaks of the Game*. It's all about the Trail Blazers."

"Good for you." She eyed Melody, who was cradling her basketball like a baby. "Are you okay, sweetheart?" She swooped her into a hug.

Melody wriggled free. "I'm fine, Mom. Lemme go." She glanced over her shoulder.

Hope noticed twin girls about Melody's age whispering between themselves at the carpool drive-through lane. "Problem?"

"No," Melody said.

Todd cleared his throat deliberately. "She's lying. The Wickeds teased her."

"The Wickeds?" Hope asked.

"He means the Johnsons," Melody said snidely.

"They told Melody that we don't belong in Hope Valley," Todd said, "because we don't have a father."

"You have a father," Hope exclaimed.

"That's what Melody said, but then they said, 'Prove it,' and food started to fly."

Hope gawped. "You had a food fight?"

Todd bobbed his head. "Yeah. On Wedges Wednesday."

"Wedges Wednesday?" Hope tilted her head, not understanding.

"All the food is served in wedges. Apple wedges. Orange wedges. Potato wedges fly like darts." Todd snickered. "It was awesome."

Melody turned crimson. "It wasn't awesome going to the principal's office."

Hope wished she had a magic wand so she could turn back time and help Melody fit in, but she couldn't. Her daughter would have to muscle through like all the other kids. She held out her hand. "Is there a form I need to sign?"

Melody fetched it from her backpack and handed it over.

Hope scanned it. The food fight fracas was laid out in black-and-white detail. Apparently, Melody had started the altercation. That was what the note said—*altercation*. She needed to be more civilized. More respectful. More...

Sighing, Hope removed a pen from her trousers, scribbled her name on the form, and handed it back. "Melody, I've told you more times than I can count that you can't let people get under your skin. They are, after all, the same age as you and struggling with many of the same issues. Maya Angelou said—"

Melody held up a hand. "I know. I know." Then she recited, "'You may not control all the events that happen to you, but you can decide not to be reduced by them.'" She huffed. "I've got Grandma's needlepoint pillow with the saying. I've memorized it. It's inscribed on my brain." She tapped her head with her forefinger.

Hope laughed and kissed Melody where she'd poked herself. "You are my darling girl."

"Yeah, yeah. Don't get mushy."

Sobering, Hope said, "You're right. Let's get going. We've got a tree to decorate."

AN HOUR LATER, HOPE folded up the rear seat of the VW and laid out the children's sleeping sacks. In all this time, she hadn't let anyone know that she and the kids lived in the VW camper, but with all her other expenses, she couldn't afford an apartment. At least when the previous owner had revamped the VW, he had fitted it with storage on the doors and more storage on the roof, and its mini kitchen worked. Hope and the children lived snugly, but they managed. When Zach left, Melody and Todd had cried. They'd bemoaned the very notion of not having him around. They'd questioned Hope as to what she'd done to drive him away. She'd sat them down and had tried to explain. Daddy was a good man, but Daddy couldn't manage money. He left because he knew they were better off without him. She sugar-coated it, for Zach's benefit, but she knew none of what she would say would help in the short run. They'd simply need time to adjust. To accept. To allow Hope to shower them with love. A holiday season without Zach had come and gone. A summer without a family vacation, too. Coping was the *new norm*.

As instrumental Christmas music played on her cell phone, Hope cleared the spot at the rear of the camper to make room for the three-foot artificial tree that she'd purchased at the dollar store.

"It's cold, Mom," Melody said.

"Throw on your parka. We can't close the doors until we have everything set up and sit down to dinner." If they moved around too much in the van with the doors closed, it would become stuffy and unbearable. They would lay out the ornaments, then eat dinner and decorate.

With a grunt, Melody obeyed. She donned her snow cap with a grumble, too.

Todd placed the box of Christmas ornaments on the floor of the vehicle. "Here you go, Mom."

Deftly, Hope removed the top of the box, and her heart wrenched when she spied enough ornaments for a six-foot tree, the same sized tree they used to have. The one Zach would chop down and tie onto the roof of the Explorer, muscles bulging, perspiration streaming down the sides of his handsome face. In Portland, the apartment they'd lived in had been huge, with three bedrooms and high-beamed ceilings. Hope had treasured seeing the tree and its sparkling lights reflected in the glass window—the window that had provided a view of the city.

"Let's lay out the smallest ones first," Hope said. "We don't want to overwhelm the little guy."

Todd pulled out the tiniest ornaments and set them on the floor of the VW, arranged largest to smallest. He wasn't OCD, but he did like order.

"This is my favorite song," Melody said as the opening notes of "White Christmas" rang out.

Hope's insides knotted as she remembered the first time she'd met Zach. At a Christmas party in college. He had crooned "White Christmas" like Michael Bublé while guiding her deftly in a box-step around the fraternity kitchen. Dance lessons, he'd confided. She could still feel his breath in her ear, the warmth of his hand at the small of her back. She remembered telling her mother the next night that he was *the one*. He was so clever, she'd said. So smart. So talented. But he hadn't put those talents to good use. He hadn't become a college math professor, as planned. He hadn't solved Barnett's or Margulis's conjectures, either. Oh, sure, they'd swirled inside his head, practically driving him crazy. However, when poker lured him to the table, the rest of his visions of solving unfathomable mathematical problems vanished. And so did he.

"Can we turn on the computer, Mom?" Todd asked.

"Not now."

"We're listening to music, bonehead," Melody said.

"Dork." Todd stuck out his tongue.

Hope Valley Trailer Park, which abutted Mt. Hope Forest, known for its hiking trails and the Hope Valley Observatory, offered showers, storage compartments, and Wi-Fi, the latter making Melody and Todd ecstatic. At least they could stream television shows through the aging laptop Zach had left behind. He'd blithely taken Hope's brand new MacBook Air. When she arrived home the day he absconded with the Explorer, she felt as if she'd been mugged. He had turned the apartment inside out. All his clothes were gone. Pots and pans were missing. Dishes. Bedding. The Sony television. And then she walked into the office they shared and discovered her laptop was gone. The one with all her expense reports, all her business models. It had taken her a month to recreate them.

"Please, Mom, it's time for the news," Todd added.

Hope sighed.

"Please."

Camping wasn't new to Hope. Her parents had rented an RV when she was seven and had taken her on a three-month tour of the United States. But living in a camper as a lifestyle? With two children? Guilt roiled through her. She had to do better. Earn more. Save more. But how? Her salary and tips at the café were not boosting her coffers. She needed a better paying job, like something in marketing, but she didn't want to move back to Portland, and life was certain to be harder and more costly there than in Hope Valley. Besides, she loved Hope Valley. It was a good place to raise children.

A decent place. And, to be honest, what she needed was a little bit of Christmas magic. Hope Valley had that in spades.

"No TV," Hope said. "Tonight is for decorating and talking like a family, remember?"

"But Steve Waldren is on," Todd whined.

"No. Sorry, Son."

"You're no fun," he said.

"Yes I am. A bunch of fun. In fact, I won the *Most Fun* award in high school. And I'm a super-duper laugher. C'mon. Tell me a Mom joke."

He twitched his nose like Hope did, one of the things they had in common and one of the things that made her adore him. "Fine. What sound does a witch's car make?" He didn't wait for her response. "*Broom. Broom.*"

Hope giggled. "Nice one. What does a gingerbread man use for linens on his bed?"

"I don't know. What?"

"Cookie sheets."

Todd groaned. "C'mon, Mom, Steve Waldren. How about two minutes?" He was a born negotiator.

"Nope. Melody, how are rehearsals going for the holiday play?" Hope asked. Melody had been cast as one of the magi.

"Fine."

"Do you like the director?"

"She's the English teacher and doesn't know much about theater, but yeah, she's okay."

Theater at this age was more about engaging children's attention. "Good."

Todd moved his hand as if it was talking. "Blah, blah, blah."

"Young man. That's rude."

"I want to watch Steve. I'll tell his parents you don't like him," he threatened.

Steve's parents did love their Stevie. Invariably, they told Hope and anyone else who wanted to listen about his exploits, although they'd been reluctant to share that his fiancée had left him during the summer to become the weather girl in Minneapolis. Lincoln had spilled that news.

"BFD," Hope said to her son, using initials a child would understand. *Big fat deal.*

Todd folded his arms dramatically. "Spoilsport."

"Cutie pie," she countered.

Melody said, "Hey, Mom, did you know the Christmas Attic is having the annual gingerbread house contest again?"

"It always does," Hope said, glad for the change in topics.

"Can we make one this year?"

Hope flashed on Zach making a gingerbread house the first year they were married. He'd used too much icing, and the roof had given way. He'd blamed her, of course, even though she was an expert, thanks to her mother teaching her how to position the pieces of roof on the house, just so. But what Hope really hated about the memory was that Zach had eaten all the gumdrops, not leaving any for her. How had she not realized then how selfish he was? How compulsive?

"We'll see," Hope answered.

"Can we order pizza tonight?" Todd asked.

It had been a tradition to order pizza whenever they'd decorated the tree. Zach had insisted. Pepperoni for him, olives and onions for Hope, extra cheese for the kids.

"No," Hope said. "Sorry. Too expensive." Even though she'd made extra tips this past week, thanks to customers being more generous during the holidays than at other times of the year, she couldn't risk spending money on something as frivolous as pizza. Medical insurance payments were coming due January first. Those held priority. "I brought home a special dinner, though. Gabe gave me burgers and salad, and I have sugar-free cookies, too." Like last year, Hope had been making sugar cookies for the decorating contest and had made it her mission to add sugar-free and gluten-free cookies as choices.

Melody clapped. "Thanks, Mom."

"Big whoop," Todd said sullenly.

"Mom, look at this silly ornament." Melody raised a snowman with the smallest head ever. "Remember when Daddy made it?"

Todd grabbed it from her. "Yeah!" he said, his mood brightening. "He said it was like the scarecrow in *The Wizard of Oz*. It didn't have a brain."

Hope laughed, but her laughter sounded hollow. She rose to her feet and closed the van door. "Dinner."

After they ate, the three of them decorated the tree. It didn't take more than thirty minutes, but throughout, they sang carols. When they put the star on the top, Hope asked them what they were thankful for. Todd said the book he got at the library. Melody said new memories.

New memories are good, Hope thought. The old ones sucked.

"What about you, Mom?" Todd asked. "What are you thankful for?"

"The two of you." She threw her arms around them and hugged them tightly. "Without you, I wouldn't be a mom."

While clearing the tiny table where they'd eaten dinner, Melody said, "Let's write letters to Santa."

Hope said that was a super idea and pulled out stationary from her box marked *business*.

"Can I write one to Steve Waldren, too?" Todd asked.

"I don't know his address."

"Sure you do. You have his business card."

"How do you—"

"Sorry, Mom." Todd's cheeks tinged pink. "I, um, was peeking in your stuff."

Hope tamped down a smile. The guilty look on his face was precious.

"Please?" he asked. "I can tell him the latest statistics."

Hope nodded. "Sure."

"Can I write a letter to Daddy?" Melody asked.

A pang shot through Hope. Last year's Christmas cards to Zach had been returned, *address unknown*. Where was he? Was he still gambling? Why hadn't he reached out to his kids? She hated him for being so selfish.

"Yes," Hope said finally.

A half hour later, she tucked her children into their sleep sacks and, as her mother had said to her nightly, cooed, "Good night, my sweet ones. Sleep tight and dream with the angels."

Then she slipped into the driver's seat to organize her wallet, one of the many business tasks she would do after putting them to bed, and spied the letters to Santa and Steve Waldren on the passenger's seat. She bundled them into her purse and then saw the ones addressed to *Daddy*. The sight sent a chill down her spine. For Todd and Melody's sake, she needed to track down Zach. Maybe instigate monthly FaceTime chats. Something—anything—so they could get to know him, and yes, she thought wickedly, maybe those interactions would erase their fantasy of him.

But where was he?

Chapter 8

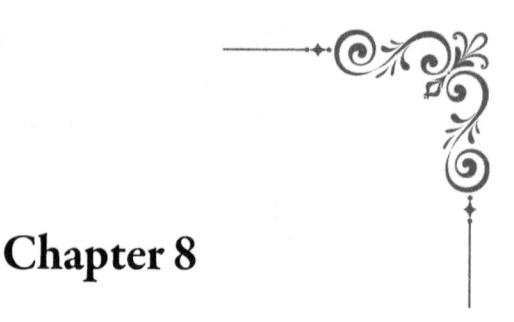

Steve sat at the KPRL news anchor desk Friday night, tightening the knot of his paisley tie, the one Gloria had given to him on the second anniversary of their meeting, the one he'd been meaning to throw out but hadn't remembered to until he'd put it on a minute ago and was already seated in front of the crew. Ripping it off would be, well, infantile, and he didn't have time to find a replacement. Instead, he did the righteous thing and soberly reviewed his notes for the evening's telecast.

Tout Trail Blazer's December stats. Check.
Chat up Portland High's center. Check.
Announce arrival of six-foot-tall co-ed at OSU. Check.

Honestly, he didn't need to reread the notes. They were imprinted on his brain like they always were. He didn't have a photographic memory but pretty darned close. So why was he sweating? He lived and breathed details. He didn't need caffeine. Didn't need to pump up his energy. All he needed was to hear, "Three, two, one . . ." and the excitement of sharing what he knew with the Portland audience did the rest.

If only you wanted to grow and strive, Gloria had carped. She was wrong, of course. He did want to broaden his horizons. There was plenty of mileage left in him before he aged-out of his career. He thought of the closing line of her letter: *It was good while it lasted, babe.* But that was a lie. It hadn't been. That was why Steve hadn't fought to win her back. Why he wouldn't fight. *Bye-bye, baby.*

An off-the-wall notion intruded his thoughts. If the bigwigs in Los Angeles made him an offer, would Gloria coming running back?

"Uh-uh, Stevie boy," he muttered under his breath. "Stop daydreaming."

Silently, he cursed his feckless agent. The guy never responded to email. Never returned text messages. If Steve wanted answers, he had to call him and catch him at just the right moment. And in December, with all the holiday hoopla? There was little chance of—

"Hey, Voice!" Brie Bryant, a reporter for the station for the past eight years, hailed him, hand overhead. She was dressed in a cocoa-colored suit that matched her complexion, her elegant braids pulled into a tight bun. She'd celebrated her fifty-eighth birthday last week, but she didn't look a day over forty, tops. "You're wanted on the phone. It's your agent."

Speak of the devil!

Steve did a fist-pump. He'd only call if there was an offer, right? Yeah, absolutely. Gloria had been wrong. *Wrong.*

Pushing thoughts of her aside, he popped out of his chair and hustled stage left to take the call. Before answering, he checked himself out in the mirror that was hanging on the wall, placed there for last-minute touch-ups. He was handsome in his own right. Strong jaw. Bright eyes. Okay, his nose was a little crooked from the fistfight with his brother all those years ago, but many said that gave him character.

"Who are you trying to impress?" Brie asked. She was standing nearby, her Nikon focused on something down and to the right. She was gifted with relating her one-on-one stories. Her accompanying photos were even more exceptional.

"Myself." Steve chuckled. "Only myself."

"Any luck with that?"

"Pretty danged successful."

"In your own mind."

"What are you taking pix of?" Steve asked.

"A spider spinning a web. The cleaning crew missed it."

Steve looked closer and realized Brie's eyes were swollen. She'd been crying. "Are you okay?"

"Yeah, sure, don't worry about me. I used some caffeine cream. This?" She indicated the puffiness with a finger. "Gone in three, two . . . Go. Answer the phone. But make it snappy. You're on in ten."

"You're a pro."

"You know it."

Steve slipped into his dressing room, kicked the glass door closed, picked up the receiver to the landline telephone, and pressed the blinking button to connect to the call. "Hey, man, how're you doing? What've we got? An offer? A deal? LA, here I come."

"Sorry, Stevie, no deal," his agent said. "Remember that kid in Denver, the Latino with the big grin? He got the job."

"No way. He's not even twenty-two. He's got no street cred. No experience."

"He looks good on camera, and let's face it, diversity is where it's at."

"He gets all the stats wrong." Steve sank into the ergonomic chair at his vanity and pounded the top of it. "Not to mention the kid's voice is squeaky."

"He's an up-and-comer. You're—"

"Don't say it." Steve grunted. *An over-the-hill loser.* Dang. He'd worked hard to cultivate his career. He could rattle off numbers in rapid succession better than anyone in the business, and his interviews with athletes and coaches were top-notch. He knew their histories, their families, their goals. "I am *not* done looking for a bigger market. Not by a long shot."

"How do you feel about Cleveland?"

Steve slammed down the phone and thumped the desk. Cleveland. As if. A perpetual gloom hung over that city. No way would he consider Cleveland. "Crap-ola!" he muttered and thought of Gloria again. Was she right? Was his career on a downward spiral? Was he simply waiting for the abyss to swallow him whole? No, he wouldn't believe it. Wouldn't accept it.

Seconds later, the landline telephone jangled. Expecting it to be his agent calling back to say he was kidding, he answered quickly. "Sorry, man. You didn't deserve that. I shouldn't have hung up on you. You were joking, right? I got the—"

"Steve?" It was his mother.

"Oh, hi, Mom." Steve leaned back in the chair, which gave a little too much. He almost toppled. Quickly, he planted his feet on the floor and anchored his elbows on the desk. "Everything okay?"

"Yes, of course. Well, no, not really. It's Lincoln. He'd like to see you. It's—"

"The holidays. Got it." Steve hadn't been home since June, and he'd only visited for one night. After his mother's last plaintive phone call, he'd made the two-hour drive. They'd eaten dinner. He'd played a game of chess with his brother. And then he'd left at the crack of dawn. He'd been meaning to return in the fall. Lincoln got edgy when he didn't see Steve for a few months, but trying to change the trajectory of his career had required his full, undivided attention. "How about I come for New Year's Eve?"

"Can't you get here sooner, Son?" she asked. "I was thinking next week."

"Sorry, Mom, I'm booked solid until New Year's." There were a couple of important donor parties he had to attend, and he wanted to be available in case an interview cropped up. No one interviewed between Christmas and New Year's.

"I'll serve a holiday meal, complete with pie."

Pie. Steve flashed on Hope and the pie he'd tasted at Aroma Café, but then he sobered. Hope, Hope Valley—yeah, not in his future. "Sorry, Mom."

"Lincoln wants to build a gingerbread house with you."

"Waldren!" Dave Zamberzini, the general manager of the station, opened the door and poked his head in. Barely five feet tall with a swatch of hair on his otherwise bald head, the man was Nero and Napoleon rolled into one. An admiral in search of a ship. A king in search of a country. Dave had only been general manager for a year, and yet Steve hated his guts.

"Coming, boss." Steve exhaled with a huff. "Mom, I'll make it happen, but I have to go. I'm due on set. Give Dad and Lincoln my love." He hung up and strode from his office.

"Don't rush just yet," Dave said, blocking Steve's progress. "We gotta talk."

"About?"

"Upper management is excited about our Spirit of Christmas giveaway."

"Cool."

"Our network and forty-nine others in our conglomerate across the country are touting the same prize."

"Double-cool," Steve said again, checking his watch. Two minutes to air. He hooked his thumb over his shoulder. "Gotta go."

"We're pitching the promo for two days, Saturday and Monday."

Not on Sundays. They didn't air on Sundays.

"Triple-cool. Cross-promotion. Good stuff." He offered a thumbs-up gesture.

"And guess who upper management has selected to play Santa Claus?" Dave aimed his pudgy index finger at Steve. "Little old you."

"No." Steve stopped in his tracks. He threw up his hands. "No, no, no. C'mon. I've played Giveaway Santa twice in the past five years, and besides I don't work Saturdays."

"This one you do." Dave snickered.

"Uh-uh. Make Brie do it. I'm not in the, forgive the pun, spirit. She can *ho-ho-ho* with the best of them."

"No can do." Dave tapped Steve's shoulder. "Tag, you're it. If you don't agree, kiss your job good-bye."

"What?" Steve's jaw dropped open. He felt like the wind had been knocked out of him. "You can't be serious."

"I'm as serious as a heart attack, buster." Dave smacked Steve's chest. "Do you think I don't know what's been going on behind my back? You, looking for other gigs. You, eager to jump ship for a bigger market. Yeah, boy-o, I know all about you. You've been putting out feelers."

"No, I haven't—"

"Cut the crap. Lying doesn't become you. But wait." Dave snickered. "Guess what I've heard? You're not sticking the landing. *Aww.*" He clucked his tongue. "It's no fun being the old man on the block, is it?"

"I'm not old."

"In this biz, thirty-eight is over the hill, bro, and you're getting close to the big four-oh. So, get this." Dave wagged a finger. "If you ask me, and if I were *you*, I'd do exactly as your boss says. Don't press your luck. Contract negotiations can be tough."

Steve pushed past Dave, who trailed him like a rabid dog. "What's the prize?"

"All fifty stations are giving away the same one." Dave slipped a piece of paper over Steve's shoulder. "Take a gander. It's way cool."

Steve snatched the paper and read: *KPRL Spirit of Christmas Extravaganza. Disneyland for a family of four for fifty families. All expenses paid.*

"Think of it. Fifty stations. Fifty families," Dave said.

Way cool, not! Steve thought. The happiest place on earth was the last place he and Gloria had gone on vacation. A month before the breakup. She'd been insistent. As anticipated, she'd complained about the room and the long lines and the vast array of junk food. Steve liked junk food occasionally. *Disneyland.* No fond memories there.

"You've got sixty seconds to say yes," Dave said. "Sixty, fifty-nine . . ."

Grousing, Steve retreated to his office, slammed the door, crossed to the vanity, and peered again at his face. This time he assessed it truthfully and saw the lines. Visible, deepening, age-defining lines. Sighing, he knew he would have to do as he was told.

Bah, humbug!

WHEN SATURDAY EVENING rolled around, Steve was edgier than all get-out. He paced his dressing room ignoring the *thank you* basket of Christmas goodies sent to him by a sponsor. He opened and slammed drawers, shunning the red-glazed donut the makeup artist had brought him. He wasn't hungry. He sure as heck didn't want sugar. He checked his eyes in the mirror—bloodshot. Tossing and turning all night about playing Santa hadn't helped. He didn't want to do it this time. It was beneath him.

But he knew he had to or Dave would lower the boom. Dave had axed over ten lifelong employees in the last year. And Steve, as much as he wanted to tackle a bigger market, liked his job. He didn't want to lose it. Luckily, Dave hadn't scrimped on the costume. The fabric was good, and the fake belly was plump. At least Steve wouldn't look like a ragtag Santa.

He tugged the fluffy white beard. Secure. Then he practiced a few *ho-ho-hos* before slapping on a fake smile and heading out to the studio. He slipped into his chair on the set.

Brie sat to his right, her eyes bright with humor. "Hey, Santa, you handsome devil, can I sit in your lap?"

"Not unless you want me to hit you with a harassment violation." She chuckled.

"Hey"—Steve loosened his wide black belt one notch and lowered his voice—"are you okay? Yesterday, you were sort of, you know, down." He twirled a finger in front of her eyes.

Brie huffed. "Let's just say I wish all my exes lived in Texas."

"Elaborate."

"Husband number two asked for a personal loan."

"And what would he have to do to earn such benevolence from you? Jump off a cliff?"

"Yeah, I wish." She snorted. "No."

"Isn't he the one who turned out to be gay?"

"No, that was hubby number one. Number two was just a piece of—" She didn't finish. "He's been out of work for a year."

"Not your problem."

"It sort of is. I made him move around for my career."

Steve nodded. "So, are you going to endow him with some of your riches?"

"I agreed to a short-term loan with an IOU."

"Good luck getting repaid."

She laughed. "Yeah, I'm an easy mark."

"Better watch out for hubby number three. He'll want to be written into your will."

That guy, the husband of two years that was supposed to be the man she loved until the day she died, had left Brie a year ago for a woman half her age.

"Fat chance." She squinted so hard he was pretty sure if she had super powers, he'd be lasered to death. After a long stare down, she rolled tension out of her shoulders and said, "How about you? Are you okay?"

"I would be if I could land a gig in a bigger market."

"Bigger isn't always better," Brie whispered with a devilish twinkle in her eye.

"And three, two, one," the assistant director said. She pointed at Steve.

"Ho-ho-ho, Merry Christmas," he crooned.

With all the enthusiasm he could muster, he read the teleprompter and recited the news about the station's Spirit of Christmas giveaway. "We're giving you two nights to qualify. Tonight and Monday. We're taking Sunday off for good behavior." He shared a wink with Brie. "Each of the two nights, I'll be collecting a name and information from a caller. At the end, the station will pick one of those two names to win the grand prize." He winked at the camera. "And what is the grand prize? Wait for it." He drum-rolled the desk with his gloved hands. "A trip to Disneyland for a family of four. That's right. A trip to Disneyland any time between January and March, all expenses paid. Why are we doing this? To gin up our ratings, of course." He chortled. "What did you expect me to say? We're doing it out of the goodness of our hearts? Nope. KPRL and forty-nine other stations are doing this at once. Why would we be so generous? Free promotion." He rubbed his thumb and forefinger together—the universal *money* sign.

A moment of panic shot through Steve. He pressed his lips together. Had he actually said the last few sentences out loud? Had he made the money sign with his fingers? *No way. No freaking way.* He glanced at Brie, who was staring straight ahead, not at him, which meant he had not given voice to his inner thoughts. *Phew.* Talk about dodging a bullet.

"We are doing this"—Steve paused for effect, and then continued reading off the teleprompter—"out of the goodness of our hearts. That's what the holidays are all about, right, folks? Give, give, give to live, live, live." The latter wasn't on the prompter but Steve went with his gut. Something about wearing the suit was inspiring him to new heights. He was feeling jolly. And, yeah, a bit punch drunk. Punch drunk on adrenaline but sober about his future. He needed this job until he had another one lined up.

"So, are you ready, Oregonians?" Steve crooned. "Check out the number on the screen and call now. And"—he held up his index finger—"don't think just because you're the first or last caller that you won't get lucky. You might!" He jutted his finger at the screen. "Tis the season. Ho-ho-ho."

Chapter 9

Hope was exhausted from work. She'd thrown on her father's forest green Pendleton and her mother's favorite sweatpants and was sitting in the VW's driver's seat using her cell phone's flashlight app to review bills while listening to the local radio station, owned and operated by Mr. Q, her former high school teacher. Every night Mr. Q read poetry or a chapter of a book. Hope found listening to him soothing. She glanced at the children's letters sitting on the passenger seat—the letters she hadn't posted—and hated herself for not following through. She'd send them tomorrow, no matter what.

"Mom!" Todd screamed from the rear of the van.

Hope startled. "What?"

"Mom, Mom, Mom. You gotta hear this."

The camper started to rock. Hope glanced over the car seat. Todd, in his pajamas and stocking feet, was jumping up and down, looking like an apoplectic cheerleader, arms going every which way.

"Hey, kiddo, settle down. What's going on?"

"Mom, it's Steve Waldren." Todd pointed at the computer screen. "He announced a contest. Can we call the station? Please?"

Melody, who was curled in her bean bag chair with her grandmother's needlepoint pillow tucked beneath one arm and reading a book, said, "We won't win. You won't get through."

Todd shot her a withering look. "You don't know that." He placed his hands together in prayer. "Please, Mom? It could be our lucky day."

Hope slipped between the driver and passenger seats and peered at the computer screen. Steve Waldren, dressed as Santa Claus, was looking directly at his audience.

"Tis the season," Steve said. "Ho-ho-ho."

"It's an eight-hundred number, Mom," Todd said. "Please, please, please." He pressed his hands together in prayer. "I'm feeling lucky."

Hope bit back a smile.

"You won't get through," Melody said in irritatingly singsong fashion.

"Melody," Hope said, "don't be a Grinch."

Melody folded her arms over her slim body. In her pink sheep-decorated pajamas she didn't look all that tough. "But, Mom, you're the one who said, 'Don't believe in pipedreams.'"

Hope winced. Zach's favorite fantasies had always involved pipedreams. She remembered the last one he'd shared, when the two of them were nestled on the couch—the couch she'd had to sell with all the rest of her furniture. *Think of everything we can do with the money I win, babe.* Zach brushed hair off her face with his fingertip. *We'll travel. We'll buy a huge house.* He ran his finger down her jawline. *Each of us will have the car we want.* He kissed her with such passion. *Just one more hand. One more...*

Hope snapped back to the present. "Tis the season," she said, and gave her cell phone to her son. "Good luck."

Todd plopped onto the floor and, tongue wedged between his teeth, stabbed in the KPRL number. He waited. And waited.

"Told you," Melody said.

Hope shot her the stink eye.

Todd ended the call and tried again. And again. Hope hated to tell him that television and radio giveaways were scams to entice fans to keep following them. No one ever won anything. No one she knew, anyway.

"Crud." Todd clambered to his feet and handed the cell phone back to Hope. "A recording came on telling me to try again on Monday."

"That means they picked today's winner," Melody said, as if she was the sage of media giveaways. "Loser."

"Melody, honestly? Cut the attitude, young lady." Hope huffed with exasperation. "Todd, I'll let you try again Monday."

"Cool!" Todd whooped with glee. "Thanks, Mom." He plunked back on the floor and planted his elbows on his knees. "Hey, Melody, Steve's doing Trail Blazer statistics. Come watch."

Melody joined her brother on the floor. Hope smiled. At least in their love of sports, they were united.

SUNDAY MORNING, WHILE on her ten-minute break at the café, Hope was rummaging through her purse for a lipstick when she spotted the letters the kids had written. She had planned to drop them in the mail, but she hadn't yet. Would she? She glanced at Melody and Todd sitting at a table in the café's kitchen doing art projects, and her heart swelled with love. They were angels. They never gave her guff. They understood how difficult it was for her to be a mom and work full-time.

"Hey, girlfriend." Zerena leaned halfway into the kitchen, a pencil tucked into her snood, order pad in hand. "Daydreaming time is over. The church crowd is filing in. Slap on that winning smile."

"Will do."

"Table four asked for you," Zerena said.

"On it." Hope swathed on lipstick without checking herself in the mirror, stowed her purse in a locker, spun the dial on the lock, and smoothed her apron.

Out in the café, she hurried to table four, her order pad at the ready. Lincoln and his parents were studying the menus.

"How are you, Lincoln?" she asked.

"Good. Very good. Very, very good. It's almost Christmas."

"Yes, it is."

"I love Christmas."

"I do, too."

"I love Christmas trees and hot cocoa and carolers."

Ellery patted his hand. "Hope needs to take our order, Son."

"Want to know the specials?" Lincoln asked. "Chili hot dog, six-ninety-nine. Steak and eggs, fourteen-ninety-five. " He never ordered a special, but he could recite each and its cost faster than anyone on the café's payroll. "Why isn't anything an even number, Hope?"

"I don't know." She had often wondered the same thing. Did an item at six-ninety-nine really seem like a bargain, compared to the same item listed at seven dollars? "Say, Lincoln, I saw your brother on television last night. He was dressed as Santa Claus."

Lincoln wagged his head. "Fake Santa. He's not fat enough. He works out."

"He looked like he was having fun." If Hope were truthful, Steve hadn't looked happy in the least, but she'd never tell her kids or his family that. She supposed losing his fiancée could have taken its toll on him, especially during the holidays.

"Fun. Funny. Funnier," Lincoln chanted. "Ho, ho, ho. Jones twenty-seven points. Boxer, eight and a half rebounds. Woodruff, seven points and eight assists."

"Yes, that was the Trail Blazers latest game," Hope said, knowing exactly who he was talking about, having caught the recap. "Good memory." She eyed Ellery and Frank. "Coffee?"

Frank nodded. "Cream. Bring a glass of milk for Lincoln."

"Juice," Lincoln said. "I like when she brings me juice."

"What kind of juice?" Hope asked.

"Orange juice."

Hope checked with Ellery, who approved. "Orange juice it is."

In less than ten minutes, she returned with their order and made sure everything was to their liking.

Before Hope left the table, Ellery clasped her wrist. "Make sure you and your adorable children come to the gingerbread house event this year, dear. It's on Christmas Eve."

Frank grinned. "It's always on Christmas Eve, hon."

"Hope missed it last year," Ellery said. "I thought maybe she hadn't seen the posters."

"How could she miss them?" Frank snorted. "They're all over town."

Last year, Hope hadn't taken the kids because she hadn't wanted to do something that would remind her so acutely of her life with Zach. This year? She had to do better. Entertain the children. Let them have fun.

"I'll do my best," she murmured.

Chapter 10

Making an effort to do what she'd promised, Hope had decided that Sunday movie night at Cascade Park would be the first special event she'd treat the children to. Hope Valley took the evenings very seriously. Especially during the holidays. Each night, the park services would show a different holiday movie. Last night, they had featured *The Santa Clause*. The night before, they'd shown *It's a Wonderful Life*.

Tonight, Hope and her children were watching one of her all-time favorites, *Miracle on 34th Street*. The park, which had cleared the grounds of snow, could accommodate a thousand people. Everyone was required to bring his or her own seating.

The air was chilly, but Hope had come prepared. She'd laid out a waterproof blanket and had placed a battery-lit candle in the middle. She'd made sure the kids were dressed warmly. Both wore parkas, sweaters, jeans, and ski hats. Granted, their clothes were a tad too small—she hadn't bought them anything new in over six months—but neither had complained. They were lying on their stomachs, elbows bent, chins propped on their hands, gazing at the screen.

Halfway through the movie, Hope asked, "Do you want a cheese or bologna sandwich?" In addition to sandwiches, their modest picnic dinner included individual bags of chips and a sugar-free cookie for each of them.

"Pizza," Todd said.

"Sorry, no pizza." Hope rolled her eyes. Todd knew exactly what she'd packed. He'd helped her. "Cheese or bologna?"

"Cheese." Todd sat up, his teddy bear tucked under his arm. "Mom, do you believe in Santa?"

"He's not real," Melody said over her shoulder. Despite her expressed lack of belief, she was facing the screen, and Hope could see she was enthralled.

"Shut up, Melody," Todd hissed. "Mom, do you or don't you?"

How Hope wanted to believe, but life had intervened and had dashed her dreams. Life was real; Santa wasn't. And yet, there on the screen was the charming, pink-cheeked Kris Kringle in court being questioned by the puzzled prosecutor, and everything in her screamed, *Yes, yes, I believe!*

"He's not real," Melody cried. "Grow up!"

"Don't. Say. That." Todd stuck out his tongue. "He is too real."

Melody lurched to a rigid sitting position. "Steve Waldren dressed up as Santa. You know who Steve Waldren is."

"Well, duh," Todd said. "I mean, yeah, he put on a costume. There are lots of people who do that. Even the Santa at the bazaar isn't real. But Santa, the real Santa Claus, is, well . . ." He shot a hand at his sister. "He's real."

"Daddy said Santa is a joke," Melody sniped. "A figment of our imagination. And we're crazy if we buy into it."

Hope jolted. Zach didn't. He couldn't have. He'd set out cookies for Santa at Christmas. He'd jingled the coins in his pocket to imitate sleighbells. He'd chewed up carrots and spit them out on the driveway to pretend reindeer had visited the house. How could he tell their daughter Santa was a figment of their imagination? How dare he!

"Melody, take it back," Hope said sharply.

"I won't. Daddy's right." Defiantly, Melody folded her arms. "I believe what he says, Todd, even if Mommy doesn't."

Hope moaned. Even when Zach was gone, he was ever-present. He'd imprinted on their children, for better or worse. She gazed at her son, so vulnerable and trusting, and whispered, "I believe Santa is real, sweetheart. Let's make it our secret."

"AFTER YOU'VE BRUSHED your teeth, Todd, snuggle into your sleep sack," Hope said in the van. "I'll read you two a story." She glanced at Melody, already in her sack, peering at a postcard from her father that she kept hidden under her pillow. Not a postcard from the present, a postcard he'd sent to the kids when Hope and he had taken an adult summer vacation a lifetime ago. Hope cleared her throat. "Melody, you pick the story."

"None of those," Melody said, motioning to the five holiday-themed books stacked on the storage box wedged between hers and Todd's sleep sacks. The battery-operated camping lantern served as their lamp. "They're all fantasy."

"Fantasy can be good for one's soul." Hope perched beside Melody and stroked her hair.

Melody turned away, clutching the pink stuffed elephant her grandparents had given her the day she was born like it was her lifeline. Hope leaned down and kissed the back of her daughter's head. Melody wriggled with displeasure.

"Stop, Mom."

"But you smell so good."

"*Eww.*"

Hope backed off. "Hop to it, Todd."

He wriggled into his sleep sack and grabbed hold of *The Polar Express*. "This one." He snatched the accompanying train beside the books and zoomed it into the air.

"I love this story," Hope said.

"I hate it," Melody carped.

"Then go to sleep. I'll just read it to Todd."

Hope read aloud until both children fell asleep and then kissed them and whispered, "Sleep tight and dream with the angels."

After dimming the light of the lantern, she tiptoed to the small basin at the side of the camper, pressed the foot pedal to pump the water through the pipe, and dripped a teaspoon of water onto her toothbrush. Most often, she brushed her teeth with a dry brush and only used the water to rinse. Tonight, she needed a little comfort.

Dressed in her nightshirt, she moved to the driver's seat, switched on the radio to a classical station, and opened her ledger, the same ledger her parents had used to balance the Curious Reader's accounting books. Inside was an envelope stuffed with the bills: medical insurance, car insurance, dental visits, children's checkups. None were past due. Yet. Hope sighed. She knew nothing in life was free, but did it all have to be so darned expensive? When she and Zach first thought about having children, they'd discussed the costs, the future. They'd decided together that it would be worth it. And it was worth it for her . . . but she couldn't deny it was hard doing it solo.

Around ten p.m., Hope felt a gleam of light on her face. She glanced out the window and recognized the North Star shining merrily, as if no one should have a care in the world. But she did, and for the first time that she could remember, she resented the star's cheerfulness.

Chapter 11

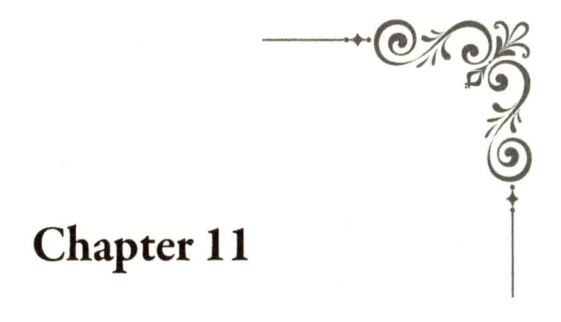

Steve used his shirttail and wiped the wrought-iron table on the terrace outside his penthouse apartment. Then he set down his laptop computer and took a long pull of his Sierra Nevada pale ale. The night air was cool, but it invigorated him.

Harker, who had brought pizza, was already sitting in a chair. "Tell me how it feels to be Santa." He snorted and smirked. "I mean, dude, do you have a craving to gain sixty pounds? Eat sweets? Drink cocoa?"

"Very funny."

"So what gives? Why do you have to play the jolly man again?"

"My boss has it in for me, that's why. He figured out that I'm looking for another job."

"Whoops."

Steve glared at Harker. "Hey, you didn't tell him, did you?"

Harker threw up both hands. "Whoa! Cool your jets, dude. I would never turn in a buddy. Besides, I don't know the guy."

"It was probably my agent undermining me," Steve grumbled.

Harker opened the box of pizza. "Want a slice?"

Steve stared at the all-cheese pizza. "Uh, bro, where's the meat?"

Harker did a double-take and threw up both hands. "Don't shoot the messenger. Not my fault. The beauty at the order counter must've forgotten it."

"Because you were making eyes at her."

Harker grinned. "Can I help it if I turn heads?" He put a slice of pizza on one of the plates that Steve had placed on the table and took a sip of beer. "Nice night."

"Yeah." Beer in hand, Steve moved to the railing and searched the sky for the North Star. Sadly, the lights of Portland often obscured the stars, and tonight was no exception. As a kid, he'd loved looking at stars with his dad. He wondered for a moment if Hope was looking at the stars and then blocked the thought from his mind. She had kids. She lived in Hope Valley. End of story.

Giving up trying to find one identifiable constellation, he took in his view of the city below. It was bathed in glitzy Christmas wonder. The sound of carolers singing "Little Drummer Boy" in the street below drifted upward, and Steve found himself humming, recalling how the rhythmic *par-um-pah-pah-pum* soothed his brother.

"Let's do this." Harker pointed to the computer. "Open that baby up. Show me what you got. You asked me here to help you with your job search. I'm ready, willing, and able."

Steve sat down, set his beer on the table, pushed the pizza box to one side, and flipped open his laptop. For two hours before Harker had arrived, Steve had explored job prospects. Granted, Zip Recruiter wasn't the best source for his line of work, but he'd wanted to see what was out there. Maybe something his agent hadn't come across. What positions for talented-beyond-belief, stats-savvy sports reporter had he found? Nothing. Nada. As in *zip* recruiter.

"Try Linked In," Harker suggested. "Let's do a deep dive. One of our Delta Taus must have some pull."

In college, Steve had joined a fraternity against his better judgment. He'd always wanted to go it alone, but friends had convinced him that a fraternity could help him down the road. One buddy had said to him, *Networking, man. That's what it's all about.*

"Networking," Harker said as if reading Steve's mind.

Steve grunted.

"Yo, dude," Harker said, spinning the computer in his direction. "You haven't updated your resume in, what, two years? Are you a Neanderthal?"

Steve hadn't felt the need.

"Okay, okay." Harker turned the computer back toward Steve. "I know you've been a lone wolf since Gloria left, and you're angry that she seared your hide, so you shut down on all fronts, but sometimes you've got to realize networking works. Reach out and they will help. Believe and they will come," Harker added, screwing up the famous phrase from *Field of Dreams*.

Even before Gloria's departure, Steve hadn't been a networking kind of guy. He'd snared the intern job at KPRL in his sophomore year of college, and that had fixed his course. Now? Was this where he wanted to be for the rest of his life? Harker was right. Steve was adrift. And if Dave fired him, what then?

He started scrolling.

"Go, Santa, go." Harker gave a fist pump. "You can do it."

"Eat grits."

"Ho-ho, hardy-har-ho." Harker raised his beer in a toast. "Speaking of Gloria . . . have you heard from her?"

"Not a word. Don't care." Steve hated how she'd chided him when he'd had to play Giveaway Santa the first time, saying he was abasing himself and denigrating his career. She'd ordered him to stand up for himself. Say no. But if he'd walked then, where would he have gone? He didn't have an *in* anywhere. He'd never applied for another position. That was when he'd reached out to his agent—his worthless agent.

Gloria. Steve sighed. Had he ever really been in love with her, or was it just the fantasy of being in love that had cemented his resolve to win her heart? She'd always done the weather right before the sports recap. She was there. Easy pickings.

Callow, Stevie, callow. You suck.

He took a pull on his beer. Their relationship was water under the bridge. He didn't miss her. He didn't miss her low jabs.

"Any leads yet?" Harker tapped the tabletop impatiently.

Steve glowered. "Cut me some slack."

Harker leaned back in his chair. "Word on the street is you've dated a few lovely lasses since our last meet."

"A few."

"Any winners?"

"Nah."

Taking another swig of pale ale, Steve thought of the women he'd gone out with. Pretty, brainless women. None had measured up to his ideal. Not that Gloria had been his ideal. On the other hand, though she was a self-centered egotist, she was smart—even if she couldn't spell Minneapolis; spelling wasn't all it was cracked up to be—and she was industrious. He liked someone who set goals.

"Have you met any of those kind, gentle women your mother wants you to meet?"

Like Hope? He said, "Nope."

"Hey, I know," Harker said. "Let's stop looking for jobs, and let's hook you up on a computer date with Mrs. Santa Claus. A woman like that would make your mom happy. A sweets-loving, cocoa-loving, gingerbread-house-loving beauty."

Steve threw his friend a scathing look. "Cut it out!" He moved to the railing again, glanced down at the street, and spotted a bunch of millennials entering a bar, most likely a handful of attractive, brainless women among them.

No, sir, Stevie boy. No more of them for you. In fact, no women at all.

He had to get his career on track. Period.

Chapter 12

Hope threw on her work blouse and trousers and tied her hair in a knot. Monday had rolled around too fast, and she couldn't dawdle. "Melody, come here and stand still," she said. "I've got to comb your hair." Melody groused, per usual, and wriggled, but Hope won the battle. After that task was completed, she said, "Now let's check your levels."

"Mo-om," Melody whined. "I'm good."

"Let's make sure." Hope did her best to manage Melody's diabetes with diet and exercise, but she still needed insulin shots.

Like a trouper, Melody allowed her mother to test and give her the required dose. When Hope was done, Melody joked, "Todd's turn."

"Not funny," Todd said.

"Listen, you two." Hope stowed the kit and tweaked the collar of Todd's polo shirt. "School's out for holiday vacation in a couple of days. I'm still trying to find daycare for you."

"I'm too old for daycare," Melody complained.

"Me, too," Todd said.

"Wrong." Hope ignored their protests. "It's the law. You cannot stay here, and you'll get super bored at the café if I bring you there and you have to sit in the kitchen alcove. Daycare it is."

"Let's find Daddy," Melody said. "He could watch us."

Find Zach. Right. As if. Hope's insides did a flip-flop. No way. Not an option. Not a possibility, honestly. "I don't have his address."

67

"He's in Portland," Melody said.

"Sweetheart, I'm not sure he's still there." The Christmas card she'd finally sent, addressed to one of his old friends, would no doubt be returned like last year's.

"I hate vacation," Todd said. "I'd rather be in school."

Melody cackled. "Weirdo."

Hope ruffled her son's hair. "It'll be fun. Promise."

After dropping the kids at school, Hope was awash with guilt. How was she going to continue to provide for them? She couldn't even find a sitter within her means. Life was unfair and she blamed Zach, but she knew in her heart of hearts, she ought to blame herself. She hadn't seen the signs of his weakness, of his betrayal, of his downfall. On the other hand, neither had her parents who had been her greatest advisors. They had adored Zach. To be truthful, she'd loved the first two years of their marriage. Right out of college, she'd invested in Pie in the Sky. Her parents had fronted her the seed money. Putting her marketing degree to work, she'd advertised like a pro and baked like a fiend. In that time, she must have made over five thousand pies, not to mention all the cakes, cookies, and eclairs that her customers enjoyed. When Melody came along, Hope took time off and allowed her sole assistant to manage the baking and sales. Zach, even though he was working full time at Tetra Tech, had handled the books.

And then Todd came along and things changed.

Zach changed.

Saving, my sweet daughter, her father had often said, *is how you create a retirement fund.* Who would have dreamed she'd have married a man who would run through everything she had without an ounce of regret? She'd never anticipated his gambling debts and his duplicity. She'd never predicted his ability to walk away without a second glance. Occasionally, Hope considered changing course and getting a job in marketing, the degree she'd earned in college. But in quaint Hope Valley? Forget about it.

"Daydreaming, Hope?" Gabe asked, catching her in a moment of reverie as she waited for an order of chocolate chip pancakes to appear.

Day-maring was more like it.

She licked her lips. "Sorry."

"What's going on in that creative brain of yours?" he asked.

"I'm thinking about my kids, Gabe." She swallowed hard. "Christmas vacation is coming up and, well, if I can't find daycare, is it okay to bring them to work? I promise they won't get in the way."

"Heh-heh." Gabe grinned. "I was just going to tell you about what my niece Khloe is up to. She's running a day camp this holiday season at the community center. She secured all the permits and has a friend on board to help. She has a head on her shoulders, that girl. She's ready to rock and roll. Your kids should go there."

"It's a nice idea, and they love Khloe, but it's probably out of my price bracket," Hope said.

Gabe put a hand on her shoulder. "You didn't let me finish. I've asked her to watch them for free. She owes me bigtime."

"Gabe, really? Are you sure?"

"Never been surer."

Hope was bubbling over with joy.

"Look here"—Gabe swooped an arm around her and pulled her close—"I can't have my best waitress running off and taking a better-paying job across the street, can I?"

"*Ahem!* I heard that," Zerena said, waltzing up to them. "I thought *I* was your best waitress. How many times have you said, 'Zerena, you are the best,' huh, Gabe?"

"Never."

"Liar."

"You're my second best," Gabe told Zerena, and then released Hope and chucked her chin. "Hope, here, is the best. The best of the best."

"Uh-uh." Zerena winked at Hope. "I am the best of the best, and don't you forget it."

"You are," Hope said. "You are my idol. I worship at your feet." She made mock-bowing motions.

Zerena let loose with a laugh. So did Gabe.

Hope grabbed the plate of pancakes with its order chit and made her way to the customer. Even from a distance, she could hear Zerena and Gabe still joshing each other.

"HO, HO, HO." STEVE paced his dressing room while tugging on the beard and plumping the stomach of his costume. He looked as much like Santa as the next guy, although he didn't have enough wrinkles and he definitely didn't have chubby enough cheeks.

Brie leaned into the room, holding the door and the jamb, her face freshly made up, the lapels of her navy suit protected by tissues. "Looking good, Santa, although I think your ho-ho-ho could use a little depth. Like so." Lowering her voice, she crooned, "Ho-ho-ho."

"Now you're a critic?"

"Just getting in the spirit." She chortled.

"How's it on the bail-the-ex-out-of-trouble front?" Steve asked.

"I've hired a lawyer."

"A wise woman."

"Move, Brie." Dave nudged her out of the way. "On the set in five, Waldren, and, FYI, you need more rouge."

Steve checked his image in the mirror. He'd added enough color already.

A short while later, he was sitting in his chair on the set. Santa's beard itched his chin, but he pushed the annoyance from his mind, and pressed onward. "The Trail Blazers were up by ten and lost it in the last two minutes," he said with enthusiasm mixed with regret. He loved his home team. Loved them. He'd made personal connections with most of the players. "By the way, folks, the last time that happened..." He rattled off a bunch of statistics. The numbers sailed through his head like a mental flowchart. When he was done, he said, "And that, as we say in the biz, is all we got for tonight. The scores. The highlights. He-e-y, we're outta here!" Steve crooned, ending with his signature sign-off.

Brie leaned toward Steve, her elbow braced on the news desk. "Hold the phone. You're not done, Santa. Isn't it time to remind the folks about the prize? This is the last night."

"Whoa! I almost forgot." Steve tapped his temple. "Santa needs a new brain."

Or a new job, he mused morosely.

"*Psst!*" Dave, standing to the side by the prompter, stuck his fingers in the corners of his mouth and stretched his lips—*smile.*

Steve sighed. If he smiled any more broadly, his cheeks would crack. "Brie, you're right. Ho, ho, ho, folks. You have another crack at winning the trip to Disneyland, all expenses paid." With bravado, he pointed a finger at the imaginary audience. "Are you feeling lucky? You know the drill. Ready, get set... Dial the number on the screen."

Ho, ho, holy crap, he thought. Gloria was right. He'd settled for less.

Chapter 13

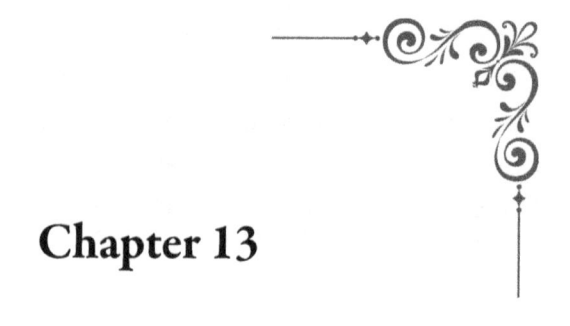

"Call, call, call!" Todd shouted.

Hope had given Melody control of the cell phone. Both kids had been at her from the moment they'd climbed into the VW after school demanding that they be allowed to listen to Steve Waldren again tonight. She'd promised, they reminded her. Despite the odds, she couldn't deny them.

"It's ringing," Melody said.

"And?" Todd rotated his hand.

"We'll get a recording," Melody assured him.

"Maybe not," Hope said, trying to instill optimism.

"Yeah," Melody sighed. "I got a recording."

Todd moaned.

"Wait!" Melody shouted. "Wait, wait, wait. The Voice—Steve—told me to hold." She eyed Hope. "Mom, did you hear me? Steve Waldren told me to *hold*."

"I heard you. The whole trailer park heard you." Hope forced a smile, knowing *hold* probably meant Melody would soon hear a recording thanking her for trying. Better luck next time.

After a long wait, Melody said, "Hi. I mean, hello. Me? You want to know my name?"

Hope gaped. Was Melody really talking to a person?

"Um, I'm Melody Lyons. Is it really you, Steve Waldren? The Steve Waldren?"

A shiver ran down Hope's spine. Had they truly gotten through? She felt like snatching the phone from Melody and speaking to Steve directly, but then a flurry of mixed emotions coursed through her. What would she say?

Melody cupped the phone. "Mom, it's him. It's really him. It's Steve Waldren." She removed her hand and said in singsong fashion, "It's nice to meet you, too, Steve. I mean, Mr. Waldren." She paused. "Okay, Steve. It's nice to talk to you. I mean—" She tittered.

Todd reached for the phone. "Let me say hi."

"No. I'm talking." Melody turned her back to her brother. "Yes, Steve?"

Hope glanced at the livestream on the computer and gawked. Steve Waldren, dressed as Santa—his beard and mustache were as white as snow, but it didn't hide his chiseled cheekbones—was talking on a telephone, and he was asking Melody about her family.

"I live with my brother, Todd, and my mother. Todd and I are big fans," Melody said. "Say hi, Todd."

"Hi!" He bellowed over Melody's shoulder. "Big fan, Steve!"

"Share the phone," Hope said, feeling proud and scared all at the same time. Her kids were going to be disappointed. The other family chosen on Saturday would win. Todd and Melody would lose. Nothing good was going to come of this. She regretted having let them call. But their faces, their sweet, adorable, grinning faces were precious.

Steve asked Todd how old he and his sister were.

"She's ten." Todd's voice cracked. "I'm almost eight."

In six months, Hope thought. *Seven and a half. A baby. They're both babies. My babies.*

Steve announced to his television audience that he was continuing the rest of the conversation off-camera because it involved personal information. He wished them all good night and signed off with his signature, "He-e-y, we're outta here!" and then his cohost, Brie Bryant, the beautiful black woman with teeth every dentist would be proud of, took over.

"Put the call on speaker phone," Hope ordered.

Todd obeyed.

"What's your address?" Steve asked.

Todd said, "We live—"

Hope snapped her fingers and took a step toward her children.

"No address," Melody chirped.

"I'm not following," Steve said.

Melody said loudly, "Our mom doesn't let us give out our address. It's private."

Relief shot through Hope. She'd taught them well. *Don't take candy from a stranger. Don't give anyone your phone number. Don't tell a soul where you live.*

"Good for you," Steve said. "Privacy is very important."

"But we live in Hope Valley like you used to," Todd blurted.

"Okay, kids, so you're from Hope Valley, huh? My folks live on Cherry Blossom Lane."

"We know," Melody chimed. "You went to Hope Valley High with our—"

Hope shook her head.

Melody chewed her lip. She whispered, "Why can't I tell him?"

"Because." Hope didn't have any better answer. She didn't want Steve to know it was her kids on the line. Sure, she'd told him about them when he'd been in town, but revealing that now seemed . . . What? Inappropriate?

"Yes, I went to Hope Valley High," Steve said. "Then I left to go to the University of Oregon, school of journalism."

"Wow," Todd uttered.

"Do you want to go to college, Melody?" Steve asked.

"You bet I do," Melody chimed. "I want to become a lawyer or an English teacher or a pro basketball player or—"

"That's great," Steve said, cutting her off as Hope had expected he would. He was a busy man. The minutiae he probably didn't want to have to deal with was over. "Now, what's your address? We need it in case you win."

Melody shook her head. "I already told you. Our mom won't let us give out that information."

"How about I talk with your mother?" Steve suggested. "Is she there?"

Hope wagged a finger and mouthed: *No.* Her heart was beating so fast. She knew she'd stammer.

"She can't come to the phone," Melody said. "She's washing her hair. She's a waitress and sometimes her hair smells like bacon."

Eau de café, Hope thought, getting a whiff of her hair.

"Okay, how about you tell me where she works, in case you win?" Steve pressed.

"Aroma Café," Todd belted. "Where your parents eat lots of breakfasts."

Hope glared at him.

"In case we win." Todd threw his arms wide.

"Aroma Café. Say, does your mom know a waitress named . . ." Steve hesitated.

Hope held her breath. Was he going to ask about her? No way. He didn't think of her. Not like she thought of him.

Steve said, "Yeah, never mind. Okay, kids, Aroma's good enough. I've got to go. Good luck."

"Bye, Steve," they screamed. Melody stabbed *End*.

Hope took the cell phone from them and pressed it to her chest.

Chapter 14

At the end of the basketball recap Tuesday night, Steve said, "Ho, ho, ho. It's time to announce the Spirit of Christmas winner." Man, the Santa suit was itchy. And it stunk. Two shows with him sweating under the spotlights hadn't done it any favors. If he worked as a drycleaner, he'd refuse the suit at the door. He turned to Brie, who looked overdressed in her royal blue sheath and dangling earrings. "My stalwart companion, do you want to do the honors?"

"Of course not, Santa," Brie said. "It's your time to shine."

Directing his focus to the camera, Steve said, "Ladies and gentlemen, boys and girls, we have the entrants from the two days." He held up two three-by-five cards filled with information. "One of these lucky families will win the grand prize. Are you ready?" He cupped his ear as if waiting to hear the audience's reply.

I'm a phony, he thought. *Big phony.*

Forcing a grin, he shouted, "Okay, then. Here we go." He folded the cards in half, dropped them into a clear glass bowl, and stirred. Then he offered the bowl to Brie.

She dipped her hand in, selected one of the two, crooned, "Fa-la-la," and gave it to Steve.

Steve raised the card and read: "Todd and Melody Lyons. Congratulations. You've won!"

Red and green confetti popped out of cannons and showered Steve and Brie. The strains of "Jolly Old St. Nick" rang out.

Steve spit confetti out of his mouth. "Todd and Melody, if you're listening, we'll be in touch." Then he gave his signature sign-off and leaned back in his chair. *Done. Finito.* He wouldn't have to wear this suit again, and he could once again look for a new job. *Los Angeles or New York, Chicago, or wherever, here I come.*

The cameras turned off and lights dimmed.

At the same time, Dave rushed onto the set. "You dolt. Those are the kids who didn't give you any information other than their mother's place of business."

"Hey, what do you want from me?" Steve spread his arms. "It's not like I could rig the thing. We had two names. One of two would win. A fifty-fifty chance."

"Voice, they're from your home town," Brie said.

He threw up both hands. "Whoa! I didn't rig it."

"Not saying you did. But maybe you know them."

Steve scratched his ear. *Lyons.* No, he didn't know anyone named Lyons.

"You need to go there," Dave said.

"Huh?" Steve coughed.

"Are you deaf? You need to go there! To Hope Valley!" Dave ordered. "Dress up as Santa and find this mother and get her permission in writing to award the prize."

"Dress up as—"

"Santa!"

"I can't go," Steve countered. "I've got—"

"Interviews?"

"KPRL donor events."

"You'll do as I say, or else."

"But—"

"Job security." Dave chopped the air. Once. Twice. Steve got the message. Or else Dave would give him the ax.

Behind Dave's back, Brie was joyfully miming his erratic movements.

Steve bit back a smile... and tamped down bile. "Fine. But Brie is going with me."

"Good idea," Dave said. "Take your camera, Brie. Document everything."

Brie gave a celebratory whoop. "Road trip!"

ON WEDNESDAY MORNING, Steve awakened and groaned. For two hours last night, he'd complained to Harker on the phone while drinking beer. Dumb, dumb, and dumber. In the end, Harker had convinced him to follow through with the road trip saying Steve needed his job. For now.

At eight a.m., Steve, yet again dressed as Santa, was on the road in his SUV with Brie. At least Dave had provided a new suit so Steve wasn't stinking up the car. Brie looked cozy, bundled in a cocoa-colored parka, cream turtleneck, and tapered blue jeans.

"You okay, Santa?" she asked between sips of coffee from her to-go cup. "A little hot under the fur collar?"

"Ha-ha. Can it!" He pressed his foot on the accelerator, teeth tight.

Brie tapped the radio station buttons until she landed on a station playing "The Little Drummer Boy." She said, "What an apropos song for you, don't you think? Dave commands. You march to his beat."

"Funny," Steve sniped. "Very funny. Ever thought about doing standup?"

"Thought about it. Passed."

"As a matter of fact, that's my brother's favorite song."

"Aw."

"Explain why you're accompanying me?" he asked, knowing the answer.

"You picked me."

"You could have opted out."

"And miss this hometown opportunity to see you grovel to give away a prize? Way too much fun. No way would I pass."

Humiliation was making Steve hungry. He pulled over at a gas station. They both got out and entered the mini mart. Steve purchased a donut.

"Want one?" he asked Brie.

"No thanks. You'd better watch the calories, Santa," she quipped. "You don't want to burst out of that suit."

"You're a laugh riot."

"You used to think so."

He and Brie had formed a good bond over the years. They had each other's backs. He loved her, but right now, he loathed her. The moment they climbed into the SUV and secured their seatbelts, Steve ground the car into gear.

"A little hostility on the road isn't smart, Santa."

"Kiss my reindeer."

"You know, I've never been a fan of Christmas," Brie said, "but driving through Oregon, seeing town after town dressed up for the holidays, I'm getting in the spirit. Your parents decorate, don't they?"

"Yeah," Steve muttered. "In all its glory. They even sponsor the town's gingerbread house contest."

"Fun! I've never made one."

"Lucky you." Steve couldn't count how many gumdrops he'd eaten over the years. If he never ate another one, he wouldn't regret it. However, he did like the way his mother beamed at the event. She truly enjoyed engaging her customers.

Brie turned up the volume on the radio. "Santa Claus is Coming to Town" blared through the speakers.

"Switch it off," Steve said.

"Touchy touchy." Brie lowered the volume. "Are your folks excited to see you?"

"Over the moon." Steve had called them before leaving. His mother promised not to let Lincoln in on the secret until Steve arrived. His brother couldn't handle anticipation.

Brie swiveled in her seat. "I think I'm going to retire."

"Serious?"

"As a heart attack. I'd like to do it while I'm young enough to enjoy it."

"I thought you were a lifer."

"Don't get me wrong, I love my job, but I'd like to worship at the altar of *Fun* for the remainder of my life. Hard to do paying rent in a big city. I think I'll move to a remote village, become a hermit, and finally publish my book of photography. It's written and ready to go."

"How do you *write* a photography book?"

"I add comments to each of the photos I've included. I'd like to publish it before I die. I've submitted it to a few publishing houses. Now it's the waiting game. And I'd like to travel. Maybe get paid to do some freelance work while I do so. What about you?"

"I've got years before I rest."

"Are you saying I'm old?"

"No, ma'am, you're mature." Steve threw her a wicked grin.

"So, tell me, why are you keen on leaving KPRL?"

He cut her a look sideways. "Who told you?"

"It's general news. You're not subtle, dude."

"Are you the reason Dave knows?"

"*Moi?* Not a chance." She pressed a hand to her chest. "I'd bet he's bugged your dressing room."

Steve groaned. Of course. That made sense.

"So why? You're a big deal in a medium market. Is it because of Gloria?"

"No," Steve said a tad too quickly. "I just need a change. Like you. And, let's face it, Dave isn't easy to tolerate."

"Tell me about it." Brie slotted her cup into the cupholder. "Have you ever considered radio? You are the *Voice* after all."

"Get out of here." Steve threw her an incredulous look. "Radio is a dying art. Podcasting could be where it's at, though."

"And how does one make money doing a podcast?"

"Not sure. Ad buys?"

"I suck at promotion."

"Nothing's easy," Steve said.

Brie faced forward and smiled, enjoying the view. "I can't believe how white the snow is. It's so beautiful and serene."

And boring, which was why Steve had left Hope Valley for college and had never looked back. He'd wanted adventure. He'd wanted to travel the world. He'd wound up in Portland. Big whoop!

Chapter 15

Wednesdays were invariably busy at Aroma Café. Hope had been bustling from the moment she'd entered the café without a moment to think about her children or her life or her dream of saving enough to start over. She was so busy that by two p.m., her feet were killing her and perspiration was swizzling down her back.

As she was serving strawberry waffles to table six—breakfast was offered all day—the door to the cafe opened. A man dressed as Santa and a stunning African American woman, who was bundled as warmly as if she was prepared to visit the North Pole, sauntered in. The woman looked familiar, but Hope couldn't place her. Santa hitched his belt over his fake belly. He was obviously too thin for the heavy suit. His gaze landed on Hope, and he smiled.

That was when she recognized the two of them. It was Steve Waldren and his co-host, Brie Bryant.

Hope said, "Help you, Santa?"

"Hey, Hope, it's me, Steve Waldren," he said under his breath. "We met last year."

"I know," she whispered.

"I've been meaning to . . ." He didn't finish and cleared his throat. "Ho, ho, ho. Merry Christmas, Hope Valley," he bellowed to the entire café and weaved heartily. "Me and my assistant are looking for Mrs. Lyons. Todd and Melody's mother. I have a prize to bestow. Young lady, can you point me in the right direction? Ho, ho, ho."

Hope faltered. "Steve, I'm . . . I'm Mrs. Lyons. Hope Lyons."

"Really? It's you?" His eyes twinkled with good humor as he threw his shoulders back and crooned, "Congratulations, Hope Lyons." He whipped a piece of paper and pen from his pocket. "You and your children have won an all-expenses paid vacation to Disneyland. All I need is your signature of consent. Merry Christmas! You are one lucky lady."

Hope yelped.

Gabe hurried from behind the counter. "Is there a problem, Hope?"

People in the café were staring at her. She couldn't find her voice. Her children won the contest? Honestly? No, it couldn't be true, could it? She hadn't let the children watch the show last night, too worried that when they didn't hear Steve say their names, they'd go to bed crying.

Gabe eyed Steve. "Santa, I'm the owner. What's going on? Why is my best waitress speechless?"

Zerena tapped Gabe on the shoulder and mock-growled. "I'm your best waitress."

Gabe didn't acknowledge her and lasered Steve with his gaze. "Speak up, Santa."

Again, Steve cleared his throat. His eyes flickered with wariness. "Gabe, sir, it's me. Steve Waldren. Hope Lyons and her family have just won an all-expenses paid trip to Disneyland from KPRL to be taken any time between January and March."

"Photo op," Brie said, aiming her Nikon at Hope. "Santa get in there. Smile."

Steve slid in beside Hope and slung an arm around her. The warmth of him, the nearness of him made her woozy.

Brie snapped a series of shots and repeated, "Smile, Mrs. Lyons. Lots of teeth."

Hope couldn't. Her lips were tight. Her throat had gone as dry as parchment paper. Suddenly, she realized she hadn't thought the whole thing through. If she accepted the prize, she'd miss work. She'd lose pay. She couldn't afford to do that. "No, thank you," she said. "It's very nice of you to offer, but no thank you."

"No thank you?" Steve dropped his arm and faced Hope. He looked flabbergasted. Pained, almost.

Gabe put a hand on Hope's shoulder. "Now, wait a sec, darlin'. Don't give it up out of hand."

Hope backed up a step. "I'm sorry, Santa . . . Steve . . . but we can't. Find someone else." She turned to retreat to the kitchen.

Steve followed her. "Wait a sec. You can't refuse the prize."

"Yes, I can." Hope whirled on him. "Read my lips. No, thank you."

Brie's mouth dropped open. Virtually everyone in the café looked stunned.

"Maybe you didn't understand," Steve said. "All expenses paid."

Hope put her hands on her hips. "What about snacks? Mementoes? Movies on the hotel television? Side trips? Silly but adorable hats? And are you going to cover my time away from work?"

Steve glanced at Brie and back at Hope.

"Yeah, no, I didn't think so, Santa. Not *all* expenses," Hope snapped. "No, thanks. We have to pass."

"But your kids will be disappointed," Steve said.

"My kids will rally." Before she could change her mind, Hope fled into the kitchen.

STEVE STARTED AFTER her.

"Hold it, Santa." Brie put a hand on his arm and held him back. "You understand when a woman says *no*, don't you?"

"Can it, Brie. This is my job we're talking about."

"Your job?"

Steve pressed his lips together, unwilling to say more. He didn't want to test Dave. Not until he had another job lined up. He scanned the café. People were staring at him, and he felt anger rise up his throat. How dare Hope Lyons embarrass him like that? And to think he'd been fantasizing about her all this time. Crap! What had gotten into her? Another notion reared its ugly head. What if Dave found out what Hope had done? Was anyone other than Brie taking photos? Or worse, videos? Would Hope's refusal go viral on YouTube? On TikTok? That's all he needed, an Internet hailstorm.

"Cut!" He mimed to Brie, ending the photoshoot.

Obediently, she capped the camera and let it hang on the strap around her neck. Then she jutted her hand to Gabe and smiled broadly. "Hello, sir. I'm Brie Bryant. KPRL."

"Gabe Greeley. Aroma Café. And please don't call me sir. I'm Gabe to everyone." He gestured toward his café. "Welcome to the best food in town. Let me find you a table."

"Gabe," Steve said, seething, "is Hope Lyons always this prickly?" He shot a hand toward the kitchen. "I mean, get real. A free trip. For her kids. Don't they deserve it?"

"Son, her husband left her high and dry. She had a life before Hope Valley. And she's struggling to make it work, but . . ." Gabe sighed. "As she made very clear, she doesn't want her kids to face disappointment. Going to Disneyland and not having the whole ball of wax? That can leave a bad taste, you know? So, what she says goes, in my book." Gabe made a thumbs-up gesture. "She's like a daughter to me. I won't argue with her, and if I were you—"

"But it's a free trip." Steve splayed his hands. "How can that be a disappointment?"

"I went to Disneyland two years ago," Gabe said. "The lines were long, and I didn't see Mickey Mouse. Not once. Plus, like she said, everything costs an arm and a leg. Want a photo on Splash Mountain? Pay for it. Want a—"

"All expenses paid!" Steve smacked one gloved hand against the other.

Gabe reiterated Hope's question, "What about snacks and mementoes?"

"And silly adorable hats?" Brie quipped.

Steve snarled at her.

Gabe said, "Give Hope some time, Steve. Maybe she'll reconsider. In the meantime, sit. Lunch is on me." He grabbed a couple of menus and led Steve and Brie to a table. "Let me chat with her."

Brie whipped open her menu and batted her eyelashes at Gabe. "What's the specialty here, handsome?"

Steve gawked. He couldn't remember the last time he'd seen Brie flirt.

"Pancakes," Gabe said. "The cranberry ones with whipped cream are my seasonal favorite."

"Done." Brie slapped her menu closed.

Steve said, "I'll have eggs, crisp bacon, and coffee. Lots of coffee."

When Gabe left the table, Brie leaned in and said, "How about a piece of humble pie, Voice?"

"And pumpkin pie, if you have it," Steve called after Gabe.

Gabe waved a hand in acknowledgement.

"Hope makes the most incredible pie crust," Steve said. "She bakes all the pies here."

"You don't say." Brie propped her elbow on the table and leaned her chin on her fingers. "When did you two lovebirds meet?"

"A year ago. When I came to see Lincoln."

"Aww."

Steve folded his arms on the table and slumped forward as another wave of crankiness scudded through him. "Can you believe it? She refused. Flat out refused."

"Not everyone likes theme parks."

"If Dave finds out."

"He won't."

"Oh, yeah? Wanna bet?" Steve flailed a hand. "How many people in here have caught it on their cell phones and sent videos to KPRL by now? Ten? Twenty?"

A waitress—her nametag read *Zerena*—set two glasses of ice water on the table and left.

Steve drank down the contents and slammed the glass on the table. "Man, she chose the wrong day to buck me."

"To buck *you*?"

"Yeah. I'm on a mission." Steve stabbed the table with a fingertip. "I intend to see it through. Or else."

Brie chortled. "Or else what, Big Man?"

"Or else I strangle that woman."

"She's quite pretty," Brie said.

Yeah, she was, Steve had to admit. As beautiful as the woman he repeatedly dreamed about. So what? And double *so what* if he'd been thinking about her on the drive to Hope Valley, clinging to the possibility that she was the waitress in question? After all, she'd said she had kids and they watched his show.

Zerena set a plate with a slice of pie on the table. "Eggs and pancakes are coming."

Steve didn't give a frick about eggs. He tucked into the pie with gusto.

Chapter 16

Hope swiped her fingers underneath both eyes to mop up tears. She hated crying. Hated feeling weak and vulnerable. She'd shed a boatload of tears over Zach and what had they gotten her? Squat.

Gabe entered the kitchen.

"What do you want?" she snapped defensively.

"Darlin'." He wrapped an arm around her. "What aren't you telling me?"

Hope melted into him, appreciating his support, but she couldn't tell him everything. She simply couldn't tolerate pity. She would muscle through this. "Nothing," she murmured.

"Liar. And let me tell you, secrets aren't good for the soul," he said. "I know. They eat you from the inside out."

"I . . . I don't have a secret," she stammered.

"Is it your no-good husband? Has he established limits for your kids? Has he said there's no fun for them unless he's there to share in it?"

"No, he—"

"As if he has any right. He ceded those the day he walked out. What kind of man does that?" Gabe released Hope and stared hard at her. "No man, I tell you. No man worth his salt."

"It's not him. He didn't . . ." She shook her head. "It's just that I've heard about Disneyland, and it's not all it's cracked up to be."

"Happiest place on earth," Gabe quipped.

"Yeah, but the kids don't need it. Not really. They've got plenty to make them happy in Hope Valley."

"Kids might not *need* something, Hope, but it doesn't mean they don't *want* it. They called in to KPRL. That means they want the prize, and they won." He kissed her on the forehead. "Take some time. Maybe go for a walk. Find your smile and think about it. In the meantime, I'm tending to Steve and his colleague."

"Colleague? How formal." Hope elbowed Gabe.

His cheeks tinged pink.

"She's quite attractive," Hope said.

"Is she?"

"And successful. She has a beautiful smile."

"Yes, she does."

Hope threw on her parka and headed outside, thankful for a moment to decompress. The instant she turned onto Main Street, she dug deep into her motives. Why had she turned down the prize? Yes, because she'd lose days of work, and yes, because there would be extra expenses not covered by the *all-expenses-paid* promise, but was there more to it? Did she want to confine Todd and Melody to Hope Valley? To narrow their horizons? Her stomach soured when she thought about what her children would do if they heard about the run-in with Santa. What if they learned they'd won the prize but she'd rejected it? They would hate her. Her personal reasons wouldn't hold sway with them. They were kids. They needed fun. They needed to dream.

Hope paused in front of an art store, her spirits sagging. She'd failed them. Failed them for not being able to turn Zach around. Failed them for not being able to make a go of it in Portland on her own. Failed...

"Excuse me," a woman said, cutting around Hope.

She looked up. It seemed she wasn't the only one who'd had the idea to get some fresh air. Dozens of people were strolling along the sidewalks. To fool herself into feeling brighter and normal, she pushed away her negative thoughts and greeted each person she passed with a smile.

At Happy Paws, she peered in the window. Four adorable tuxedo cats were roaming the kitty condo. Plenty of customers were milling about. At Cathy's Closet, the owner was tweaking a display model, fitting it with the latest in upscale winter jumpsuits. Beyond the owner, Hope spied at least six eager women waiting to ring up their purchases. At the Art Guild, two customers seemed to be arguing over an oil painting of Mt. Hope dusted with snow.

Sweet Place was as busy as Hope had ever seen it. A long line of customers picking up pre-ordered cakes or pies had formed on one side of the raspberry-pink shop. An equally long line of people had formed on the opposite side to put in new orders.

"Hey, Hope." Denny Benton stepped out of the bakery. He looked merry in his red sweater and green scarf. The pink box tied with green raffia that he was carrying looked festive, too. "How are you?"

"Pre-occupied. What did you buy?"

"Cookies for my mom." He jiggled the box.

"You and she are close."

"Sure are. Ever since Dad passed. She's having an early Christmas party this year so she can go on a cruise with a bunch of girlfriends."

"That sounds like fun."

"My mom always has a great time, no matter what she's doing. She's that kind of person."

Like my parents, Hope reflected. How she missed them. How she could use their wise counsel now.

"Where are you off to?" Denny asked.

"I'm walking through town to mull over a problem."

"Want me to join you?"

Hope shook her head. "Don't take it personally, but I need to figure this out on my own."

"I'm a good problem solver and an even better listener. My mom says—"

"That's sweet, Denny. Thanks for the offer. But no. And I bet your mom is looking forward to receiving those cookies. Plus, I just remembered, I have to buy a book." Hope picked up her pace, leaving Denny standing in front of the bakery. From a discreet distance, she glanced over her shoulder. He looked perplexed.

At the Curious Reader, Hope turned in and drew in a deep breath. Visiting the store always stirred memories for her. Her mother reading to her young customers. Her father whistling as he opened a new shipment of books. The *cha-ching* of the cash register. Nothing had changed in the shop since her parents had owned it. It still featured floor-to-ceiling bookshelves on the walls and moveable bookshelves placed helter-skelter. As usual, placards touting the most popular books stood atop each of the moveable shelves. For the season, the owner Isabel, a former librarian who'd always dreamed of owning a bookshop, had positioned miniature Christmas trees alongside the placards. Twinkling lights lined the edges of the ceiling. Instrumental strains of "O, Tannenbaum" was playing merrily through a speaker at the register.

Isabel said, "Hope, how lovely to see you." As skinny as a licorice whip, she looked even thinner in her thigh-length sweater over denim leggings. "Did you see the sign?" She nudged her wirerimmed glasses higher on her nose. "We have a two-for-one sale today."

Hope brightened. In her Christmas budget, she'd planed a book apiece for her children. Getting two for each would make their holiday that much merrier. It wouldn't squelch the pain of not winning the Disneyland trip, but it would be a start. Why, why, why did it have to be Steve Waldren delivering the prize? She'd hated turning him down. The pained look in his eyes nearly made her reconsider.

"Isabel!" an elderly customer cried from across the store. "Help." She was carrying a stack of at least twenty books.

"Oh, mercy," Isabel murmured. "That woman does this every time, even though I tell her to bring her purchases to the counter. Roam to your heart's content," she said, and raced to assist.

Hope found herself breathing easier as she studied book titles. By the time she'd found two for Melody and a sports-themed book and graphic novel for Todd, she was at peace, convinced she had been right to have turned down the prize.

Life was filled with disappointment, but that didn't mean joy couldn't be found in simpler things.

Chapter 17

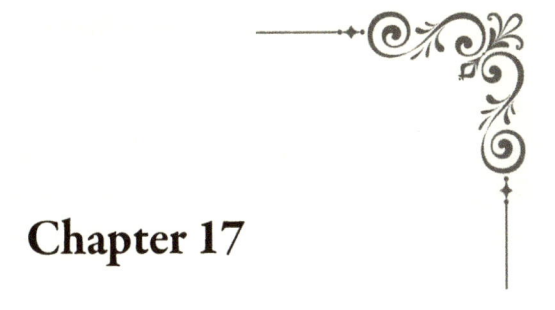

Steve hung around the café for another hour, but Hope didn't return. He learned from the waitress that had served him that Hope had texted she was going home for the day. When he pressed for her address, she said she didn't know where Hope lived. Outside the restaurant, Brie gave Steve guff for scaring Hope away.

"You came on strong, Voice."

"Stop calling me Voice."

"She's a mama bear with cubs. You have to tread softly."

"I won't be deterred. In the morning, I'm gonna return and use my inimitable charm to persuade her to say yes."

"Inimitable. Big word."

"Inimitable," he repeated, convincing himself he could accomplish his mission. Heck, he had to. And, honestly, didn't her kids deserve the prize? Wasn't she the bad guy in this scenario?

Dusk was settling in and a light snow was falling as Steve drove Brie to her bed-and-breakfast, a charming Victorian-style establishment a couple blocks from his parents' house. Yes, he would be staying with his folks, but he didn't want to arrive there in the Santa suit, so he begged Brie for permission to shower in her room—he stank of frustration; she didn't disagree—and then he shrugged into the jeans and green sweater he'd stowed at the top of his overnighter, spritzed the Santa suit with an odor-eliminating spray brought specifically for the task, and he and Brie continued on to Cherry Blossom Lane.

He parked on the street and at the foot of his parents' walkway paused and drank in their handiwork. As always, their home was decorated with love. The towering pine tree was decked out with colored lights. All the windows were trimmed with holly. A fake Santa was affixed to the roof, tiptoeing near the chimney with his big red sack over his shoulder. And good old Rudolph was perched beside Santa, his nose blinking merrily.

Brie whistled. "Wow. Your folks go all out. I should've worn a more colorful outfit if I'd known." She'd donned a white sweater over leggings and boots.

Steve chuckled and opened the front door. "Merry Christmas!"

"Stevie." His mother hurried to embrace him in the foyer.

The aroma of something savory wafted into the foyer. An early recording of Frank Sinatra crooning "It Came Upon a Midnight Clear" was playing in the living room.

"It's so good to see you," his mother said. She was wearing her lucky gingerbread sweater, the one she'd knitted when she was pregnant with him. On numerous occasions, she'd claimed that he'd been a tough pregnancy and had tossed and turned as though he would never be satisfied. The knitting had gotten her through the ordeal.

Life hasn't changed much, has it, Stevie boy? he thought. *You're still a pain in the—*

"You look so handsome." His mother kissed his cheek. "Brie," she said warmly, giving her a hug. "I wish you were staying with us, too."

"Thank you, Mrs. Waldren, but I'm a bit of a night owl. I need my own space."

"Call me Ellery. We're not formal."

Booking a room at the inn would have given Steve the privacy he craved, but he couldn't do that to his folks. He would be staying in his old room, adorned with the same décor as when he'd been in high school, his journalism awards prominently displayed. He'd almost begged off, not eager to get into lengthy all-night discussions about his career and Lincoln, and well, life in general. He definitely didn't want to talk about Gloria. His mother had pressed him for weeks about their split, and he and Harker had exhausted that topic *ad finitum*. She was doing well in Minneapolis. That was all he knew.

"Frank," Ellery yelled over her shoulder. "Frank, they're here! Look it's Steve and Brie." She turned on her heel and led the two of them into the house. "Frank!"

Brie stopped in the middle of the foyer and glanced at Steve, her eyes wide.

He nodded. "Yep, even inside the decorations are over the top, but my folks love getting into the spirit."

"All we had growing up was a wreath and a fake two-foot tree. This is so cool!"

Steve hadn't spent a lot of personal time with Brie, but he liked her. At moments like these, he wished he knew more about her.

"Merry Christmas!" Steve's father appeared at the end of the hall in a cardigan sweater over a buttoned-down shirt. He was carrying a plate of cheese and crackers and assorted olives. "Son." He hugged Steve with his free arm and released him, then shot a hand out. "Welcome, Brie."

"Mr. Waldren," Brie said, shaking with him.

"Call me Frank," he said.

Ellery jutted a hand. "Doesn't Brie look fabulous, Frank? She's so pretty. Your skin is glowing. You'll have to tell me your beauty treatments." She clutched Brie's elbow and drew her further into the house. "White suits you, dear."

Steve paused in the foyer and drank in the rest of the decorations. Running lights everywhere. A Christmas train—his father's handiwork, fostered by Steve's love of trains at the age of five—circled the upper perimeter of the living room, its soft whistle whooshing under the music. Stockings were hung by the chimney with care. There weren't any gifts in them yet. No matter how old Lincoln and Steve got, their mother insisted that Santa filled the stockings on Christmas Eve.

Steve sighed. Yes, indeed, Christmas was a beautiful tradition at his family's household. If only he felt an ounce of *fa-la-laughter*. *Hope*, he thought. Could he persuade her to take the prize, or would she shoot him down again and ruin his life?

"Steve! Steve! Steve!" Lincoln hurtled the last four stairs and landed with a thump inches from Steve. He was wearing a snowman-themed Christmas sweater. His hair looked like he'd used an eggbeater to comb it. "I knew you'd come!" He threw his arms around Steve and hugged. Hard.

Steve didn't resist. He hugged back, but jokingly said, "*Oof!* Bro. I need to breathe. Have you been working out?" Steve was the only person Lincoln would hug. His mother and father envied the contact.

"Yeah. Weights," Lincoln said, releasing him and flexing his muscles. "Repetition is good."

"Repetition *is* good," Steve said, and offered a fist.

"It's all good," Lincoln said. "Good, good, good now that you're here." He banged his knuckles against Steve's, and they both fluttered their fingers, saying "Pow!" in unison. Steve had taught his brother the greeting when he was a toddler.

For a half hour, Steve, Brie, and his family sat in the living room drinking eggnog, snacking on appetizers, and chatting. Brie did her best to regale Steve's parents with her first impression of the trip to town. The glistening snow. The lack of traffic. The magnificent elk that had stared at them from the side of the road. The town's wonderfully festive decorations.

"Can you tell she's in love with Hope Valley?" Steve quipped.

"What's not to love?" his mother replied.

At seven, they retired to the dining room. The rectangular walnut table was set with the twelve days of Christmas placemats and napkins Steve had given his mother four years ago. A pair of red-and-green nutcrackers flanked by pillar candles served as the centerpiece. His mother told Brie to sit beside Steve. Lincoln sat opposite them. Steve's father took the far end of the table.

"A feast is coming," his mother announced. "You'd better be hungry."

Since Steve wasn't going to be home for Christmas dinner, having told his mother that he could only stay a couple of days, she'd prepared a complete holiday dinner, including turkey with all the trimmings. The aroma of the savory sage stuffing yanked Steve back to his junior high school years when his father had asked him to help make the dish. Steve had misread the word teaspoons as tablespoons. Big mistake. But that was what had steered him into learning how to cook and bake, and he'd gotten better at measurements over the years. In truth, he really did like making cookies. He hadn't given Hope a line last year.

"These sweet potatoes," Brie gushed, heaping a second portion onto her plate after she polished off every bite of her meal. "I've never tasted anything like them."

"It's my recipe," Lincoln said.

Ellery confirmed that it was. "He added the marshmallows all my himself. An entire bag."

Brie tittered.

After the main meal, Steve rose from the table and helped his mother clear the dishes and put them in the dishwasher. Then he carried out the desserts, a choice of cherry cheesecake or Yule log. Steve had to laugh. Both were large enough to serve twelve.

"It's not as if any of it will go to waste," his mother argued. "It'll all get eaten."

"No pie?" Steve joked.

"I figured you'd have eaten a piece at the café already, you liked it so much on your visit last December."

Steve winced. He hadn't told his parents about playing Santa to deliver the prize. He hadn't said Hope turned it down flat, either. He'd only mentioned that he'd stopped at the café in an effort to show Brie around.

"Brie," Ellery said as she rounded the table offering homemade whipped cream, "what are your plans for the future?"

"Future?" Brie eyed Steve, an impish grin spreading across her face. "As a matter of fact, I was talking about that very subject on the way here. I'm thinking of retiring."

"Retiring?" Ellery clucked. "Why? You're so young."

Brie scoffed. "Nice of you to say, Ellery, but I'm pushing sixty."

"No way. You don't look a day over forty."

"Ha!"

Ellery pressed Brie for more details. What would she do? Where did she want to travel? As they talked, Steve leaned back in his chair. He didn't want to retire, and he sure as heck didn't want to be fired. Slyly, he texted his agent from beneath the table: *Anything?*

"So, Steve," his father said, "let's discuss the elephant in the room. You didn't come to town just to see us. You brought Brie. So what's the deal, Son?"

"I—" Steve hesitated.

Brie said, "He's supposed to give a prize to the winner of KPRL's Spirit of Christmas contest. A Hope Valley local. And he tried, but she didn't want it."

"Why didn't she want it?" His father snickered. "What was it? Two tickets to a Trail Blazer's game? If so, I'd have passed, too. The team's been on a losing streak since early November."

Brie said, "No, it's an—"

"All-expenses paid trip to Disneyland!" Lincoln blurted. "Steve's been pitching it on TV. Didn't you see that, Da-a-ad? Where's your head been, in the clouds?" he added, using a line their father had used for years on Lincoln . . . to center him.

Frank whistled. "I must have missed that."

"He falls asleep in front of the TV," his mother said to Brie.

"Do not."

"Do, too."

Lincoln said, "I want to go to Disneyland."

"Yes, dear, we know." Ellery patted his cheek, then set the cream aside, and took her seat. "So what happened, Steve? Why did she refuse?"

"He dressed up as Santa," Brie quipped. "It turns out she's afraid of mall Santas."

"I didn't look like a mall Santa."

She chortled.

Steve huffed. "She was rude about it."

"She wasn't rude," Brie said.

"Yeah, she was."

"Okay, changing subjects," his mother said sweetly. "Brie, is there anyone special in your life?"

Steve leaned forward on one elbow. "Yeah, Brie, do tell."

Brie's eyes widened, making her look like a deer in headlights.

"Steve, stop," his mother said. "Don't tease."

"Who's teasing? Brie is about as close to the vest as anyone I know when it comes to talking about her personal life. Three disastrous relationships, and, *wham*"—he smacked his hands together—"she bans men from her life."

"Disastrous is a bit harsh," Brie countered.

"Is it?" Steve cocked an eyebrow. "You've been moping about your last husband for a long time."

"You're one to talk," she sniped. "The weather girl leaves for a better paying job, and you pine about her for a year."

"Six months. She left in June."

"Six months. Half a year." Lincoln held up a finger with each pronouncement. "Twenty-six weeks. One hundred and eighty-two days."

Ellery chuckled. "We know, dear."

Brie bit back a smile and took a sip of the chardonnay she'd brought as a housewarming gift.

"I'm not pining," Steve said.

Brie said to Ellery and Frank, "Definite bouts of pining." She pulled a pouty face. They laughed.

More jabs continued through dessert. Frank soft-balled a few to Steve, who ribbed Ellery, who joked with Lincoln in just the way she knew she could without riling him. Lincoln laughed more openly than Steve could remember. Maybe his little brother was coming around.

Don't kid yourself, Stevie boy. He knew as well as his parents that Lincoln would always struggle. Society, even social do-gooders, didn't understand him and never would.

As Ellery and Brie removed dessert plates from the table, Steve's father said, "So tell us more about this woman who turned down the prize. Who is she? What does she do?"

"She's a waitress at Aroma Café," Brie offered before leaving the room.

"Do we know her?" his father asked.

"It's Hope Lyons," Steve said sullenly.

Lincoln said, "We love Hope."

"She refused me!" Steve cried.

"Hope?" Ellery hurried in, wiping her hands on her apron. Brie followed her. "Did you say it was Hope? Steve, darling, Hope is the sweetest girl in the world. She couldn't have been rude."

"She was taken aback," Brie said.

"Taken aback. Bah. *Rude.*" Steve folded his arms.

"She's kind to everyone," his mother went on. "Never a harsh word. Always a smile."

"She's very good with Lincoln," his father said. "You saw her when you visited last year. So even-tempered. So patient. Why she even plays knock-knock jokes with him. Right, Son?"

Lincoln gave their father a thumbs up. "Hope gets me."

Steve guffawed. "She *gets* you?"

"She knows what I need. All the time."

Ellery put her hand on Steve's shoulder. "Did you consider that Hope might be . . . proud?" She worked her tongue in her mouth, deliberating. "After all, she's a single woman raising two kids. Her husband left her—"

"Gabe told me, and I get it, and, yeah, it sucks." Steve splayed his hands. "But, c'mon, doesn't she owe it to her kids to say yes to the prize? It's Disneyland!"

Lincoln said, "I want to go to Disneyland."

Steve snarled. "I know."

"What's the big deal if she doesn't accept the prize, Son?" his father asked.

"I'll lose my job."

Brie gasped. "What? Are you kidding me? Is that what Dave meant when he said *job security*? And doing this?" She mimed axing. "He was threatening to fire you if—"

"If I didn't get her to sign off. Yeah." Steve slapped his napkin on the table. "Can you believe that? Fire me for something I can't control!"

"Why, that . . ." Brie hissed something under her breath.

"Let us talk to Hope," Ellery said.

Steve shook his head. "No, Mom, thanks, but this is up to me. I'll give it another try. Tomorrow. After she's had a night to think about it." Steve wondered when Dave would call for results. For pictures. So far he hadn't. But if Steve didn't nail this tomorrow . . .

"That's the spirit." His mother kissed the top of his head.

"I want to watch the news," Lincoln announced, and bounded from the room.

Brie yawned. "I'm going to head back to the inn."

"I'll walk you," Steve said.

"Uh-uh." Ellery grabbed Steve's shoulders. "Your father will walk her. You spend time with your brother." She spun him in the right direction. "Put your sour side away." She gave him a squeeze. "Lincoln needs you. And, truth? You need him."

Chapter 18

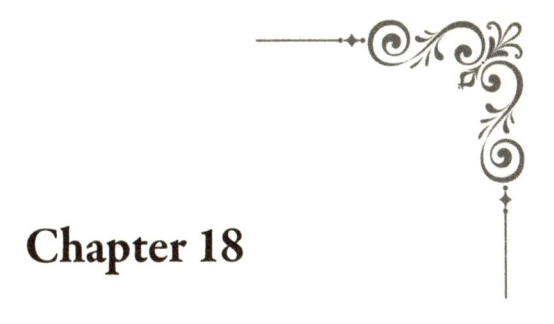

Steve joined Lincoln in the den, a welcoming space filled with comfortable chairs and a few more of Steve's trophies. Like the living room, the den was decorated with Christmas to the *nth* degree. Stuffed Santas sat on shelves. A mantel was filled with nutcrackers, a strand of twinkling white lights at their feet. Snow globes—Lincoln's yearly gift to their mother—crowded the upright piano. Steve's favorite was a scene of a small village that reminded him of Hope Valley.

Lincoln picked up one of Steve's trophies and boomed, "The Voice."

Steve chortled. "Yep, that's me." If he didn't get that prize signed off on, his voice would be toast. He switched on the television, an old plasma TV that had seen better days—his parents had wanted to replace it, but it was Lincoln's favorite—and he started surfing through channels.

"Stop," Lincoln ordered when KPRL appeared. "You aren't there."

"Right, buddy. I'm here."

"Who's taking your place?"

"The weekend guy."

"But it's not the weekend."

Steve could have kicked himself. Lincoln could be so literal. "The sub," he amended.

"He's no good."

"Sure he is."

"No, he's not. Turn it off." Lincoln moved to the radio on the table by the brown leather sofa and switched it on.

Mr. Q, an eccentric guy with a rich baritone, was discussing the weather. Steve remembered him from high school. He'd been Steve's science teacher. He retired to run the radio station three years after Steve graduated. Soon, Mr. Q would talk about sports and rehash the news. He did it all day, every day. He was devoted to keeping Hope Valley up to date, their mother had said of him.

Steve noticed Brie standing in the archway, studying him and his brother. She and his father hadn't left yet. Steve raised his hand subtly.

She smiled. "You're a good man, Charlie Brown."

Steve contemplated that. If his brother's condition frustrated him but he didn't let it show, did that make him a good man? Maybe. He wasn't sure. "Don't tell anyone," he said. "It could ruin my reputation."

She put a finger to her lips. "It's our secret. G'night."

"Night."

"Night, Brie!" Lincoln cried. When she disappeared from sight, he said, "The radio station is for sale."

"Is it?" Steve raised an eyebrow.

"I don't want Mr. Q to sell it. I won't be able to visit."

"Sure you will."

"No, they won't let me."

"They *who*?"

"The new owners. Mr. Q likes me. He says lots of statistics, same as you." Lincoln tapped the chessboard agitatedly. He'd been home-schooled, but for the last fifteen years, he'd regularly visited the radio station. The place soothed him. "Mr. Q doesn't mind when I ask questions."

Probably because Mr. Q was a scientist who loved probing the unknown. "It'll be okay, dude," Steve assured his brother. "Whoever buys it will be just as welcoming."

Lincoln screwed up his mouth. "You don't know that."

"Mom and Dad will make sure the new buyers allow you into the studio. Promise."

"But what if they don't?" Lincoln's voice skated upward. "What if..."

Steve gripped his brother's hand. "Hey, Linc, it's not going to sell tonight. We're good. *You're* good."

Lincoln calmed down.

"Somebody nice will buy the station, and everything will go back to normal," Steve said, not believing a word of it. The station would probably fold. Who wanted to own an antiquated business with such a small outreach in this day and age? Did it make a profit or run a deficit? "In the meantime, you can watch me on KPRL."

"But you're not there."

"Not right now. But I will be. When I go back to Portland."

"I don't want you to go."

"I know." Steve released Lincoln's hand. "But I have to. That's where I live. That's where I work."

"You could work here. You could buy the radio station."

"Ha! With what? Two cents and a rabbit's foot?" Steve had a decent nest egg, but he hadn't been able to save much over the past few years. Gloria's engagement ring had set him back, and living in Portland wasn't cheap. A bigger and better paying job would help build up his cash reserve for sure. But all of that was a pipedream if he didn't get Hope Lyons to accept the prize. Dang! Why had Dave put him in this untenable position?

"Let's play chess," Lincoln said, and moved to the small game table by the window. He sat in his preferred chair, braced his elbows on his knees, and stared at the chessmen as if expecting them to move on their own.

Steve sat opposite him and mirrored his brother's body language. Lincoln moved his centermost white pawn two spaces forward.

"Really? That's your opening gambit?" Steve teased.

"Yeah." Lincoln screwed up his face, knowing Steve was messing with him. "Make something of it," he taunted.

Steve grinned. At times, his brother acted so normal that Steve forgot he was challenged. Steve moved his rightmost rook pawn one space forward.

"What's bothering you?" Lincoln asked.

Steve met his brother's steady gaze. It was unnerving. "What do you mean?"

"You aren't yourself. You're angry. Something"—Lincoln twirled a finger at Steve—"is eating at you."

"Is that psycho mumbo-jumbo?" Steve joked. "Something you heard at a session?" His brother went to monthly group meetings with other guys like him. To talk. Just in case their caretakers or parents weren't getting the whole picture.

"No. It's not mumbo-jumbo. When you're mad, you talk through your teeth." Lincoln mimicked Steve. "Like. This. Through. Your. Teeth. Why?"

Steve stared at his brother. Nailed. "It's Hope Lyons. She rubbed me the wrong way."

"Ow," Lincoln said.

"No, not that kind of rub," Steve said. "She irked me."

"Irked?"

"That means made me mad. See, I want to give her and her family the prize, but—"

"The Spirit of Christmas prize. To Disneyland."

"Right, but like I said at dinner, she refused."

"I want to go to Disneyland."

"Exactly. Who wouldn't?" *Other than me.* Steve scrubbed the back of his neck.

"I'll talk to her."

"Thanks, bro, but I've got this."

Lincoln gripped both sides of the chess table, looked left and right, and then lowered his voice. "Hope is sad. She's in a bind."

"What kind of bind?"

"A chess bind."

Steve understood the term. It was a stranglehold, hard for an opponent to break.

"You have to try again," Lincoln said. "Be kind."

Steve thought for a long moment, and an idea formed. As challenged as Lincoln was, maybe he'd landed on an endgame.

AFTER HOPE TOSSED THE trash from their dinner into the trailer park's bins, she clambered into the VW still pondering what she was going to tell her children about the set-to with Steve . . . with Santa.

"Mom," Todd said, "you look sad. Do you need a joke?"

"Yes, please."

"Why did the picture go to jail?" he asked, and without waiting for Hope's response said, "Because it was framed."

Hope mock-moaned. "That's a good one."

"I heard it at school."

She squeezed his shoulder. "You're one funny guy."

"Can we watch TV?" he asked.

"Sorry. No. It's books-by-flashlight night."

"Aw, c'mon," Todd griped. "Just one show."

"Books."

Hope had loved reading by flashlight as a girl, tented beneath her blankets, the scent of baby shampoo and lavender soap lulling her to sleep. Sure, her kids liked to read, but she hadn't made reading an adventure for them. That stopped now. An early Christmas present was in order.

"Melody, I went to the Curious Reader today," she said.

"Really?" Melody's eyes widened.

"I bought you the Lisa Leslie book." Hope dug into her tote bag, withdrew the book, and handed it to Melody.

"Oh, Mom." Melody squealed with delight. "Thank you. It's just what I wanted."

The book featured a fictional all-star basketball player who took the Olympic team to a gold medal. It had been on Melody's wish list for months.

"Thank you. Thank you." Melody pressed the book to her chest.

"And for you, Todd—"

"Please, Mom, I don't want to read tonight." He tugged on Hope's arm. "Just one show. Steve Waldren is on."

"No, he's not," Hope said.

"Yes, he is," Todd said. "Let's find out who won."

"No, he's . . . on the road." Hope didn't say he was here in town. She also didn't lie and say he was sick. "Someone is standing in for him."

"How do you know?"

"I just do."

"Mo-o-m," Todd whined. "Please. Let me watch anyway."

"No." Hope was the boss. What she said *went*. Tomorrow, after Steve gave up on her and her family and picked the other night's winner for the Spirit of Christmas prize, she'd let them watch KPRL again.

Todd plopped on the floor, elbows planted on his thighs, chin in his hands.

"Todd, lose the 'tude, and I'll give you your book. You'll like it."

He perked up. Hope held it out to him.

"Wow! The LeBron book? So cool." Todd bounded to his feet.

"Flashlights," Hope said.

Both children obeyed.

Thrilled that she'd found a distraction, she tucked them into their sleep sacks, kissed them goodnight, and whispered, "Have fun reading. And then sleep tight and dream with the angels."

Chapter 19

Hope awoke Thursday with a kink in her neck, but when she heard gold-crowned sparrows chirping merrily outside and caught a glimpse of sunshine glistening on the new dusting of snow that lined the VW's windows, she dared to feel optimistic. Buoyant, in fact. Quietly, she slipped into her work outfit, set out the children's clothes, and prepared a protein-rich breakfast. When everything was ready, she cried, "Rise and shine! Get up and get dressed, kids. Hop to it."

"Mom, I wore this last week," Melody said holding up the blue plaid shirt.

"I know, and you looked adorable. It's freshly-laundered."

As Hope did every morning, she checked Melody's insulin and brushed and styled her hair. Todd was allowed to finger-comb his.

On the drive to Hope Valley Elementary, the children chatted about the upcoming day camp and what they planned to do: arts and crafts, baking, music jam. Hope had listed all the possibilities on the way home from school yesterday. When she'd added that Gabe's niece Khloe was going to be in charge and she would be one-on-one with them this coming Saturday, two days before camp started, that had sealed the deal.

As the kids hopped out of the VW and slung on their backpacks, Hope said, "I'll return in a few hours to see the holiday play. Todd, you'll sit with me."

"Okay."

Weeks ago, using items she'd picked up at a second-hand store, Hope had cobbled together a costume for Melody, who was as over the moon as a ten-year-old could get about a red scarf.

"And Melody, remember—"

"The scarf knot goes at the back of my head," Melody chimed, holding up a thumb. "Got it."

AT AROMA CAFÉ, HOPE was wiping down the counter with a clean rag while doing her best to avoid eye contact with Denny. He had come in for coffee and a slice of pie.

Zerena sidled to her. "Denny has a crush on you," she whispered.

"Yep."

"What're you going to do about it?"

"Nothing."

"He's cute. Single. And he has a steady job."

"Not interested."

"He even loves his mother." Zerena made smooching sounds.

"Maybe a tad too much," Hope snarked.

Zerena snorted and elbowed Hope. "C'mon, don't you want someone to grow old with?"

"I had somebody. He split."

Zerena sighed. "If you're always putting on the brakes—"

"I'm fine on my own."

"Just saying." Zerena sashayed away.

Denny waved his chit at Hope, ready to pay.

She threw the rag into a bin beneath the counter and ambled to him. "How was everything?" She didn't offer a smile. Didn't encourage him. Denny was nice but he wasn't . . .

Hope paused. He wasn't what? Steve Waldren?

"Best pie in town, as always," Denny said.

"Don't tell the owner of Sweet Place." Hope winked and regretted the gesture because Denny winked back.

Then he grew serious. "Say, did you get things sorted out yesterday?"

"Sorted . . ." Jogging her memory, Hope recalled her excuse not to let him walk with her. "Yes. I did. I'm good to go," she lied. She wasn't. Melody and Todd were going to find out what she'd said to Steve and despise her. But Denny didn't need to know that.

"Great." Denny drummed the counter. "Hey, I'm still counting on that date sometime."

"It's always good to be optimistic," Hope said, kicking herself for such a coy reply.

"Yes, indeed. Helen Keller said, 'Optimism is the faith that leads to achievement.'" He waved on his way out.

Hope knew the quote. She'd even believed it at one time in her life.

"Morning." Brie Bryant sauntered into the café and took a seat at the counter. She was wearing one less layer than she had the day before. Her multiple braids were swept over her shoulders. "What a lovely morning."

The sun was out, but the weather was crisp.

"It is," Hope said cheerily.

"Coffee, please. No cream. No sugar." Brie perused the menu briefly before setting it aside. She glanced around as if looking for someone.

Please, please, please not Steve, Hope thought. She didn't want to face him again. If only he hadn't been the one to offer the prize. She liked him. She would've liked to have gotten to know him better. Now she wanted to avoid him at all costs.

"How do you like Hope Valley?" Hope asked as she set a mug of freshly brewed coffee in front of Brie.

"It's magical. The lights, the decorations, the look of peace and goodwill on everyone's faces. I haven't celebrated Christmas in years."

"Why not?"

"Long story short, my folks gave up on Christmas when I was ten. It was just too hard to decorate, buy presents for me and my four brothers, and make everything seem happy when they were miserable and ready to divorce. And then husband number one soured it even more."

Number one implied there was a second husband and perhaps a third. Was Brie expecting Hope to ask about that?

"But now," Brie said, "in this town, this café? It's the whole ball of wax!" She flourished a hand. "I can't wait to put up a tree in my apartment when I get home."

"Good for you. That's the holiday spirit."

"I'm going ornament shopping after breakfast. There has to be someplace in town—"

"The Christmas Attic is *the* place," Hope cut in. "The Waldrens own it."

"Well, silly me. Why didn't I know that? I had dinner with them last night and they didn't mention it. But I didn't ask. Bad me. I must be more curious in the future. No one needs a narcissistic anything." Brie leaned forward on her elbows and cradled her coffee cup in her hands. "By the way, Steve—"

"Is narcissistic?"

"That's not what I was going to say. In fact, he's far from it."

"It doesn't matter. Save your breath," Hope said. "I'm not changing my mind."

"Okay, okay. A stubborn woman is like a bronco. Hard to break."

"I'm not stubborn. I'm . . ." Hope sighed.

"Between a rock and a hard place."

Hope nodded.

Brie took a sip of her coffee. "Yum. Is this Kona coffee?"

"Mm-hm. Gabe dreams of seeing the USA when he retires. Hawaii is first on the list. He has it shipped in."

"Ooh, I've never been there, but I know I would love it." She sang the opening words to the Hawaiian Christmas song "Mele Kalikimaka" while doing a hula move with her free hand.

Hope wanted to travel with her kids, too. Not to Disneyland. Maybe to visit all of the national parks. She and Zach had talked about doing that. Someday she would. Someday. After she got her pie shop on its feet again. After . . . She pushed the bittersweet musings aside. "The Kona coffee is Gabe's way of bringing the islands to us."

"What a thoughtful guy."

"You have no idea."

"You two seem close."

"He and my dad were good friends."

"Were?"

"My parents passed away."

"I'm sorry." Brie didn't press. She took another sip of coffee. "Where is your handsome boss, by the way?"

Handsome? Gabe? He was nice enough looking, but Hope had never pegged him as handsome. "He's in the back."

Brie glanced in that direction. Hope smiled. Did Brie like him? Gabe had seemed keen on her, too. Hope wondered if she should—

No. She was not a matchmaker. Gabe and Brie were from two different worlds. Gabe was a small-town guy. Brie was worldly. If he was going to settle down with someone new, it should be someone from Hope Valley. Someone who loved the same things he did.

"He's making the icing for the cookie decorating contest," Hope said.

"Which is when?"

"Sunday." Hope grinned. "My kids are looking forward to it. They can't win, of course. No employee's child is eligible. But they love to participate. My daughter is quite the artist. My son goes heavy on the icing."

Zerena swooped next to Hope and slung an arm over her shoulders. "Guess what, girlfriend?"

"What?"

"Roman asked me to go ice skating."

"To which you said yes."

Tears blossomed in Zerena's eyes. "No."

"*Yes,*" Hope said more forcefully.

Zerena shook her head.

"Why not?" Hope persisted. "You rock at ice skating." Zerena excelled at all sports.

"That's just it. Roman has never been on skates. He thought it would be fun for us to try." Zerena licked a tear that slipped across her lips. "I don't want to show him up, and I didn't want to tell him that I—"

"Men." Brie rapped her knuckles on the counter. "They have such fragile egos." She aimed a finger at Zerena. "You need to tell this Roman—" She eyed Hope. "Who is Roman?"

"The chef."

"Aha, your chef." Brie glanced toward the kitchen. "He's very ooh-la-la. That smile? Worth a million bucks. Plus he can cook. He's a keeper!"

"Tell me about it." Zerena shook her head. "I burn toast."

"Do not pass up this opportunity," Hope said.

"So what do I do?" Zerena asked, a pleading whine in her voice.

"I want to go on a date with him. Anywhere. Just not skating."

"The tree-lighting ceremony is Sunday night," Hope said.

"The town has a tree-lighting ceremony?" Brie thumped the counter. "Of course it does. That's a perfect first date. And *trés romantic*."

"Great idea." Zerena squeezed Hope's arm and returned to her station.

Brie aimed a finger at Hope. "I've heard about you. Gabe says you always know the right thing to say to make people feel special."

"Exactly when would he have told you that?" Hope cocked her head.

"Last night, after dinner at the Waldrens, I stopped in for a cocoa to go."

A cocoa to go that turned out to be an opportunity to chat, Hope mused.

Brie smirked like the proverbial cat who'd eaten the canary. She sipped more coffee and said, "By the way, Ellery and Frank Waldren raved about you last night. You are high on their list"—she motioned above her head—"of favorite people."

"I'll bet Steve didn't rave."

Brie snickered. "Let's just say he's disappointed he couldn't romance you into a *yes*." She sputtered. "I didn't mean *romance* romance. I meant—"

"I know what you meant."

"Anyway," Brie continued, "like I was saying, I moseyed over here for a cup of cocoa to help me sleep..."

"Uh-huh." It was Hope's turn to smirk.

"And Gabe and I got to talking. He says you're a wizard with Lincoln Waldren. He said not many could handle serving him, but you make Lincoln feel comfortable so he doesn't get ahead of himself, and that helps his folks."

Hope smiled. "Lincoln is challenged but he's so sweet. Now, his brother is—"

"A looker."

"Yes." Hope felt a flutter in her stomach.

"But not sweet."

"He was sweet when I met him last year."

"You met him? Do tell. Steve didn't mention that, but he can keep his private life private."

Hope filled her in on the chance meeting, and Steve telling her he liked to bake. "But this prize thing—"

"Has made him intense." Brie sipped her coffee. "In his defense, he's got a few challenges of his own."

"What kind of challenges?"

"No. Uh-uh. I'm talking out of turn." Brie swatted the air.

Hope remembered back in high school how her girlfriends had gone on and on about Steve being so talented and so-o-o smart. He had been a terrific basketball and baseball player, although not major league-worthy, plus he'd been the star reporter for the school newspaper. He had the gift of gab and could get anyone to cough up a good story. She recalled the one time they'd met, when she was selling pies to raise money for the sports teams, and he'd thanked her for her service. For a nanosecond, like her girlfriends, she'd developed a small crush on him. Then he graduated and life went on.

"I really want you to know that Steve means well," Brie said.

Means well? Hope flashed on Zach, who had started out with the best of intentions—how often had he told her he'd *meant well*—only to succumb to his habit, ultimately breaking her and her children's hearts.

"Meaning well and doing well aren't the same thing." Hope picked up a wet towel, slapped it on the counter, and began to wipe with fierce intensity. End of discussion.

Chapter 20

Steve's cell phone jangled at noon, jarring him awake. He sat up in bed, hit his head on the bookshelf above the headboard, and grumbled. He'd been trying to sleep in because Lincoln had kept him up playing chess until two a.m. prattling on about Kasparov versus Topalov, 1999, and Byrne versus Fischer, 1956, and all the other historic games. Lincoln might not be socially adept, but like Steve, he could cycle through stats in his head like a champ. What was Steve supposed to say to the brother he hadn't seen in months, he was tired? No, he'd muscled through. Now, he swiped his mouth with the back of his hand, scanned the phone's readout, saw Dave's name, and scowled.

Forcing a lightness he didn't feel, he answered, "Hi, boss."

"Good morning, sunshine. Did you deliver the prize? Brie hasn't sent photos yet." Dave drank a sip of something and let out an *ahh*. "I've been texting her, but she's not answering."

Maybe she didn't want to admit mission failure, either, Steve thought, or she was protecting him, which made him wince. He didn't need protecting, and he sure as heck didn't want her to jeopardize her job on account of him.

"FYI, it's not okay to ignore my calls or texts," Dave warned. "You two are not on vacation. *Capiche*? I expect normal work hours."

"Yeah." Steve cleared his throat. "However, lest you forget, Brie and I don't come in until two in the afternoon. We work nights."

"Not when you're on assignment." Dave sounded like he was cutting food of some kind. The knife rasped against the plate. He began chewing something.

Steve waited.

After a long, unbearable moment, Steve heard the silverware clank on the plate.

Dave said, "You didn't get it, did you?"

"Get what?"

"The agreement. In writing."

Steve hesitated.

"Did you even find the mother?" Dave asked.

"Yes, but, it's complicated."

"Look, pal"—Dave diced something loudly; *chop, chop, chop*—"we announced this family as the winner. We need this family. Not another one. Not a runner up. The bad publicity could hurt KPRL. Got me? So put on that Santa suit and get this mother to accept the prize or else you lose your job. It's as simple as that. You're not getting any younger, boy-o. Do you hear me? Not any younger. Tick-tock." He ended the call.

Steve scanned his text messages. None from his agent and none from Brie. Irked, he tossed his cell phone on the nightstand and threw off the Trail Blazers' comforter. He clambered to his feet, his toes instantly chilled by the hardwood floor, and slogged into the bathroom. He turned on the shower. Knowing it would take a full minute to warm up, he studied his face in the mirror.

Nope. You're not getting any younger, boy-o. There are no jobs coming your way. It's do or die time. Get this stubborn, beautiful woman to sign. Or else.

———— ❦ ————

FOR THE LIFE OF HIM, Steve couldn't shake his brother. Lincoln wanted to go wherever Steve went. At one thirty in the afternoon, Steve once again donned the Santa suit, and he and Lincoln strolled toward Aroma Café. Carolers were singing "Deck the Halls" in front of a Sweet Place. A pushcart vendor hawking handmade Christmas décor was moving along the sidewalk, her smile bright and inviting.

"I like Christmas time," Lincoln said. "Don't you?"

Steve grunted.

"You do." Lincoln elbowed him and guffawed. "I know you do."

Near the cafe, a little girl in a green coat rushed in front of Steve, blocking his path. Breathlessly, she said, "Hi, Santa. Can I tell you what I want for Christmas?"

Her mother looked at Santa expectantly.

Steve sighed. This was the last distraction he needed, but looking at the girl's face, seeing the optimism that flooded her gaze, he crouched down. "Okay, young lady, but I have an appointment. So make it quick."

"I want a brother."

In spite of himself, Steve chuckled. "I'm not sure I can do that. I'm in charge of toys, not real human beings. How about I get you a boy doll who can stand in as your brother until—" He glanced at the mother who, bundled in her puffy parka, appeared more than a few months pregnant, and mouthed *Boy?* She nodded. "Until a baby brother comes along. Okay?"

"Okay."

Her mother said, "What if the doll has brown hair and eyes like yours, sweetheart? Would you like that?"

"Uh-huh." The girl nodded.

Steve said, "Done. Brown hair and eyes." He tapped his temple. "On Santa's nice list. I'm assuming you're nice."

"Very nice!" she chimed.

"Okay, then. Merry Christmas. Ho, ho, ho." He held up his white-gloved hand for a high five.

The girl slapped it.

Steve rose, and said to Lincoln, "Go inside the café. Move."

As they entered, Brie, carrying bags from the Christmas Attic and three other shops, hurried to them. "Ho, ho, ho," she crooned. She had dressed for the weather in a white parka, white turtleneck, and black trousers tucked into boots. She'd even donned eye makeup, which she usually didn't do unless the studio's makeup artist put it on for her. What was up with the look? Who was she trying to impress?

"You've been shopping," Steve asked.

"Tis the season. I love this town."

"You look rested."

"I slept great."

In fact, Brie seemed more relaxed than Steve could remember. How he wished he could feel that way.

"Dave called," Steve said. "You didn't return his text messages."

"And admit defeat? As if. I thought by staying quiet, I could buy you a little time. Let you figure out your next move." She waved a hand at the Santa outfit. "Red suits you."

Steve scowled. "Have you seen Hope Lyons?"

"Recently? Nope."

He approached the fresh-faced hostess, *Trudy* her nametag read, and asked her to seat them at Hope's station. Trudy said she would if she could, but Hope was at her daughter's holiday play. She wasn't going to return today.

Steve sagged. *Swing and a miss. Major strikeout.* "Let's go," he said to Brie and his brother.

"Where?" Brie asked.

"I don't know. For a walk. I need to clear my head."

"No." Lincoln stamped his foot. "I'm hungry. I need to eat. Mom wants me to have lunch."

Steve sighed. "Yes, she does, and I promised I'd feed you. Table for three, Trudy."

"This way, Santa." She seated them in Lincoln's preferred booth and said their waitress would be with them shortly.

A few minutes later, Steve swiveled in his seat and scanned the café. "Where's our waitress?"

"Huh?" Brie asked. She was sitting opposite him and Lincoln scrolling through photos on her cell phone.

"Our waitress. She's a no-show."

"Patience is a virtue, Santa," Brie replied.

"And time is money," he retorted.

"Gold is money," Lincoln said. "Silver is money. And pennies are money, though they aren't worth a red cent, Dad says."

Brie snickered.

Gabe sauntered to the table and handed the three of them menus. "Hiya, Santa. Hi, Lincoln." He straightened the lapels of his red jacket and adjusted the knot on his tie. "Hello, lovely lady."

Brie batted her eyelashes. "Hi, you. You weren't in earlier."

Steve cocked his head. "You came in before, Brie?"

"Yep," she said.

"When?"

"At nine. I needed coffee before I went out to buy one of everything."

"Was Hope here then?"

"Yes, why?"

"Why do you think?" Steve asked, unable to keep frustration from his tone. He twirled a hand. "Did you even think to get her to accept the prize?"

"I don't do your bidding."

"But—"

"She and I chatted, but no, I didn't get her to accept."

"Because?"

"It's your job."

No, fooling, Steve thought glumly. *Literally, his job.*

"I'm hungry," Lincoln cut in.

Brie turned to Gabe, her gaze twinkling. "What's the special?"

"You," Gabe responded.

"Ha-ha," Lincoln said. "*You.*"

Steve gawked. Gabe was the reason Brie had donned makeup? She liked him? Given her track record, Steve would have guessed she was over and done with romance, not to mention Gabe was nothing—*nothing*—like her exes. He was a good, kind man. Nothing studly about him. Nothing self-centered, either. Steve remembered meeting Gabe's wife. She was as affable and sweet as he was. They had been a perfect pair. Him and Brie? Steve couldn't see it, but what did he know? He and Gloria had been a bust.

Brie said, "Where pray tell, Gabe, is Hope's daughter's holiday play?"

Steve blinked and did a mental forehead slap. Why hadn't he thought to ask the question? He blew Brie a kiss. She was a godsend. "Yes, kind sir," Steve said solicitously. "Pray tell, where?"

"Hope Valley Elementary."

Brie mock-groaned. "Well, that was a no-brainer."

Lincoln said, "A no-brainer. *Heh-heh.* Without a brain, you're dumb. Unless you're the scarecrow in *The Wizard of Oz*. He didn't have a brain, but he was smart."

Right about now, Steve was feeling pretty darned stupid.

Chapter 21

A half hour later, after downing a stack of red velvet pancakes—his brother had ordered them for everyone—Steve, Lincoln, and Brie drove to Hope Valley Elementary. It was a well-tended school with a wealth of trees. According to a school placard, the PTA had raised funds for a brand-new auditorium. A banner displayed the name of today's event: *Hope Valley Elementary Extravaganza*.

Steve parked in the school's lot, and the three of them headed for the auditorium. A light snow was drifting down. Steve dusted off his Santa suit. Brie held out her palms to enjoy the white flakes. Children, guided by adults, were lining up beneath the columned portico in front of the auditorium. Steve didn't see Hope among them. Some kids were craning their necks at him, and he realized that, dressed as Santa, he was yet again garnering a lot of attention.

To keep up the pretense, he waved and bellowed, "Ho, ho, ho."

Children tittered. Adults smiled indulgently.

The doors opened, and the line of people began to move inside.

"Why are we here?" Lincoln asked.

"To give Hope the prize," Steve said.

"But she doesn't want it."

"I'm going to change her mind."

Steve guided his brother to the end of the line. As they passed through the entryway, a student handed them flyers for the play.

Lincoln browsed it. "Steve, this play is about the birth of Christ. With Mary and Joseph and the sheep."

"That's right."

"I like sheep. I count them when I can't sleep."

"Me, too." Steve ushered his brother across the foyer.

"Baa," Brie crooned, following.

"Cut it out," Steve said.

"Face it, Voice, you're a big mush," she whispered.

"Only for my brother."

Following the throng inside, Steve felt a tad nervous. Yesterday, Hope had dismissed him. He didn't want to upset her today, but he needed to convince her to take the prize. Could he sweeten the pot? Throw in a few extra bucks? Would that be considered a bribe? Would KPRL or the prize authorities frown on that tactic?

The collar of his Santa suit started to feel tight. The beard began to itch. He wasn't nervous about seeing Hope. No way. He'd never had a case of nerves. Ever. Okay, maybe once or twice as a gawky teen, but not as an adult.

The auditorium was dim. The stage was aglow with lights. The people ahead of him began grabbing all the available seats.

"There's Hope," Brie whispered.

"Where?" Steve asked.

She pointed.

Hope was sitting in the third row flanked by a boy and another woman. Hope's lustrous honey-blond hair was unleashed from its snood and hung loosely down her back.

Knowing his mother would chastise him if he distracted her during the affair, he said, "Let's wait to approach until it's over."

"Fine by me," Brie said.

"Can we sit anywhere?" Lincoln asked. "I like to sit far away."

"I like to sit close," Steve whispered.

"But Mom says—"

"I'm not Mom. Stick with me, buddy. And remember, we whisper inside."

"He always bosses me," Lincoln complained to Brie.

"Not true," Steve said. "You bossed me at the diner."

"Café," Lincoln corrected.

Brie cackled.

Steve flashed on the first time he'd escorted his brother solo to a movie. A Disney classic. Entranced after the first showing, Lincoln had asked to watch the movie a second time. And a third. When the movie queued for the fourth time, Steve muscled Lincoln out. Lincoln went kicking and screaming, calling Steve a *mean bossy boss*. Luckily, the theater manager knew Lincoln and didn't threaten to have Steve arrested for child abuse.

Stealthily—if someone in a Santa suit could move stealthily—Steve led his brother to the row two back from Hope's. She was talking animatedly to the boy. Her son Todd, he presumed. His hair was russet, but even in profile, Steve could see he had Hope's smile.

The lights grew dim. On stage, a director began guiding the costumed children onto the stage. They were humming "Silent Night" as the music played through the auditorium's speakers. The décor featured a manger, two palm trees, and a blue-black backdrop filled with a multitude of stars.

"I like the stars, Steve," Lincoln whispered.

"So do I."

Steve slipped into his seat, and a wealth of emotions washed over him. He'd gone to Hope Valley Elementary, and he'd enjoyed performing in the shows. In eighth grade, he'd considered becoming a professional actor, but he'd known then that he didn't have the talent. He was a numbers guy, not a creative guy. He knew sports, not art. And he had a voice that would work well on television, but he couldn't sing worth a lick.

"Is Brie getting us popcorn?" Lincoln asked.

"No popcorn. It's not a movie theater." Steve looked around. Brie had settled into the last row, probably considering her future. She wanted to retire. Was she contemplating retirement in Hope Valley? Gabe and she were flirting, but was what they were experiencing real? Sustainable? Steve decided to give her space and not razz her. Yes, that was against his nature, but what the heck. It was Christmas. He could be magnanimous. "I'll get you some caramel corn afterward. At Sweet Place. Okay?"

"Okay."

Steve recalled his many visits to Sweet Place. The caramel turtles, the bonbons. How many butterscotch suckers had he licked in his youth? Idly, he wondered what kinds of sweets Hope liked and pushed the notion from his mind. She probably preferred sour tarts.

"Mom," Todd said to his mother loudly enough for Steve to hear, "KPRL should have announced the winner by now. Can we watch the show tonight? Please? I've got to find out if we won. We had a fifty percent chance. One out of two, Mom. One winner for Saturday, and one winner for Monday. Fifty-fifty. Those are really good odds. An ace pitcher doesn't get those odds."

"Yes, sweetheart, we'll listen later." Hope caressed her son's hair. "But, understand, if the other people won, it's okay. We have a good life, right?"

"The best." Todd leaned into his mother, gave her a squeeze, and gazed at her with adoring eyes.

Steve's insides snagged. Hope wasn't hard-hearted. She was simply a mom protecting her kids. Even so, he wanted her children to learn that they had won and believe that sometimes good things did happen. How could he do that without throwing Hope under the bus and making her out to be an ogre?

"Ladies and gentleman," the director announced from the stage. "Welcome."

"He has a nice voice." Brie slid into the seat next to Steve.

"Not as good as my brother's," Lincoln said like a true fan. "He has the perfect radio voice, don't you think? I like radio. Radio waves were first discovered by physicist Herman Hertz. The first transmitters were made by Guglielmo Marconi. The—"

"Enough with the radio facts," Steve said.

"But I like radio."

"I know you do. But we can't talk about it now. The show is starting. *Shh.*"

"Welcome to Hope Valley Elementary's Holiday Extravaganza," the director continued. "This afternoon's event will include a number of skits and songs designed to bring the holiday into your hearts. Enjoy."

"Enjoy," Lincoln echoed loud enough for all to hear.

Steve shrank down in his seat.

Chapter 22

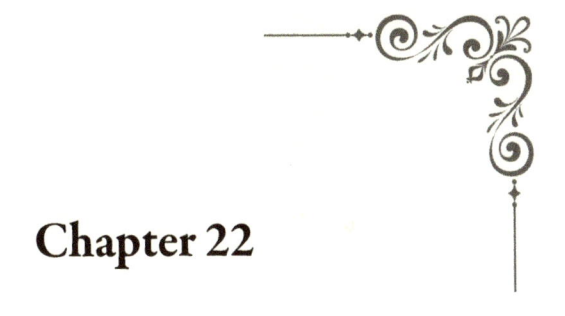

Hope couldn't believe the joy she was experiencing watching Melody perform. Her daughter was glowing and totally in her element.

"Mom," Todd whispered, "she's pretty good, right?"

"Right."

"So maybe being an English teacher isn't her calling."

"Her calling?" Hope grinned. "Where'd you hear that?"

"Mr. Q said it. After he gave up being a science teacher, he searched for his calling. It's like . . . it's like a career or something that you absolutely have to do. His was radio."

"That's a good explanation."

"Do you know your calling?" Todd asked.

"I do." To resurrect her pastry shop. If Zach hadn't—

No. She wouldn't go there. Bitterness solved nothing.

"Your sister and you can do whatever you want to, Todd," Hope whispered. "The future is yours to make of it what you will."

"I want to be a sports announcer like Steve Waldren."

Hope winced as she flashed on her encounter with Steve at the café. He'd been so earnest. He'd probably never considered what extra expenses were involved with a trip to Disneyland. Brie had alluded that he might get into trouble because Hope had turned down the prize.

Not my problem, she thought and focused on the stage.

"Can I?" Todd asked.

"Can you what?"

"Become a sports announcer like Steve?"

"If that's what you want, you go for it." She ruffled her son's hair. "Now, *shh*, let's watch the play."

"STEVE, THIS IS TAKING a long time," Lincoln whispered.

"Yes, it is, bro, but basketball games take a long time, too." Steve patted his brother's arm. "Aren't you enjoying the sheep?"

"Yes, and I like the camel."

"Me, too." Steve had winced a time or two when a child had sung a sour note, but he'd smiled when the magi had presented their gifts, and he'd downright laughed when the camel had waddled out. The rear legs hadn't been able to keep up with the front legs. The director had leaped into the action to help the young actors to their feet.

When the play ended, the audience went wild with appreciation. Steve decided to bide his time while Hope approached her daughter and congratulated her on a job well done.

"What now?" Brie asked.

"Caramel corn," Lincoln said.

"Not yet, buddy," Steve said. "First, let's move outside, and we'll catch them when they come out."

"Catch who?" Lincoln asked.

"Hope and her kids. That's why we came."

"Are we playing tag?"

"No. We're—" Steve exhaled.

"When are we going to Sweet Place?" Lincoln asked.

"After," Steve said.

"After what?"

"After we give Hope the prize."

"The prize to Disneyland."

"Right, bro. Now you've got it!" Steve followed the audience members out of the auditorium. Kids gawked at him and whispered *There's Santa*. He ignored them and herded Lincoln and Brie under the portico to wait.

Ten minutes later, as the sun was sinking in the sky, Steve started to worry. Had Hope seen him? Had she eluded him? Was his moment of opportunity gone?

"There's Hope!" Lincoln cried.

"Where?" Steve whirled around to search the crowd.

"In the VW camper." Lincoln spouted off statistics about VW models, including Rabbits, Jettas, and Beetles. "Of course, a Beetle isn't really a Beetle. It's not a bug. But they do call it a bug—"

"Stop! Zip it, bro!" Steve grabbed his brother's hand. "Come with me."

"Where are we going?"

"On an adventure."

Lincoln resisted. "I don't like adventures."

"Yes, you do."

"No." Lincoln pulled free and stamped the ground. "Remember when we went to the stream on an adventure? It wasn't fun."

Steve did recall. At age thirteen, he'd wanted to go fishing in the middle of winter. Lincoln wanted to tag along, and when they got to the stream, Lincoln slipped and fell into the icy water. Talk about a disaster.

"This is a different kind of adventure," he said. "A safe one. We're going to follow Hope and her kids to their home."

"And then what?" Lincoln asked.

I'm getting her to say yes, come hell or highwater.

"I'm going to pitch Hope a softball," he said. "One she'll catch and throw back."

"We didn't bring any softballs," Lincoln said, taking Steve literally.

"It's a metaphor, bro."

"Stalker," Brie mumbled good naturedly, and began humming "Little Drummer Boy."

Lincoln joined in the humming. "I like this song."

"I know you do," Brie said, and raised her voice.

"Can it!" Steve ordered.

Brie tittered.

"Can what?" Lincoln asked.

"Nothing. C'mon. Hurry."

The three of them climbed into Steve's SUV, and he tore out of the lot. "Seatbelts," he ordered.

"Hope turned left at the light," Brie said.

"On it. When we get to their house, Brie, you watch Lincoln, and I'll make contact." He caught sight of the VW and slowed a tad. All he had to do was keep it in his sights. "In private, away from the glare of café customers, I'm sure I can convince her to come to her senses."

"Because you're such a smooth talker," Brie joked.

"Because the kids will make her see the light. Once they hear they've won, how can she refuse? She'll be persona non grata if she declines, and I'll be the hero. Santa the hero." Steve pounded his chest and let out a Tarzan-like yodel.

Lincoln plugged his ears. "Too loud."

"Sorry, buddy."

"Steve," Brie said, "maybe this idea—"

"Don't dissuade me. We're talking about a free trip. For a family of four. To the happiest place on earth." He cast a sidelong look. "C'mon. Their dad ditched them. Don't these kids deserve some fun?"

"As much as you deserve to keep your job, I suppose," Brie said. "Even so, pressing her in front of her kids, well, it's cruel."

"Steve is not cruel," Lincoln said. "He's my brother."

Brie said, "I fear one does not rule out the other."

Chapter 23

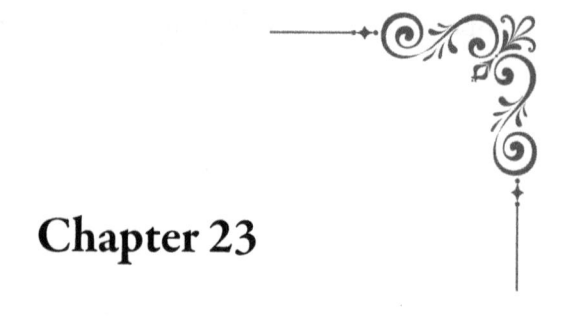

"There. She's slowing. Slowing. Whoa!" Steve choked. "Where'd she go?" He craned his head out the driver's window. The sky had turned dark, but stars weren't glimmering yet, and the friendly neighborhoods of Hope Valley had receded. "Brie? Anything?"

"Sorry, Santa, nothing."

"Stop calling me, Santa."

"Dress like a Santa, look like a Santa, you're the big red guy. Own it." She snickered.

A sign read *Hope Valley Trails ahead*. Another read *Hope Valley Trailer Park, next right*. Steve exhaled with frustration. Where in the heck had the VW disappeared to?

"I don't see any houses," Lincoln said from the back seat. "Or Christmas trees."

"Actually, eyes right. There's a tree with white lights." Brie was peering out the passenger seat window. "At the entrance to the trailer park."

"Did she turn in there?" Steve asked.

"Must have."

"They live in a trailer?" Lincoln said. "Cool."

Steve veered right, and in a matter of seconds, saw the VW's taillights. He followed at a safe distance. When the van came to a stop at a vacant site, he hung back, idling.

Hope parked and popped out of the VW. Deftly, she hooked it up to the park's shore power connection.

"Aw, crap, the VW is their home?" Steve ran his fingers through his hair. What was he supposed to do or say now? Talk about awkward.

Lincoln said, "I think it's cool."

"Stop with the cool," Steve hissed. "I don't care what you think."

"That's not nice." Lincoln huffed.

"No it's not"—Steve parked the car and glanced over his shoulder at his brother—"but right now I need to do the thinking. Not you." He tapped on the steering wheel, straining his brain trying to come up with the appropriate words.

Nice place, Hope. No way.

Ho, ho, ho, you're a year-round camper, I see. Uh-uh, hokey.

"Santa!" Brie knuckled his shoulder. "Chill. Get out, knock on the van's door, and turn on the high-wattage smile. You can sell sawdust to a lumber mill. C'mon. You got this." She pulled her camera from her tote and waggled it. "If that's not enough incentive, remember your career depends upon it."

"Eat dirt," he growled, as he deliberated. Maybe he should—

"I can do it!" Lincoln bolted out of the car.

"Bro, wait! No!"

HOPE BEGAN SETTING the table for dinner. Peanut butter sandwiches and a few sticks of raw carrots would have to suffice. She watched her daughter pour water into three glasses. "You were really good today, Melody. Did you have fun?"

"Mm-hm."

"I think there's a spring play. Do you want to try out for it?"

Melody hitched her shoulder. "Maybe."

"What's the theme?"

"Spring," Melody said. "Duh."

"Mom, help!" Todd was trying to get a connection on the computer. "The Wi-Fi isn't working."

"Give up then and wash your hands."

"I want to see Steve Waldren. You promised."

Hope had prayed Todd had forgotten about that. Shoot. "Don't worry. If we can't get online tonight, in the morning we'll call KPRL, and we'll ask what happened. Okay?" She scrubbed his hair with her knuckles. "How does that sound?"

"Really? Nah, you won't call," he said skeptically.

"Yes, I will. I'll let you dial."

By then, Steve will have chosen the other family for the prize. Case closed.

"First thing," Todd said.

"Yes."

Hope was sad to disappoint her children—to lie to them—but she had to if she was going to have a shot at rebuilding her business, their lives, their future.

Someone knocked on the van's door. Hope startled and stared at it. No one had ever visited them. She'd paid her site fee. She moved to the door and said, "Who's there?"

"Ho, ho, ho. It's Santa."

Hope raised an eyebrow. She didn't recognize the voice. Someone in the trailer park was playing a trick. "Go away!" she shouted.

Todd whooped! "Mom, Mom, it's him. He's here. Steve's here!" He leaped to his feet and flew to the door. "I'd recognize his voice anywhere. He found us."

Melody followed, as excited as her brother. "Mom, open the door."

Hope gawked. Who was playing such a dirty trick? Todd was right. Whoever it was had sort of sounded like Steve, but she knew it wasn't. The timber was off. It wasn't Zerena or Gabe. No one knew where she lived. Had someone from the café who'd seen her decline the prize followed her to the trailer park? Another thought rippled through her. What if Lincoln had learned she'd turned down the prize? What if he'd convinced his parents to take part in finding her? No. No way. They wouldn't.

Another knock. Another *ho, ho, ho.*

And then it dawned on her. Someone at the café must have told Steve about Melody's play. It was him outside. He must have tailed her from the school. Shoot! Why hadn't she paid attention?

She listened hard and heard Steve chiding his brother. "Why'd you do that, bro?"

"Ow!" Lincoln cried. Steve must have swatted him.

"I was ready to ditch the idea. Ready to turn around. But you... you... Dang it."

"Don't swear," Lincoln said.

"Fine," Steve muttered. "Sorry." His brother couldn't handle even moderately bad language. It threw him into a tizzy. "Move. Out of the way. Please."

Fury rising up her throat, Hope cranked open the door. "What the—"

"Hi, Santa!" Melody chimed, at the door in a flash.

Todd, too. "Hi, Steve. I mean, Santa."

Steve edged around his brother. "Ho, ho, ho," he crooned with great bravado.

Brie sidled next to Steve, her camera at the ready.

"Hi, kids." Steve raised his gloved hands into the air. "Santa—" He halted, peering at Hope and then past her. His eyes widened. He swallowed hard, and his cheeks flushed hot pink.

"Please leave," Hope said, teeth clenched, his embarrassment becoming hers.

Steve bobbed his head. "Yeah, okay. We're going. Sorry to have disturbed you. Brie. Lincoln. Turn around. Get back in the car." He prodded them while continuing to gaze at Hope. "Look, I'm sorry. I thought I was following you to your house. I had no idea you were—"

"Hi, Hope," Lincoln said, inserting his head between Brie and Steve's. "We're on an adventure."

"Hi, Lincoln," she said as sweetly as she could muster.

"You live in your car. It's cool."

Steve leveled him with a gaze. "It's not cool, dude."

"Yes, it is cool," Hope said in a tempered tone, tamping down all the anger that was welling up inside her. "But it's not a car, Lincoln. It's a camper, and it's hooked up in a trailer park."

"Cool."

She directed the next bit at Steve. "FYI, we are not homeless."

"Wait," Steve protested. "That's not what I was going to say."

"We're not living in a box on a street. *This* is our home. Not everyone can afford all the amenities of life, which include food, plus wheels, car insurance, health insurance, and you name it. I do the best I can. We're fine. We're happy."

"Got it," Steve stammered. "We're leaving. We're sorry to have disturbed you."

Brie said, "Hope, you rock."

Lincoln said, "We came to give you the prize. Steve tried once but you said no, and he wants to try again."

"Lincoln, stop." Steve grimaced. "I told you—"

"Again, Mom?" Melody shot a scathing look at her mother. "Lincoln said, 'Again.'"

Hope sighed. Her daughter was quick on the uptake, she'd give her that.

"Is that true?" Todd asked.

"Uh-huh." Lincoln pointed from Steve to himself. "My brother tried to give your mom the prize at the café yesterday, but—"

"We won!" Todd grabbed his sister's hands and jumped up and down. "We really won!"

With all the bouncing, Hope worried the VW's floor would give way. "Stop!" she shouted. "No jumping. Melody. Todd. Stop!"

They settled down instantly, looking chagrined.

"What's wrong, Mom?" Melody asked, her voice tiny and scared.

"Sit on your bean bags. Both of you." Hope shot out her arm. "Don't move."

They scurried to them and hunkered down.

Hope scowled at Steve—*Santa*—and shoved him from the door. Lincoln moved backward, too. Brie edged to the right.

Hope stepped outside and slammed the VW's sliding door. "Steve—"

"I'm sorry," he blurted. "It was wrong to come here. Wrong to—"

"I already told you *no*."

Steve blanched. "Yes, but I thought I could—"

"No, you didn't think."

"I think," Lincoln said.

Brie knuckled him and said, *"Shh."*

Lincoln curled his lips inward and mimed locking a key.

Hope sighed. "Look, Steve, single parents with overwhelming debt are the working poor. As I said a minute ago, we can barely afford things like insurance and medicine, let alone rent. We make choices. This is my choice. And it's my choice not to take the prize because there are all sorts of extra expenses KPRL hasn't factored in, as I explained to you."

"Got it," Steve said.

Did he really? Maybe he did this time. He seemed to be listening. Processing.

Hope willed the knots in her shoulders to unwind, but they wouldn't obey. "Please leave."

"Hi, Hope," Lincoln said, as if on auto-reset.

She softened. "Hi, Lincoln. Having a good time?"

"I'm with Steve. On an adventure."

"So you said."

Steve cut his brother a look—a slightly bewildered but definitely kind look—and turned back to Hope. He seemed flummoxed. Actually, tongue-tied.

Brie said, "Hey, Hope, couldn't your kids use some sunshine in their—"

"Drab lives?" Hope cut her off.

"I wasn't going to say that. I . . ." Brie exchanged a horrified look with Steve.

"Listen, Brie," Hope began, "and you listen too, Lincoln and Steve."

"Santa," Steve said with forced joviality that he clearly didn't feel.

"Santa." Hope heard the edge in her voice. *Santa.* As if a benevolent jolly elf had ever existed. She did not believe in the guy, no matter what she'd told her son. Okay, maybe when she was five, she'd believed. But after her parents died and after what Zach did, the blinders had come off, and naive belief vanished. "My kids eat right. They enjoy school. They love sports. Heck, they adore watching you on TV." She shot a hand in his direction. "You. The Voice. Mr. Statistics. They can rattle them off like you can."

"Me, too," Lincoln said over Steve's shoulder.

Steve said, "Quiet, bro, c'mon."

Lincoln locked his lips for a second time.

In spite of herself, Hope smiled. *Brothers.* In a nanosecond, she wiped the smile off her face and continued. "They adore how Hope Valley decorates for Christmas," she went on. "They love the tree-lighting ceremony. And the gingerbread house event. They do not need a trip to the happiest place on earth to make it better."

Steve dramatically clapped a hand to his chest. "Santa Claus is going to be crushed if you don't—"

"No. Stop. No pretending to be Santa Claus. There is no—"

"Mom!" Melody whipped open the door, tears spilling down her cheeks. "Don't say it out loud. Please." She hitched her head toward Todd who was dutifully sitting on his bean bag chair. "I might not believe in you-know-who, but he does. Mom, please."

"You could hear me?" Hope asked.

"Uh, yeah, you were yelling."

Lincoln wedged past Hope and climbed into the VW. He sat on the floor beside Todd's bean bag. Seconds later, Todd was showing Lincoln his collection of basketball trading cards.

Steve motioned to the two of them. "Isn't that sweet?"

Hope folded her arms across her chest and gave him the side eye. "What's in it for you, Steve? Do you get a bonus if I accept? No, wait. Let me guess. Will you lose your job if you don't make this deal? Ha! As if."

Steve blanched, and Hope felt as if she'd struck a nerve. Would he lose his job? No way. He was the Voice. He was an icon.

Regardless, she pressed on. "Maybe you're the one with a drab life, Steve. Maybe—" Hope shuddered. Had those horrible words actually flown from her mouth? She hadn't meant to utter them. She wasn't cruel. Her mother had often cautioned: *You can never take words back.* "I'm so sorry. I didn't mean—"

"It's okay. I deserved it. We're out of here." Steve turned on his heel. "Brie, Lincoln, let's go."

Lincoln gave Todd a fist bump and clambered off the floor. He scooted past Hope. "I like statistics. Steve does, too."

Hope offered a weak smile. "I know."

"And I like snickerdoodles and cocoa and—"

"Lincoln!" Steve barked. "Out."

Lincoln leaped from the VW.

After Hope closed the door, she glanced at her children. The sorrowful, grief-stricken, angry looks on their faces told the whole story. She was a monster. But someone in the family had to be a realist, right? Someone had to plan for the future.

Chapter 24

Steve climbed into his SUV and said, "Fasten your seatbelts."

"It's going to be a bumpy ride," Brie chimed ala Bette Davis.

Steve threw her a dirty look. "Don't start with film quotes."

"I buckled my seatbelt," Lincoln said.

"Brie?" Steve asked solicitously.

"On it, Santa."

"Don't call me that!"

"Then lose the danged suit." Brie threw up her hands in surrender. "Geez, you're cranky."

"For good reason."

"We shouldn't have followed her," Brie said.

"But we did, and look what happened. Crud."

"Don't swear," Lincoln said.

"*Crud* is not swearing."

Steve pulled onto the main road and squinted at the headlights of oncoming cars flaring in the windshield as he thought of what he'd just witnessed. Hope and her kids living in a VW that wasn't much bigger than a closet. Why? What had brought her to that? Her ex had left her. Got it. Didn't she receive alimony? And what was all the talk about insurance payments? Steve got his plan through work. Didn't the café provide insurance for its employees? Maybe not. Steve was hip enough to know that most hourly workers didn't get coverage. Feeling like a heel, he ran a hand down the back of his neck. How could he fix this? He had to make it better.

"That was sad," Brie whispered. "Seeing them, you know." She twirled a hand. "The place was so small."

"Of course it's small," Steve said. "It's a van."

"A camper," Lincoln corrected.

Brie was reviewing images on her cell phone, not making eye contact with Steve. "You get why she's mad at you, right?"

"Honestly, she didn't seem upset about her arrangement," Steve said, lying to himself. He had forced her to face reality. What a jerk he was. He glanced in the rearview mirror and saw Lincoln tap-tapping the window. Though Steve despised the irritating noise, he didn't make his brother stop. Lincoln was agitated.

"She has a lot of pride, Steve," Brie said.

"Rightly so."

"Hope makes the best sugar cookies," Lincoln said.

"I'll bet she does," Steve replied.

"And pies. You like pie, Steve."

"Yes, I do. And you're not wrong there. I've tasted her pies." Steve paused for a moment, the word *pies* stirring a memory. A year ago when he saw her at the café, he mistakenly called her Holly, and she corrected him. She mentioned that they'd met. She was from Hope Valley, she said, so he assumed they'd bumped into one another somewhere in town, but then she added that she'd owned a pie shop. Where? He wracked his brain to fill in the gap.

"Her tree was pretty," Brie said.

Steve didn't disagree. It couldn't have been three feet tall, yet she had done the best she could, complete with strings of popcorn. He had fond memories of making those as a boy. Lincoln always woke with a stomach ache the next morning.

"Mom says Hope is a gem," Lincoln said.

"A gem?" Steve grinned.

"Uh-huh. She always smiles, and she's kind to everyone. She's a gem. A diamond in the rough. A treasure. A–"

"Okay, got it." Steve shook his head, amused. He could hear his mother saying that about Hope. She always saw the best in people. And, yes, Hope probably was a gem.

Man, oh, man. Why had he followed her home?

ON FRIDAY MORNING, Hope said, "Let's get going, kids. Last day before Christmas break." She was doing her best to add warmth and mirth to an otherwise bleak day.

But the kids weren't buying it. They were sad. They'd gone to bed teary-eyed. Melody had tossed and turned all night and had cried out *Daddy* at one point. Todd had mumbled in his sleep about Santa.

"We have to get on the road," Hope said, buttoning her white shirt.

Neither Melody nor Todd had eaten breakfast. They had stared at their microwaved oatmeal with disgust.

"Todd, what are you doing?" Hope asked. He was in the passenger seat, bending forward, mumbling. "Is your tummy okay?"

"Yeah, I'm good."

He sat up abruptly. She heard something fall to the floor, and quickly, he clambered into the rear of the camper looking like he'd gotten his hand caught in the cookie jar. Whatever he'd been up to, probably sneaking a dollar from her money clip to use in the school's vending machine, she decided to let it slide. This time.

"Hop to." She handed them their lunchboxes. Bologna and cheese again. *Ho, ho, merry nothing.* "Tick-tock."

"For Pete's sake, don't rush us, Mom," Melody carped. Her hair was a rat's nest but she'd refused to let Hope run a brush through it. Todd's wasn't much better, standing on end as if he'd rubbed a balloon across it.

"You had a bad night," Hope said. "I get it. Sit in your seats. Put on your seatbelts."

"No, Mom, *you* had a bad night," Melody said, doing as told. "You were horrible to Steve. Dad would have let us take the prize. Dad would have made sure we had a happy Christmas. Dad—"

"Stop!" Todd yelled. "No, he wouldn't. Dad's mean."

"No he's not."

"Yes he is. He left us. He's not coming back."

"Don't say that!" Melody wailed.

"Well, he's not," Todd said. "When was the last time you saw him? I . . . I . . ." He fought for breath. "I can't remember what he looks like."

Hope covered her mouth with the back of her hand and sucked back a sob.

"Does he have dark hair or red hair like me?" Todd demanded.

"Rusty red, you dope. Just like yours. Don't you remember?"

"No," Todd said softly, and tears leaked down his cheeks. "I don't remember anything."

Hope's chest heaved. Why had she buried pictures of Zach at the bottom of her keepsake box? It was wrong of her to do so. Her kids didn't hate him. She did. They were allowed to dream about and idolize him.

"Daddy is going to show up this year," Melody said, clipping off her words. "He is."

Hope gaped at her daughter. Since when had Melody, the pragmatic one, become the dreamer?

"Just like Santa will show up?" Todd asked. "Ha! As if." He folded his arms. "Yeah, yeah, I know Santa doesn't exist. Nathan Atkinson told me. Santa isn't real. And you know what? Daddy isn't real either."

"He'll bring presents," Melody said.

"No, he won't. You're lying!" Todd busted out of the VW, leaving the door open. Cool air rushed in.

Hope wilted, wishing she could have prevented what Zach had done. She'd often wondered whether she was the reason he'd gone down the rabbit hole of gambling because he'd fallen out of love with her. Because he'd needed to put distance between them. Sometimes she wondered if he'd felt the need to prove himself, believing a career as a mathematician wasn't sexy enough. Except she'd done everything she could to keep their marriage vital. Private dinners on the terrace. Long walks at night. Arranging for sitters so they could spend occasional weekends at a bed-and-breakfast. Until she realized her actions weren't lighting any fires between them. That was when she'd become a doormat so Zach could feel like a big man. He hadn't hit her. Ever. That would have been a dealbreaker. But she'd let him call her a failure and weak and cloying. Her pie shop had prospered, but she'd allowed the digs. *Whatever you say, Zach. Run through all our money, Zach. I still love you, Zach.*

Hope stiffened. No, no, no. She wasn't like that. Not anymore. And she never would be again. She would stand up for her rights. She would fight for her kids. They were all that mattered.

She told Melody to stay put, and then she ran out into the cold to find her son.

Chapter 25

Steve's cell phone rang Friday morning at seven a.m.. He sat up in bed, this time avoiding hitting his head on the shelf, and looked at the readout. *Unknown Caller.* Not Dave. Not his agent. On the off chance it was someone from Los Angeles calling him directly, he answered.

A boy said, "Hi, Steve, it's me."

"Who's me?" Steve asked, sort of recognizing the voice but not being able to put a name to it.

"Todd Lyons. We met last night."

Whoa! The kid. Steve rubbed his jaw, fully awake now. Had Hope put her son up to this? Was she going to accept the prize after all? Would she save face if her son said yes instead of her? Okay, sure. Whatever it took.

Steve said, "Hey, what's up, Todd?"

"Not much. I just wanted to talk about the Trail Blazers' lineup."

Huh? Steve rolled the kinks from his neck. Was this kid for real? He wanted to chat at—Steve checked the time again—yeah, seven. His eyes weren't deceiving him. Didn't Todd have school? "Uh, sure, kid, okay. What do you think of the lineup?"

Todd launched in, getting all the names and statistics right. Over the course of five minutes, he and Steve agreed on a number of items, including that Boxer wasn't so hot of late.

When a lull occurred, Todd said, "Well, gotta go. Nice talking." And he hung up.

For a long minute, Steve stared at the phone, slightly puzzled. The kid had no endgame. No request. He hadn't lashed out at Steve for embarrassing his mother. Was it a trick? Scratching his jaw, he mumbled, "Cute kid," and scrambled out of bed to wash up.

Under a shower of steaming hot water, he tried but failed to come up with a solution that might appease Dave. The truth was always best, he decided, and after dressing for the day, he called his boss. In less than two minutes, he recapped last night's fiasco. "She was embarrassed. I was mortified. My timing—"

"Sucked," Dave inserted. "You know you need her to sign on the dotted line."

"Yeah. I'll get her to accept the prize today. Promise." Even if he had to personally cover the expenses Hope was so worried about. He'd stewed over Hope's reasoning until about two a.m. before deciding that was the solution, legal issues aside.

"You know, boy-o, giving it to someone in her position will be a ratings boon, now more than ever."

"Ratings . . ." Steve wagged his head. "No, Dave, man, we can't mention her situation. We have to keep it under wraps."

"Sure, sure. Now, go make me proud."

At noon, Steve, Brie, and his family made their way to Aroma Café. Outside, a quartet of madrigal singers decked out in turn-of-the-century regalia were singing "O, Come All Ye Faithful."

Steve put his hand on the door to open it and paused. Even though he'd dressed for the weather in a long-sleeved shirt, vest, and coat, a chill cut through him. It had nothing to do with the possibility of seeing Hope and being on the receiving end of her wrath again. In fact, it had to do with the reality that for most of the night he'd had recurring dreams of her. Stroking her lustrous hair. Kissing her lips. He was smitten—no two ways about it—but he was also a pragmatist and knew she'd never have eyes for him. Not after what had happened at the trailer park.

"Hold on, Son." Steve's mother gripped his elbow. "Don't go in yet. Let's listen." Her cheeks were rosy, her eyes bright with delight.

His father said, "Lincoln loves listening to carols."

Lincoln was toying with his red scarf, transfixed by the singers.

"Me, too," Brie chimed.

"Sure, fine." Steve stamped fresh snow off his feet and peeked into the café. He didn't see Hope. If she wasn't there, he'd fail. Probably for the best. He'd head back to Portland, alert the other semifinalist, and beg Dave not to fire him. He'd get down on his knees if he had to. He wasn't above groveling. Not at this stage of the game.

"Lovely. Truly lovely," Ellery said when the singers concluded. She tapped Steve's arm. "Okay, let's go inside."

Steve opened the door to Aroma Café, allowing the others to go in first, then he entered. Warm air washed over him.

While removing her overcoat, Ellery said, "Look! Our booth by the window is available."

"Their booth," Brie whispered to Steve. "How cute is that?"

He tried to think of one place in Portland that he could call *his*, but he drew a blank. Yes, he went to Café Au Lait, where he knew all the baristas, and he and Harker often went to Piccolo's, but they didn't have a regular booth, table, or stool. A year ago, he'd gone to Pie in the Sky weekly, but since it changed hands, it wasn't the same. He paused as a memory tried to break through. Was that where he'd met Hope? She hadn't mentioned living in Portland, but he'd never asked. Was that the shop she'd owned? He tried to remember the face of the owner but couldn't. Admittedly, most often he went in with his gaze fixed on the pies in the display cabinet. If Hope had been the owner, had she mismanaged the venture? Had it tanked and forced her into bankruptcy, thus propelling her family to live in a camper? Was that why her husband ditched her? No, that scenario didn't sound feasible.

Fresh-faced Trudy was seating a group of six, so Ellery signaled Gabe. Beaming, he grabbed a few menus and ambled toward them. Steve could see why Brie was attracted to him. Gabe had an ease about him, as if life was good all of the time.

"Good morning, Waldren family and lovely lady," Gabe said, guiding them to the table. "How is everyone on this fine day?"

"Great," Brie replied. "Business seems to be good."

"I can't complain. Holidays make everybody smile." He winked at her.

Steve scanned the café for Hope and spotted her near the kitchen picking up an order, her ponytail in the snood-style net. From what he could see of her silhouette, she looked tired, distracted. A pang of guilt shot through him. It was his fault. Despite her son's upbeat attitude on the phone earlier, Steve imagined her kids had given her a hard time after she'd sent Steve, Brie, and Lincoln packing. Driving a wedge into her relationship with them hadn't been his intention. Not for a second. He'd simply wanted her to take the prize so he could keep his job and move on with his life. *You were selfish, Stevie,* he chided. *Selfish with a capital S.*

"Steve, there's Hope," Lincoln said as if reading his brother's mind. He slid into the booth and scooted toward the window.

Brie slid in next to him, and then Steve sat down.

"I'll send a waitress over," Gabe said as he handed out the menus.

"Send Hope," Lincoln blurted.

"Sure thing. Merry, merry."

As Gabe moved away, Lincoln said, "Mom, we went to Hope's camper last night."

Steve shushed Lincoln.

"Her camper?" Ellery glanced at Steve. "What does he mean?"

"Nothing, Mom." Steve fanned the air.

"Hope and her children live in a camper," Lincoln said.

In a VW camper not big enough for one, let alone three, Steve thought, although Hope had arranged it with care. He'd liked the way she'd hung the children's art everywhere.

"At the trailer park," Lincoln added.

Ellery frowned. "I had no idea. Did you, Frank?"

He shook his head. "I wonder if Gabe knows."

"She's not upset about it," Steve said, surprised to find himself fighting Hope's battle. "She's making do."

Lincoln opened his menu. "Brie said she's proud."

"She is," Brie chimed.

"Proud and pretty and powerful and playful," Lincoln said.

Brie chuckled. "I didn't say all that."

"And perfect and pleasant," Lincoln continued. "And—"

Ellery patted Lincoln's hand. "You certainly know a lot of words that start with the letter P."

All of which did apply to Hope, Steve mused, studying his brother, wondering whether he'd been prattling or whether he'd intentionally chosen those words. Lincoln, oblivious to Steve's stare, was perusing the menu even though he had it memorized and probably knew the moment he'd awakened what he wanted to eat.

"How did you learn about, um . . ." Frank hesitated. "About Hope's situation?"

"We followed her," Lincoln replied.

Quickly, Steve explained. "She was at her daughter's school play, and we went there to offer her the prize again."

"But she drove away before we could, so we followed her," Lincoln said, continuing the story. "It was a no-brainer."

Ellery blinked. "A no-brainer?"

"Dumb. Stupid. Idiotic. Senseless. Sil—"

Steve reached behind Brie and flicked his brother's shoulder. "Cut it out with the synonym salad."

"Ow." Lincoln rubbed his shoulder.

"Boys." Ellery eyed Steve.

He shrugged and returned his gaze to the menu.

"What did Hope say?" his mother asked.

"I was the one who told her kids they won," Lincoln said proudly. "But Hope told us to leave."

Steve stewed. If only he'd anticipated Lincoln bounding from the car.

"She turned it down again?" Frank asked.

"She was mad," Lincoln said.

"Not mad," Steve said sullenly. "Upset."

"Mad," Brie mumbled.

Ellery raised an eyebrow. "You told her it was an all-expenses paid trip?"

"Well, you know, Mom, it isn't, really." Steve said. "When you add up all the out of-pocket things that crop up on a vacation, like extra snacks and mementoes and hats and stuff, it's not cheap." He recalled buying all of that and more when he'd gone to Disneyland with Gloria. "KPRL isn't paying for those things."

"They should," his father said.

"*Should* and *will* are two different things."

Steve glanced over his shoulder and spied Gabe speaking to Hope. She looked in Steve's direction. What her gaze conveyed made him shiver. Feeling duly chastened, he lowered his head. How he wished she wasn't so good with her kids and—yeah, his brother was right—pretty. Even frowning, she was stunning. And those eyes, when she wasn't staring daggers at him, were incredible. He'd never seen any like them before.

Hope strode to their table, pad and pen in hand, and offered a big, albeit *forced*, smile. "Good morning, Waldrens. What will it be? Lincoln, I'm guessing you want the raspberry white chocolate pancakes."

He looked incredulous. "How did you know?"

"Because I'm psychic."

Lincoln heehawed. "Psychic. Clairvoyant. Second-sighted. Telepathic." He elbowed Brie.

She guffawed with him, then said, "I'll have the same. You only live once. Extra whipped cream."

Hope eyed Steve. Her nose twitched ever so slightly as if she was suppressing . . . what? A sneer? The impulse to clock him? "How about you?"

"Eggs," he said. "Look about last night—"

"How would you like them? Scrambled, fried, or soft-boiled?"

"Scrambled. With crisp bacon. About last night—"

"And for you, Ellery?" Hope asked, turning her attention to the others.

"Same as Steve," Ellery replied.

"I'll have the raspberry pancakes," Frank said, "like Brie, with extra whipped cream."

"Dear," Ellery chided.

Frank patted his stomach. "January second, it's back to the treadmill."

Ellery laughed and kissed Frank's cheek. Steve envied them. He and Gloria hadn't had that kind of—

No. Steve stiffened. *No.* He hadn't realized until she was gone how detrimental she'd been, undermining him at every turn. *You lucked into this job. You never really had the talent. You're a flash in the pan.* That last one had hurt the most. He had a career ahead of him. A long career.

"Steve?" his mother said. "Answer Hope."

"I'm sorry. What did you ask?"

"Coffee?"

"Yes. Black. And a slice of pie. You choose. Say, did you ever live in Portland?"

Hope slipped her order booklet into the pocket of her apron. "Be right back with those coffees."

"Hope, wait. I wanted to ask . . . " Steve licked his lips. "Actually, what I wanted to say was . . ."

A few strands of hair had escaped her snood. They made her look carefree. Did she want to be? Had life made her wary? *Duh, Steve. Of course it had. Especially if she'd gone through bankruptcy.*

"Speak up," Hope said.

He couldn't. He was tongue-tied.

"Funny," Hope smirked. "You were never at a loss for words in high school."

He tilted his head. "So that was where we met. High school."

"I was a freshman, you were a senior. We met at an event to raise money for the athletic teams. My girlfriends all knew you."

"I'll bet they did," Brie said snarkily.

"No, not like that. By reputation." Hope hurried to say, "No. That's not what I meant, either. Steve was a big deal. Popular. He was a star reporter—" Her cheeks blazed red, which made her look ridiculously gorgeous and vulnerable. She chewed on her lip before starting again. "What did you want to ask a moment ago, Steve? Whether I'll reconsider accepting the prize because yes, I'll take it! You're right. My kids could use some sunshine."

In their drab lives, Steve thought, replaying her retort in his mind.

"Great," he said. "That's great. I mean it's really, really great." He was blathering. He never blathered. "I'll make it happen. You won't regret it. And if there are extra expenses, the station will pay for them. You won't be out a dime." He smiled, pleased with how the promise had rolled off his tongue.

Hope smiled, too, although her cheeks seemed to be twitching. With excitement? With concern about what she'd just agreed to?

"We have some contracts to sign," Steve said. "You'll have to commit to a travel schedule."

Gabe sneaked up behind Hope. "She's got whatever time she needs!"

"Excellent." Steve clapped his hands.

Lincoln did, too.

But when Hope turned away, Steve could see her shoulders quivering, as if she was doing everything she could to hold it together and not cry. The notion made his heart snag.

Chapter 26

After serving all her orders and following up to make sure her customers' needs were met, Hope paused by the register to catch her breath. How could she have said yes to Steve? Was she insane?

"Hope," a woman said.

Hope turned. Brie was approaching her. Was something wrong? Hope had served breakfast. She'd brought Steve a slice of apple-raisin-pecan pie. She'd readied the bill and delivered the change. The Waldrens had even made their way out of the café. Through the window, she spied Steve air-sparring with his brother on the sidewalk. Both were laughing, so what was the problem?

She brushed a hair off her cheek. "Yes, Miss Bryant?" She gripped the register to steady herself. "Is everything okay?"

"Please, call me Brie." She glanced over her shoulder and back at Hope. Softly she said, "You can trust Steve to get you the extra money."

"Really?"

"Yes, your story is newsworthy."

Panic shot through Hope. "What? No, no, no. I won't agree to a story. That's not part of the deal. Steve didn't mention a story. I can't—"

"Everything okay, girlfriend?" Zerena asked as she whisked past Hope with an armload of breakfast plates.

"Uh-huh. Yes." Her heart was hammering her chest. "Go deliver your order. I'm good." When Zerena departed, Hope said to Brie, "No. If this is contingent upon Steve telling my *story* or anything about my living situation, he may not. There will be no pictures of my kids. No photographs of the camper."

"But—"

"No. Do you hear me, Brie?" Hope blew a hair off her face. "No, no, no. On second thought, we don't want the prize." She slashed the air with one hand. "I withdraw my acceptance."

With two hands, Brie clasped Hope's mid-air. "Calm down."

Hope yanked free. "If publicity is part of the deal—"

"Please. I didn't get to say everything. Listen. This is important. You represent so many women in this country. Single women working hard to make ends meet. Women with kids and a job and no savings. Our audience needs to hear about you. Connect with you."

"Your audience likes sports," Hope countered.

"Not my audience. I do human-interest stories. And KRPL has hundreds of thousands of viewers who want to know about their neighbors. Their successes. Their struggles. People who will find inspiration from heroes like you." Brie's gaze glistened with tears. "You're keeping afloat. Your kids are happy and balanced. I meant what I said last night when I said, 'You rock!' Other women will feel the same as I do." She offered a supportive smile. "Here's what we'll want to know. What happened? To your family? To your husband? Gabe said he left you. Why? Where is he now?"

"No." Hope swallowed hard. She would not demean Zach. He was still the father of her kids. If her story went public, Zach, wherever he was, would take the heat and her kids would suffer. None of them deserved that. "No. N-O." She brandished a hand. "We don't want the trip. We don't need it. Our lives are private and off limits. That's final. How could Steve even think I'd go for that?" She strode toward the kitchen, seething with anger. At herself, for being duped. At Steve, for enticing her with empty promises. Did he think by offering extra money he could persuade her to share her story for TV ratings? Uh-uh, no way.

"Hope, wait." Brie pursued her. "Steve didn't—"

"Save it!" Hope whirled around and touched the snood at the nape of her neck. Strands of hair were loose. She must look a mess. Frantically, she tried to stuff them in and failed. She glanced out the café's windows. Steve had stopped sparring and was peering into the café. He waved to her and grinned broadly. She didn't respond. "Look, Brie, I'm sorry, but I can't—I won't—do this."

"Listen, we don't have to discuss your marriage, okay?" Brie spread her arms wide. "We can focus on your dreams. You have dreams, don't you? Waitressing isn't your end-goal, is it?"

Hope thought of her meager savings. On the ten dollars a week she was saving.

"Maybe a little exposure would make your dreams become a reality," Brie said.

"Like going to Disneyland, where dreams come true?" Hope sniped.

"I was thinking, what if we talked about your dreams and investors came forward?"

Brie seemed so intent that Hope wanted to trust her, but the rational side of her brain screamed *Impossible!*

"I'm talking about sharing the dream you had when you got married," Brie said. "Or before you got married. The dream that fizzled when life came at you fast. You're still trying to make it happen, aren't you? C'mon. I know you are. What is it?" Brie clasped Hope's arm and peered into her eyes. "What is your dream?"

"I used to own a bakery in Portland," she whispered, surprised to give voice to it. "When my husband . . ." She shook free and shivered. "No, I'm sorry, Brie. If telling my story is what it will take to get KPRL to cover all the expenses, then we're out. We won't accept."

"But Steve will lose his job if you don't."

Hope gasped. "So I was right last night?" She recalled the horrid things she'd said to him. Now, they didn't sound so awful. He'd been in it for himself after all. She peered out the café's window. Steve had his arm around his brother and was happily chatting with his parents, looking for all intents and purposes as if he had this prize deal—his job security—all sewn up. Well, he didn't. Not by a longshot. Hope refocused on Brie. "Now, it makes sense. This is all about Steve. Not me. Not my family. *Him*. *His* job. *His* future. He sent you to be his emissary."

Brie shook her head. "You're wrong. I was the one who—"

"I don't owe Steve anything." Hope planted her hands on her hips. "If protecting my family's privacy negates the deal, then so be it. Good-bye."

"Hope—"

Zerena drew near. "I have mace, girlfriend."

Hope smiled weakly. "Please inform Gabe that I need a breather." She untied her apron, tossed it on the counter, and bolted through the kitchen and out the back door.

Chapter 27

Hope loved her town. She loved the people and the good vibes, and for a full five minutes she strolled Main Street drawing in soothing breaths. When she calmed down, she returned to the café and tended to three more customers before leaving to pick up her kids at school. They were standing at the drive-through location when she arrived. Neither looked happy. Todd's nose was caked with dried blood, as if he'd gotten into a scrape. Melody wouldn't make eye contact.

"Last day of school," Hope said as they climbed into the van and strapped on their seatbelts. "No homework, but I have a long shift, so you're going back to work with me. Gabe said you can eat whatever you want. I've got some projects planned for you, and—"

"Not hungry," Melody said, staring listlessly out the window.

Todd grunted. He was peering into the book Hope had given him but he wasn't turning pages.

"When I'm done, we'll swing by the pizza parlor," she added. She could afford pizza this one time. To ease their disappointment and heartache.

"What didn't you understand about not being hungry?" Melody carped.

"Tone," Hope said automatically, then pressed her lips together, deciding not to address the elephant in the VW. She knew what was wrong. She had let her children down. If only Steve's deal had been simple. No story. No photographs. No pressure. They could have gone to Disneyland. They could have had fun. Hope would have figured out how to pay for a treat here and there by dipping into savings and postponing her dream.

She pulled into the lot behind Aroma Café, and the children scrambled out. "Stay in the nook in the kitchen," she advised.

Todd showed Melody something hidden in his palm. Her eyes went wide. Hope decided that whatever their secret was, she'd let them have it. For all she knew, it was a dead bug.

Two hours later, after the sun had sunk below the horizon, Hope removed her apron and tossed it into the hamper. "Kids, let's take a walk around town. See the lights. Window shop."

"For what?" Melody shot her a look. "We can't afford anything."

"Snow is falling," Hope said. "Let's lick snowflakes. That'll be fun, right?" She took hold of Todd's hand. "Maybe there will be carolers. We can sing along. And then we'll get that pizza I promised."

"Yeah, okay," Melody muttered.

"Fine," Todd said, sounding as disheartened as his sister.

"Bye, Zerena," Hope said as they neared the exit, doing her best to sound perky and upbeat.

"Wait, wait!" Zerena cried. "Hold up. I didn't tell you." She sidled close to Hope and peeked over her shoulder. Whispering, she said, "Roman and I are going to the tree-lighting ceremony. Woot!"

"That's great."

"I don't know what to wear."

"Something warm. Something blue. Blue is your color. And don't worry." Hope squeezed her friend's arm. "He won't care what you're wearing. He already thinks you look hot in waitress gear. I've seen him ogling you."

Zerena bussed Hope's cheek. "Where are you off to?"

"Window shopping," Melody and Todd said in monotone unison.

"Have fun!" Zerena gave Hope a questioning look at their lack of enthusiasm.

She mouthed, *We'll talk*, and bustled the children outside.

The moment Hope, Melody, and Todd exited the café a swarm of people leaped from nearby vans or SUVs. Not just any people. Reporters and camera people.

No, Hope thought. *No, no, no.* Her insides seized. *Crap!*

"Mrs. Lyons," a woman with a shag haircut called. "Why did you say no to the prize?"

"Won't your children be disappointed?" a man with a red beard yelled.

"Don't you feel like the Grinch?" Shaggy asked.

"Or Scrooge?" Red Beard grinned lasciviously.

Hope swallowed hard. How had these vultures found her? How had they learned that she'd said no to Steve Waldren? Did he sic them on her? She couldn't imagine him doing so. What did he gain by embarrassing her? For all his faults, she hadn't pegged him as spiteful. Did Brie Bryant do it? No, Brie had acted remorseful when they'd parted earlier.

"Mrs. Lyons," Shaggy yelled.

"Mrs. Lyons," Red Beard echoed.

Hope muttered. If the newshounds had approached her without her children in tow, she would've spoken her mind and used colorful language. Zach had taught her a host of bad words.

"Go away!" Hope shouted and hustled her children toward the café.

"Hey, Mrs. Lyons." A thin reporter with a snake tattoo slithering up his neck blocked the entrance. His equally thin cameraman aimed the lens at Hope. "Talk to me." His sibilant voice crackled. "Don't you feel guilty for depriving your kids? Why don't you say yes? C'mon, say yes into the microphone."

"Mom?" Melody was shivering. "What's going on? Why are there cameras? Say yes to what?"

Snake shoved a microphone in Todd's face. "How about you, Son? Got something to say?"

Todd mewled and curled into Hope.

"Get. Out. Of. Our. Way," she yelled, each word louder and crisper than the first. "Do not test me." As snow drifted around them, she grabbed her children's hands and forged down the sidewalk, trying not to slip.

Snake bellowed, "What's it like living in a car?"

He knew about the camper? How could he? Only Steve, Brie, and Lincoln . . .

Anger bubbled inside of Hope. Whoever had told them was toast. Burnt toast.

"Did you say no because you were worried about KPRL's liability?" the woman she'd dubbed Shaggy shouted.

"C'mon, hon. Disneyland," Red Beard crooned. "Everyone loves Disneyland. Say yes."

Hope hated when anyone called her *hon*. The guy had to know her name was *Hope*. Why not use it? She'd been named for her grandmother, a beautiful woman with a calm yet indomitable spirit. How she wished she possessed an ounce of that spirit now. But she didn't. Every fiber was quivering. She wanted to run. To hide. To take a swing and draw blood.

Shaggy shouted, "Think of your children!"

"How about you, little girl?" Snake pursued Melody. "What do you think your mom should say?"

"Mo-om," Melody whimpered, and tucked her head beneath Hope's arm.

How dare you, Steve Waldren! Whether or not he was behind it, it had all started with him.

"Mom!" Todd shouted. "Look!" He pointed to the Holiday Bazaar up the street. It had been set up in the expansive public parking lot beyond Sweet Place.

"Great idea," Hope said. "Let's go." They could get lost among the shoppers. "C'mon, don't dally." *Dally? Honestly?* Dally had been one of her mother's favorite words. Fine, she would channel good old indomitable Mom. "Let's find you two some new Christmas stockings."

"Really?" Melody gasped. "You know the one I want."

Hope did. The bazaar had an online presence. Melody had searched it a few days ago and seen an adorable green-and-white striped stocking with a cartoonish red reindeer hand-stitched into it.

Todd said, "I want candy cane ice cream. Can we buy ice cream, Mom?"

"Yes, we'll have a backward dinner tonight." Hope didn't care about the cost. But first she had to lose the reporters. As deftly as a secret service agent protecting the president, she steered the kids beneath the bazaar's archway of pine boughs and into the grand tent.

STEVE EXITED GOOD SPORTS with his brother and drew to a halt. What the heck? What was going on down the street? Why were Hope and her kids running? *Oh, crap.* They were being pursued by a pack of reporters. *Crap, double-crap. No, no, no.* Where had the wolves come from? They were going to ruin everything. Okay, sure, Hope had said *yes* to Steve earlier, but then she'd told Brie *no,* yet even though she'd turned down the prize a second time, he knew he could persuade her to say *yes* again. He had it all worked out on how he'd approach her in the morning. He'd sweettalk her. She'd listen. She'd come around.

"Dang it!" he muttered.

"Don't swear," Lincoln chided.

"Bro, chill. I'll be right back. Stay here." He took off at a gallop.

"I'm coming with you!" Lincoln hurried after him. "Mom said I'm supposed to stick with you. Stick like glue. Stick like tape. Stick like gum."

Good old mom, Steve groused. "Okay, c'mon."

He jutted a hand behind him. Lincoln grabbed hold. Steve couldn't move as fast with his brother in tow, but he couldn't leave him, either.

In high school, Steve had participated in baseball and basketball, but by college he hadn't been brawny or tall enough to be truly competitive, so he'd switched to track. He'd been good at hurdles. Short sprints, too. He cut in and out of people on the sidewalk, yelling, "Merry Christmas," every time he or Lincoln bumped into someone.

The gaggle of reporters turned right into the Holiday Bazaar. So did Steve.

Chapter 28

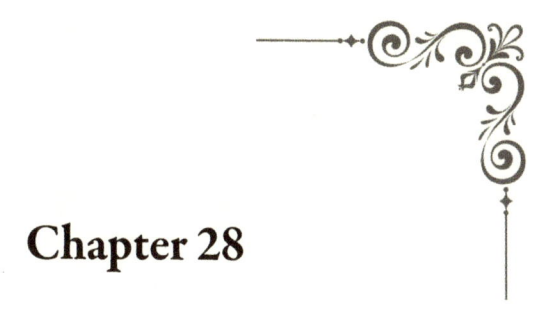

Hope entered the bazaar, her children's hands fisted in hers. The place was teeming with people. "Winter Wonderland" was blasting through overhead speakers. Booths were arranged in aisles. As Hope weaved her kids through them, she peeked over her shoulder. Snake and Shaggy and their cameramen were hot on her tail. Red Beard and his camerawoman were trailing them.

"This way." Hope maneuvered Melody and Todd around a cluster of adults with children. Near the décor aisle, she said, "Duck, kids. Hide with me." She steered them beneath the table of the vendor selling handmade stockings.

As they huddled, Hope said, "Remember, you two. You have each other's backs. You are each other's advocates. No one, other than me, will stand by you like the two of you will."

"Yes, Mom," Melody said.

Todd echoed her.

When Hope was confident she'd eluded the reporters, she said, "Okay, let's get up. But be alert." She scrabbled to a stand and scoured the area. The reporters and camera crews were gone. But she wouldn't give up her vigil.

STEVE SHOT THROUGH the arch of twinkling boughs and pulled to a stop. Lincoln collided into him and apologized.

The scent of pine, cocoa, and cotton candy was intoxicating. Lights twinkled everywhere. Steve held a hand above his eyes to block the glow and scanned the area. Hundreds of people were mingling about. All were smiling. There were three aisles of booths. Which one had Hope and her kids gone down? He spied the reporters to his left, on the hunt. He trailed them and slowed when the heavily-tattooed reporter pulled to a stop and mimed *Cut* to his cameraman. When the shaggy-haired female whacked her cameraperson on the shoulder, and the remaining red-bearded reporter bent over, clutching his chest, Steve whirled around. Were they done? Giving up? Were there others? He didn't see any more predators.

"Steve, look!" Lincoln pointed away from the reporters. "Candy apples. Can we get one?"

"Go for it." He handed Lincoln a five-dollar bill. "I'll stay right here."

Lincoln trotted away.

Steve wiped snow off his face and hopped up and down trying to get a view of each aisle. He couldn't see squat. He hustled to a workman on a ladder who was fixing a string of dormant lights and motioned to the ladder. "Can I climb up?"

"Not now. Too busy."

"Twenty bucks is in it for you."

The workman scuttled down and held out his hand. Steve paid him and moved the ladder backward about five feet. He clambered to the top and surveyed the activity. He couldn't spot Hope or her kids anywhere. And then he did. In the décor aisle. Scooting from beneath a table.

BREATHING EASIER, BELIEVING the newshounds had dispersed, Hope took in her surroundings. What a wealth of joy surrounded them. Vendors populated each aisle, their booths decorated to the max and filled with handmade goodies. Felt elves. Stuffed snowmen. Elaborate snow globes. Glittery ornaments. Due to their limited funds, she hadn't ventured into the bazaar in years, but it hadn't changed much since she was a girl. Fondly, she remembered strolling through the bazaar with her mother and caressing each item.

"Melody and Todd, you can pick one thing apiece," Hope said. "Under twenty dollars."

"The stocking I told you about for me," Melody said. "This one." She lifted it off the vendor's table.

Hope paid for it. While waiting for the vendor to wrap it, she glanced nervously over her shoulder. No reporters. Nobody gawking. Maybe if she and the kids spent a long enough time in the bazaar the reporters' thirst to question them would abate. They didn't know where she lived, did they? Surely Steve wouldn't have given out her address. None of the creeps had mentioned the trailer park. One had said she lived in a car, not a camper. Silently, she prayed it wouldn't dawn on them to stake out the café and follow her.

"Take your time deciding, Todd," she said, as she mulled over what to do. "Take all the time you need."

QUICKLY, STEVE CEDED the ladder to the workman and grabbed Lincoln, who was merrily biting into a candy apple.

"Did you get a napkin?" Steve asked.

"Uh-uh."

"Dope."

"You're the dope. Can I keep the change?"

"Knock yourself out."

"That would hurt."

As they passed another food vendor, Steve swiped a napkin. "Next time think ahead."

"Next time, you think ahead," Lincoln sniped. "Where are we going?"

"I want to catch up to Hope."

"She's here?"

"Yep. With her kids."

"Why do you want to catch up to her?"

"Because."

"Because why?"

Steve glanced sideways at his brother. Lincoln was not being cheeky on purpose. He truly wanted to know. "Just because." He didn't want to go into detail.

"Mom says *because* is not a good answer."

"It's the only one I've got." He turned back to get a bead on Hope and gasped. "Oh, no! She's gone!"

"I see her." Lincoln pointed. "By Santa's Village."

Relief swept over Steve when he spotted her, too. "Good eyes, bro."

The village was stationed at the far end of the bazaar. The land was a riot of red, white, and green, and dusted with fake snow. Elves with huge pointy ears, floppy hats, and striped costumes were guiding children into a long waiting line. A booth serving hot cocoa stood to the right. Another booth offering caramel corn and cotton candy was to the left.

Santa, seated on an ornate gold chair, shouted, "Ho-ho-ho!" to a child approaching him.

Lincoln said, "He's a better Santa than you."

"Ah, man!" Steve slapped a hand to his heart, overacting. "How can you say that to your very own brother?"

"He's happy, and he's smiling more."

"I smile."

"It's a fake smile." Lincoln mimicked him. Lips tight. A sneer in his eyes.

Steve grunted. "Okay, that's enough critique. I need you on my side."

"I'm on your side. I'm on your right side."

"Yes, you are." Steve grinned. "But now, I need you to be quiet." He put a finger to his lips and beckoned his brother. "Follow my lead."

"I already am."

Chapter 29

Steve drew near to the village. Red velvet ropes helped form the line to Santa's throne.

"There," Lincoln said softly, pointing.

Melody and Todd were standing near the end of the line, looking as excited as everyone else. Hope, holding a gift bag, lingered outside the ropes, nervously glancing over her right shoulder and back at her kids, alert for sightings of the reporters, no doubt. Perfect. Steve had time to talk to her without the children being within earshot.

"Stay here," he said to Lincoln and, wiping perspiration from his forehead, proceeded toward Hope with caution. He slipped up on her left. "Hey. Having fun?"

She startled, hand raised as if ready to fend off an attack. She lowered her arm. "You." She said it accusatorily, venom in her tone.

"Yep, me." Steve splayed his hands. "I'm sorry. I didn't mean to scare you."

Lincoln said, "Yes, he did. He told me to be quiet."

Steve threw a peeved look at his brother. So much for him following orders.

"You," Hope repeated, cheeks flushed, eyes wary. "You . . . You're the reason reporters are pursuing me and my kids. You gave them the story. *My* story. You told them I lived in my car."

"No, I didn't. I'm not sure how—"

"It had to be you. Brie wouldn't have done that."

Steve didn't think Brie had. She'd been extremely contrite about scaring off Hope. He said, "I didn't. I swear." He crossed his heart and elbowed his brother. "Tell her, Lincoln. I didn't contact any reporters. I've been with you."

"Steve's been with me. He bought me a new lure." Lincoln hoisted the bag from Good Sports. He had a huge collection of lures—over two hundred by now—but Steve could never say no to buying him one more. "Want to see? We got a green gummy one. It's really cool." Lincoln pulled it from the bag and shook it in Hope's face.

She recoiled.

"Do you believe me now?" Steve asked, surprised by how much he needed Hope to say she did. He wanted her approval. He wanted her to trust him.

She sighed. "Then who sent those reporters?"

Steve wagered a guess. Dave. He probably thought the newshounds would embarrass Hope into accepting the prize or, hearing that they'd chased her, shame Steve into being more forceful. Either way, it stunk, and Steve wasn't going to let him get away it. He wasn't sure what he'd do. Quitting wasn't an option. But he had to do something.

Steve said, "I think you're safe for now. I saw three teams exit the bazaar."

Hope heaved an exhausted sigh, and Steve's heart wrenched. She looked so vulnerable instead of her proud fierce self, and it was his fault.

"Hey"—he nodded to the bag she was holding—"I see you've done some shopping."

Hope glanced at the bag and back at him. "Melody wanted a new Christmas stocking."

Lincoln said, "Santa leaves presents in stockings."

"Sometimes he does," Hope replied.

"Every year." Lincoln nodded as if his truth were the only truth.

Hope smiled warmly at him. "Yes," she said. "I suppose for you, Lincoln, he does."

Steve sighed. His mother was right. Hope had a kind word for everyone. Everyone but him. "Listen, Hope, about pressuring you earlier, I've gotta admit I was happy when you said yes, but I understand your concern about finances, and I promise we can come up with the extra bucks you'll need—"

"Stop, Steve." Hope held up a hand. "Brie told me how the station would find more money for me because the stakes would be higher if you told my story, but that's exactly why I told her no."

"Wait. Hold on." Steve ground his teeth together. He hated being the last to learn something. "What story?"

"KPRL wants to make me the poster child for women that struggle."

"No." Steve moaned. "No, that's not true."

"She said you want to call out my ex-husband for being a louse."

"No. She's wrong. I never said we'd do a story. She must have come up with that idea on her own. That's not—" He swiped his hair with one hand. *Dang it, Brie. What the heck did you do?* No wonder she'd hightailed it back to the bed-and-breakfast after telling Steve that Hope made an about-face. She knew she'd blown it.

"I'm sorry, Steve, but no matter what, I will not allow KPRL to flaunt my family in front of TV cameras for ratings. As for my ex, he's . . . He's off limits." Hope pressed her lips together. "Look, we didn't work out, but that's no reason to drag him through the mud. Plus that would only make my children suffer. They adore him, or at least the memory of him. And, for your information, I am not a poster child for anything. Women who find themselves in my predicament, struggling to make ends meet, choosing insurance over housing, food over clothing, do what we can to survive. Life isn't fair, but we muscle on. Got it?"

"I get it. I do. I never . . ." Steve paused. He really *did* get it. He didn't want to undermine Hope. If anything, he'd want to shine a spotlight on her courage.

"Brie asked if I had a dream, and I do," Hope said. "A big dream. But going to Disneyland is not going to make that dream come true for me or my kids. Hard work will. Saving for the future will. Not living in a fantasy world believing someone will come along and rescue me. Do you understand?"

Steve wanted to reached out. He didn't. He held back. She looked so determined yet fragile, and he knew—he sensed—that if he made a move to comfort her, she'd bolt. "Your kids have a good fifteen minutes in that long line. How about a cup of cocoa? I'd like to hear about your dream."

"I want cocoa," Lincoln said.

Hope looked at Lincoln and back at Steve. "Sure. I could use a cup of cocoa."

"With extra whipped cream," Lincoln said. "And a peppermint stick."

"Wait with Hope, Linc," he said, and sauntered to the cocoa stand. He paid for the beverages and returned, handing one to Hope and another to his brother. "So what is your dream, Hope?"

She took a sip of cocoa, her nose twitching as if assessing the drink by its aroma, and tilted her head, her gaze once again wary. "My dream."

"Yes." Under her scrutiny, Steve felt an ache in his chest. An ache to know everything about her. "I really want to hear."

"I'll tell you my dream," Lincoln cut in. "I want to own a radio station."

"Yes, I know," Steve said, "and you want me to be the voice for it."

"You're the *Voice*," Lincoln grinned. "Mom and Dad are so proud."

Hope bit back a smile and took another sip of cocoa. A film of whipped cream stuck to her upper lip. She licked it off. Steve had the sudden urge to kiss her, but tamped down the impulse.

"Mr. Q is the voice of KQHV," Lincoln went on.

"I know Mr. Q," Hope said. "He was my science teacher."

"Mine, too," Steve chimed.

"He's really smart," Lincoln continued, "but he's retiring."

"That's too bad," Hope said.

"Enough about me or my brother," Steve cut in. "Lincoln, suck on your peppermint stick for a while, okay, bro?"

Lincoln took him literally and slurped the stick out of the cocoa.

"So, Hope," Steve began cautiously, "what is your dream? To run for president?"

Hope coughed out a laugh. "You've got to be kidding me. You're taking that tactic? Trying to charm me?"

"Is it working?"

"Ha! President? Not on a bet. No, Steve, I do not have impossible dreams. Besides, who would ever want to be president?"

"I sure wouldn't," Steve replied, and laughed.

"Me, either." Lincoln mimicked Steve's laugh, though Steve was certain his brother didn't have a clue what he was chuckling about.

Steve blew on his cocoa, looking at Hope over the rim of his cup. "So . . . your dream."

Hope glanced at Santa's Village. Reflection from the twinkling lights graced her face, giving her an angelic glow. "I want to own my own bakery again."

"Was it Pie in the Sky in Portland?" he blurted.

"Yes."

"That's where we met."

"Yes."

"But I didn't remember."

"Completely understandable," Hope said. "You meet a lot of people. I was one of thousands and behind the counter. In essence, faceless."

Steve couldn't grasp how humble she was. "Why did you sell it?"

"I had to." She shrugged one shoulder, as if it meant nothing, but he sensed it did.

"Why?" he blurted, and quickly waved a hand. "Don't answer. Delete that. Stupid question. I get it. Your husband walked out, and it became too much for you to run a business and take care of the kids."

"No, that wasn't it."

"It's still open."

"That's good to hear. I invested a lot of time and energy building up the business."

"The pie crust isn't as good as yours."

Hope scrunched her nose in a pixie-like way. "That's a shame, but I have to admit I didn't sell the new owner my recipe." She glanced to where her kids were standing.

Steve followed her gaze. Melody and Todd were talking to Santa. Both looked euphoric. He sipped his cocoa, waiting for more. Hope didn't continue.

"Couldn't your parents help you out?" he asked.

Lincoln said, "Her parents died years ago in a car accident."

Hope's eyes grew misty.

"Oh, man, I'm sorry," Steve said. *Slick, boy-o. Super slick. Open mouth, insert both feet.* He was stunned that his brother knew more than he did, but Lincoln did pay attention. He might not be able to spit out everything that cycled through his brain, but he was bright. "I had no idea."

Hope said, "They left me an inheritance, but . . ."

Steve gagged on his cocoa, the truth becoming clear. "No. Say it isn't so. Your husband ran off with the money?"

"More like ran through it."

"How? Did he start a losing business venture?"

"He was . . . is . . ." Bitterness and regret flickered in Hope's eyes. "No. I'm not telling you more about my sob story. I wouldn't want a reporter to hold your feet to the fire to get it out of you."

"Hold Steve's feet to the fire." Lincoln chortled. "Ouch!"

"I wouldn't . . . They wouldn't . . ." Steve stopped blathering and nodded in understanding. He was seething, ready to kill Dave. Short of that, he'd remove every one of his boss's fingernails to the quick.

"At the café, I get the chance to bake my mother's specialty pies," Hope said. "It's good enough."

Steve had never been okay with *good enough*. Hope Valley, as beautiful as it was and as much as he loved his family, had never been good enough. He'd had big dreams and had intended to achieve those dreams. It was why he'd moved to Portland and had made plans to land an even larger market. Now, however, standing alongside Hope, he was questioning those decisions, those dreams.

"What about a small business loan or a startup loan?" Steve asked. "Those aren't too hard to get, I hear."

"They are if you had to declare bankruptcy." Hope sighed, resigned. "I'm saving up what little I can from tips. My paycheck goes to regular expenses."

Lincoln said, "I wish I had enough money to buy the radio station."

Hope turned to him. "Hold on. You said Mr. Q was retiring. You didn't say he was selling."

"Yup. KQHV is for sale."

Hope frowned. "I had no idea."

"It's okay," Lincoln said. "He's getting old."

"He was a terrific science teacher," Hope said. "Steve, did you take biology with him?"

He nodded.

"Remember when he made the class dissect a frog?" Hope's gaze lit up. "He cracked such corny jokes."

Steve snorted in spite of himself. "What kind of shoes should someone wear when dissecting a frog?"

"Open-*toad*," Hope answered, and offered a giggly *ribbit*.

The sound tickled Steve. "Mr. Q's a good guy."

"A good guy," Lincoln echoed.

"Maybe you can save up to buy it, Lincoln," Hope suggested.

"I can't." He wagged his head. "I don't have a job."

Hope looked at Steve. "Couldn't your brother cut Christmas trees or serve cocoa or do dozens of odd jobs around town?"

Steve appreciated her naivete. "He could, but he'd bottom out. He doesn't interact like other people, as you've probably noticed. He gets distracted."

Hope said, "I bet if you were his boss, he'd be attentive. He adores you."

Lincoln slung an arm around Steve and pulled him close. "You da' boss," he said with a rapper's accent.

"Yeah, I am, and don't you forget it." Steve caught Hope watching her children as they left Santa and said, "They're cute kids. You know, Todd—"

"Likes statistics." Lincoln knuckled Steve's arm. "Just like my brother. He's really smart. He knows everything about every sport in the whole wide world."

"Steve," Hope said, her cheeks were flushed, her gaze fervent. "If you promise to keep the reporters that you swear you didn't sic on me at bay, then yes, I'll accept the prize. Re-accept the prize." She let out an exasperated sigh. "I'll take it!"

Joy shot through Steve. And something else he couldn't put his finger on. Was he wishing for a future with Hope? Nah, no way. That was not going to happen. But it was definitely elation he was feeling, and for now, that was good. "I vow I will do everything I can"—he said, crossing his heart with his finger—"to protect your privacy."

And he meant it.

Chapter 30

Hope blamed the hot cocoa for why she'd said yes to Steve again, but if she was honest, she knew it hadn't been the cocoa. It had been his attentive gaze. Those hazel eyes. He'd acted as if he was really listening to her. *Getting* her.

"Mom," Melody said, "are you listening?" She had hold of Hope's hand and was dragging her back into the bazaar's shopping mecca. Todd had a grip on the hem of Hope's coat.

"Yes, I'm listening."

"No, you're not. You're in la-la-land. Santa had the most incredible baritone voice."

"That's nice."

Hope hadn't told the children about the prize yet. Steve and Lincoln had slipped away before the kids exited Santa's Village, so the children hadn't spotted them.

"He knew all about sports, too," Todd said.

"He told Todd there's a collectibles seller at the bazaar," Melody said. "That's what Todd wants to spend his money on."

"Okay." Hope smiled, loving how her daughter was looking out for her brother.

At the vendor's, Todd gleefully purchased a single baseball card for a dollar.

"Pizza!" Todd announced when he accepted the bag from the seller.

During dinner, the talk turned to statistics. On the drive home, Hope glanced at her children's sweet, expectant faces. She deliberated telling them about the trip and decided to save the news for after camp tomorrow. They'd celebrate in the proper way with dinner and cookies and the party poppers she'd purchased at the dollar store to save for a special occasion.

But at dawn, she rose with doubt once again swirling inside her. Was saying yes the right choice? Was it bad of her to have waffled? If she said no again, Steve would think she was a flake. He wouldn't understand. But she had so many expenses, so many obligations.

No, she rebuked herself *No.* She'd said yes. The answer would remain yes.

Without waking Melody and Todd, Hope hurried to the showers in the trailer park. The water was tepid, but after running from the reporters, she needed to cleanse herself of the stench of fear that clung to her. When she returned to the VW, she dressed for work.

An hour later, Hope drove the kids to the community center. It was a white-and-brown, one-story expanse with multipurpose rooms, an outside area with tables for eating, and a playground where kids could work off pent-up energy. In other words, perfect.

Gabe's niece Khloe, a natural beauty with carrot-orange hair and a pert turned-up nose, came out to meet them. She smiled broadly and opened her arms wide. "Hello, Lyons! Welcome, welcome."

Though Melody and Todd knew Khloe, both looked reluctant to exit the camper.

"Go on," Hope encouraged. "She's excited to spend time with you."

Melody grabbed her backpack and basketball, and Todd, already wearing his backpack, fetched one of his prized comic books.

"I have so much planned for you two today," Khloe said, as they joined her on the sidewalk. "Art, crafts, and music jam."

"Music jam. Yes!" Todd gave an emphatic fist pump.

"Maybe we'll even shoot a few hoops, Melody," Khloe said.

"In the snow?" Melody asked skeptically.

"Sure, why not? It's not that deep."

"Um, okay." Dressed in her pink parka and pink snow hat with pompom, Melody looked younger than ten.

"First, cocoa." Khloe looped an arm around them.

"Sugar-free," Melody said.

"Sugar-free! Done." Khloe guided them along the path to the entrance. "Wave bye to Mom."

They obeyed.

An hour later, as Hope was wiping down the counter and almost giddy about Steve and the prize, Gabe approached her.

"Hey, darlin', are you okay?" he asked. "You're staring into space."

Hope snapped to. "Yes." *No more daydreaming,* she chided herself. She had customers. "I'm fine."

"No, you're not. Tend to those tables then come back here and talk to me."

"Gabe . . ."

"Don't *Gabe* me. Do it."

Hope nodded. After she made sure everything at each of her tables was okay, refilling coffee cups and delivering second servings of cocoa, she returned to Gabe. "I'm fine, really," she murmured.

He nabbed her elbow, guided her to a stool at the counter, and forced her to sit. His face was filled with concern. "Spill."

"Here?"

"No one is listening. Everyone has his or her life to manage. Talk."

"I did something bad yesterday."

"Something bad, as in illegal?" He raised an eyebrow. "Are you going to prison?"

"No. Nothing like that." Nervously, she weaved her hands together.

"*Phew*. I was worried. You've got the look of a criminal," he teased, twirling a finger in front of her face. "Kidding." He touched her shoulder. "Okay, so what did you do?"

She threw her arms wide. "I said yes to Steve Waldren. I accepted the prize."

"I know. I was there. I gave you time off. Have you forgotten?"

"Yes . . . No . . ." Hope rubbed her neck and chuckled. "I've got mush brain."

"I like when you laugh."

Me, too, Hope thought. Years ago when she'd met Zach, she'd laughed at the silliest things. Goofy faces. Funny movies. But then life changed, and her laughter ebbed.

Gabe perched on a stool beside her. "I'm glad you said yes about the trip. You deserve something good in your life."

"But then I said no."

"No?"

"To Brie. Because she said KPRL would want to go public with my story."

"Your story?" He looked perplexed.

"About being homeless."

"Homeless?" He look dismayed.

"Not homeless, per se. We live in my VW at the trailer park."

"Why?"

"Zach left us high and dry." Deciding it was time to loop Gabe in fully, she explained her predicament. "Brie said because I'm a single mother who struggles, the station would pay me to talk about my story."

"How did she find out?"

"Steve and she and Lincoln followed us from the school to the trailer park."

Gabe nodded. "Go on."

"Brie said they'd want to talk about Zach, and I put my foot down and said if that meant no prize, then no prize. But then reporters found out somehow, and they chased me and the kids, but we eluded them by running into the bazaar."

Gabe's mouth fell open.

"I ran into Steve there," she went on.

"Why was he at the bazaar?"

Hope wasn't sure. Had he seen her being chased? Had he come to rescue her? She shook her head. "I don't know, but he bought me cocoa, and we talked, and he said he'd make sure KPRL honored our privacy—no story. So I said yes again." She fought tears.

"That wasn't bad."

"Yes, it was! Oh, Gabe, I know you gave me time off, but if I accept the prize, I'll miss work."

He wrapped her in his arms and cradled her head like her father used to. "You'll go in January. We're slow then."

"I can't afford to lose wages. I've been scrimping. Every last penny. I've been trying to save to . . . " She couldn't put words to her dream. She didn't want Gabe's pity.

"You won't lose wages. You've earned two paid weeks off."

Hope wrinkled her nose. "Ha! You don't give anyone paid vacation."

"Well, it's about time I did." He winked.

Hope remembered how her father or mother would wink at her whenever they'd wanted to perk her up. She missed them so much. Gabe hadn't replaced them, but he was all she had.

"Maybe if I did give paid leave," Gabe went on, "I'd have more loyal employees."

"You have the best, and they adore you."

Brie appeared over Gabe's shoulder. "Yoo-hoo, Gabe? I was wondering..." She hesitated. "Sorry, Hope." She looked mortified. "I can tell I've interrupted a serious conversation."

Gabe flashed a smile, clearly happy to see her. "We're talking about vacations," he said. "Have a seat and give us a minute. I'll be right with you." He patted the stool next to him.

Brie didn't hesitate. In fact, she was acting as if she belonged. Worry shot through Hope. Didn't Gabe realize Brie would be heading back to Portland soon? Was she going to break his heart?

Gabe hailed Zerena. "Coffee for the pretty lady." He refocused on Hope. "As I was saying, a bonus or paid vacation goes a long way. You deserve it, and I'm doing it. See? You're starting a trend. Making me a better guy. A magnanimous guy. I've always loved that word. Magnanimous." He stressed the second syllable and patted her cheek.

Hope smiled.

"Are you taking a vacation, Hope?" Brie asked, apparently not understanding Gabe's request to give them a minute.

"She is," Gabe said. "And she's going to Disneyland."

Brie gaped. "You're saying yes again?"

"She already did," Gabe chimed.

"Last night," Hope said. "To Steve. At the bazaar."

Brie whooped.

"Except Gabe will be one waitress short, and—"

"I can take your shifts." Brie waved a hand. "I used to waitress when I was putting myself through college. Gabe, will you let me help out?" She batted her eyelashes.

"You live in Portland," Hope retorted. "It's not an easy commute."

"I won't live there for much longer." Brie rose to her feet and planted a fist on her hip. "I've decided to officially retire January first and move to Hope Valley. I love it here."

Hope gawked at her.

"So, Gabe," Brie said sassily, "can I sub for Hope?"

He grinned. "Absolutely."

A moment of sensual electricity passed between them. Hope was dumbfounded.

Without breaking her connection with Gabe, Brie said, "Go to Disneyland with your kids, Hope. It'll be fun."

Suddenly Hope couldn't breathe. Her chest felt cinched with duct tape. "I need some air."

"Sure. Take all the time you need," Gabe said. "Say, why don't you go for a drive? Open the windows. Drink in the beautiful weather."

Hope couldn't leave the café fast enough. On the sidewalk, she stood shivering, wondering whether the universe was conspiring against her. *Get real, Hope. Conspiring to make you happy? To make your kids happy?* She glanced over her shoulder at Brie and Gabe, chatting like old friends with him leaning in to her and Brie blushing like a schoolgirl, and a rash of resentment cut through her. All of this merriment and Christmas spirit and fellow man helping out another fellow man was not real. She had to keep her guard up. If Zach had taught her anything, it was that.

Feeling as wound up as a Jack-in-the-box, she slogged to the parking lot and climbed into the VW. She headed to the north end of town and decided to tour the streets to check out the merry decorations. As she drove, she thought of Melody and Todd and smiled. She was doing the right thing. They deserved a trip. They deserved joy.

But then, out of nowhere, the VW started coughing. Not just coughing. Juddering and sputtering. "Crap," she muttered under her breath. "No, no, no."

Hope cycled through the possibilities. She wasn't out of gas. She'd filled up two days ago. Was it the fuel system? The catalytic converter? During her teens, her father had shown her how to change her oil, check the radiator, and more. He'd said he never wanted her to be a damsel in distress. So why did she feel stressed to the max now? She couldn't be without the VW.

Frustrated, she drove to the mechanic, a sweet guy who had been in business since she was a girl. He took a quick look and declared that she needed a mass airflow sensor. He could swap it out right away, and it wasn't too expensive, but Hope did the calculations and knew the cost would empty her savings account. Even so, she agreed. She had to.

As she waited for the car, she thought again of Melody and Todd. Yes, they deserved a trip, but, more importantly than that, they needed their mother to provide food and insurance and a place to sleep. Gabe's generous offer of two weeks paid vacation would cover the basics, but it would not provide for unforeseen extras—like the van they lived in conking out.

Hating how reality had once again reared its ugly head, she cursed Zach . . . and then she called Steve. When he answered, she blurted, "I'm sorry, Steve. I can't accept the prize. I know I said I could last night, but I can't. My van. It died. I . . . I'm sorry."

"But—"

She ended the call and sobbed.

Chapter 31

"Dang it!" Steve tossed his cell phone on the kitchen counter and paced, glaring at the phone. What the heck had changed her mind? "Dang it!"

Lincoln, who was sitting on a stool watching their mother make cookie dough, stiffened.

"Steve," Ellery warned, wiping her hands on her snowman-themed apron. "Don't swear around Lincoln."

"Don't worry, Mom. I won't swear," he said. "*Dang it* isn't swearing, and *dang it* is as bad as it will get, but dang it and double-dang it!" A slew of sailor-worthy curse words ricocheted inside his brain.

"Would you like some cocoa?" she asked.

"No, Mom, I do not want cocoa. Cocoa will not solve this problem."

"Don't raise your voice, either," she said.

"Sorry."

"What is the problem, Son?"

"Not a danged thing!"

"Steven Richardson Waldren!" she barked.

Lincoln began tapping the rung of his stool with his toe.

"Sorry, sorry." Steve mimed zipping his lips and in a soft voice said, "Nothing, Mom. Really. Nothing I can't handle." He pecked her cheek, gave his brother's shoulders a hard squeeze, and hurried to his room.

Seconds later, his mother knocked on the door. "We're going to decorate the tree tonight."

"It's already decorated," he said.

"Not with our personal ornaments. You know the tradition. The night before the tree-lighting ceremony, we add the ornaments that you and Lincoln made over the years." She opened the door, moved to where he was sitting on the bed, and sat beside him. "I know you haven't been here for the entire Christmas season in a while, but the traditions haven't changed. I'll make your favorite cookies as a bribe. Chocolate crinkles."

"Fine."

"Want to help me make them?"

"Not this time."

"Don't brood. You'll get wrinkles." His mother kissed the side of his head and tiptoed out of the room.

Steve lowered his face into his hands. Not because she'd made him feel guilty. She hadn't. At least, she would never mean to. No, this was all about him. His career. He was done. Over the hill. Toast. Why had Hope said no again? There had to be a reason. Whatever it was wouldn't matter to Dave.

"Rip off the bandage," Steve whispered. "It won't hurt as much." He pulled his cell phone from his pocket and saw that he'd missed a call. Not from his agent. From an unknown caller. A telemarketer, most likely.

Sighing, he dialed the station and asked for Dave.

Seconds later, his boss came on the line. Steve pressed Speaker, set the cell phone on the bed, and, while stretching his arms and torquing his torso, calmly and coherently explained the situation. Hope said yes at first, but then she said no. But then she said yes after he went to her camper. Dave said he knew all of that. So Steve continued. After accepting the second time, she said no to Brie because she didn't want KPRL to tell her personal story. Plus, she didn't want her ex-husband dragged through the mud. And then, out of nowhere, reporters showed up and chased her and her kids into the Christmas bazaar.

He thought he heard Dave chuckle, but he might have imagined that. He continued. "I saw the jackals, so I raced after her. She eluded them and me. But then I spotted her and her kids at Santa's Village, so I cozied up to her, and she said yes again."

"Good job."

"However, something changed between then and now, and, well, she said no again."

"What? Why?"

"I don't know. Something about her van. I'm sure she has good reason."

"You blew it, Waldren! Blew it!" Dave shouted, as emotive as Mt. Vesuvius. "Do you hear me?"

"I hear you, boss."

"Yeah, about that. It's the last time you get to call me that. You didn't get the winner of the prize to say yes. You epically *failed*. Therefore, you're fired."

"Fired?"

"You heard me. F-I-R-E-D."

"Dave, be reasonable."

But Dave wasn't listening. He was continuing his rant, ridiculing Steve, making snide comments about Steve's performance and his relationship with the weather girl.

"Dave, c'mon, man, I've given the station nearly two decades of my—"

"I. Don't. Care. Come into the station and clean out your belongings. You're finished."

Steve sighed, realizing Dave wasn't lying because the man truly relished his role as career killer.

"You know what?" Steve said, summoning his gumption. "You are a class-A jerk. Sending those reporters to hound Hope. Don't deny it. I know it was you. Did you think you'd embarrass her into saying yes to the prize?"

"Duh."

Steve could've kicked himself. Why had he mentioned Hope's living situation to his boss? "I repeat, you're a jerk, Dave. A jerk with no soul. A class-A jerk with no moral compass. You disgust me. Do you hear me?" Steve didn't comprehend until he'd finished his diatribe that Dave had hung up on him.

After he found his calm, Steve contacted his agent and begged him to find him a new position. Anywhere. It didn't have to be a big city. He simply couldn't go cold. If his resume had a gap, he would never work again. Any job he accepted could be explained away by Steve saying he'd wanted a respite from the bigger markets and wanted to see what working in a smaller one was like. But he couldn't afford a *gap*.

When his agent said he'd do the best he could and ended the call, Steve stabbed in Harker's number. Harker answered after the first ring. Steve laid it all out. Hope's surprise turn-down. Dave's toxicity and duplicity. His agent's lackluster support. "I've given that guy fifteen percent of everything I've earned for years."

"Dude, that sucks," Harker said. "But this could be good for you."

"How so?"

"You get to start fresh. A chance to find your passion."

Steve grumbled. He was passionate about his current job. At least he thought he was.

"It took me five jobs to find this one," Harker said. "But the punches to the gut, the loss of confidence, how much I suffered . . . You know it was worth it."

Steve did. Harker had gone through a rollercoaster of emotions after dumping job three and four. Steve had been his sounding board.

"And now I love what I'm doing. I love the company. Love my boss."

"Because she's a looker," Steve retorted.

Harker snickered. "Take a deep breath, pal, and reassess in the morning. I've got your back."

Steve hung up and stared at himself in the mirror. Oh, he was reassessing all right. Tired eyes. Weary smile. Cheeks blazing with anger. But if he admitted it to himself, there was also regret. How he'd wanted Hope and her family to take the trip. Not because it would have saved his career but because she and her kids might have experienced a moment of joy.

Hope. He pictured her face. Her winning smile. Her deep-rooted sadness. She'd suffered too much. Why had she said no again? If he reached out, would she—

His cell phone rang. He stabbed Send without looking at the readout, thinking it was Harker prepared to give him one more pep talk. "Yeah?"

"Hi, Steve, it's me again. Todd. Did you see what Jones and Woodruff did last night? Both rocked it at the stadium."

Steve agreed.

"Jones had thirty-six points and Woodruff thirty-four," Todd went on. "Woodruff usually averages twenty-six per game, and Jones averages twenty-six-point-nine with seven-point-two rebounds."

"Seven-point-three," Steve corrected.

"Yeah, three. You're right. Anyway, it was so awesome, and well, that's all I called to say. Okay? Bye." Todd ended the connection.

Steve chuckled, stunned that yet again the kid hadn't asked about the prize. He'd just wanted to talk stats. Steve wondered if Hope knew her son had called him and determined that she didn't or she would've put the kibosh on it. He remembered having secrets at Todd's age. He wouldn't rat him out.

Spurred by Todd's enthusiasm, for a few minutes Steve streamed ESPN to see highlights of last night's games, and then, giving into fatigue, flopped onto the bed, covered his eyes with his forearm, and instantly fell asleep.

"Steve?" His mother tapped on the door.

He glanced at the bedside clock and was startled to see it was already six p.m. Where had the time gone? "Come in, Mom."

Ellery opened the door. She was no longer wearing an apron. She'd put on makeup and had swapped out the shirt she'd been wearing for a cherry-red Christmas sweater adorned with jingle bells. "The cookies are ready, and Lincoln has unwrapped the box of our personal ornaments. He would like you to join us."

"Mom, I was fired."

"I'm sorry, Son." She took a long moment before crossing to him and sitting on the foot of his bed. She rested a hand on his toes. "You'll be fine. You always are."

That wasn't true. Steve had only needed to land one job, and he did it right out of college. He didn't know if could rally.

"Will you join us?" she asked.

"Sure, Mom."

Chapter 32

Steve changed into a white shirt and slacks. An hour later, he couldn't believe he was actually having a good time with his family. Hanging the glitter-frosted ornament he'd made at the age of eight brought back a poignant memory, how at the time he thought he was quite gifted in the art department. Every snowflake was a touch of perfection. Lincoln's was mostly globs of glue coated with glitter. Granted, Lincoln was four at the time of its creation. Even so, Linc had been thrilled to see his ornament hanging alongside his big brother's work of art.

With each addition to the tree, their parents applauded like Steve and Lincoln were still kids. Man, they were cute, he thought. In love for over forty years. Had they ever quarreled? Had they ever questioned their commitment? He and Gloria had never been in love like his folks, and if he was honest, the lack of real love in his life was eating at him. He wanted to treasure and to be treasured. He didn't believe in everyone having a soulmate, but Gloria had never been his, so maybe his was still out there.

"Stevie, pass the cookies," his father said.

Steve glanced at the half-empty platter and moaned. Had he actually downed three chocolate crinkles? He needed to have more impulse control. He couldn't afford to put on weight. Every ounce showed on camera. "Sure, Dad."

On the record player—his father was and would always be a vinyl guy—Dean Martin was crooning "I'll Be Home for Christmas." His mother was humming along.

When she switched the LP to the Drifters' upbeat rock version of "White Christmas," Lincoln started dancing around the living room, steering an imaginary woman in his arms.

"C'mon, bro," Lincoln said. "Grab Hope and dance."

"What?" Steve shook his head. "You're nu—" He stopped short of saying *nuts*. "Ha-ha, Lincoln. Funny. Hope wouldn't dance with me in a million years. She hates me."

"She does not," his mother said. "How could she? You're handsome, smart, and funny."

"Uh-uh, Mom, she hates him," Lincoln said.

"Lincoln, sweetheart, why would you say that?" Their mother was frowning, trying to understand.

Lincoln continued dancing. "She didn't like the reporters."

"What reporters?" Ellery's brow furrowed. "Frank, do you know what they're talking about?"

Frank, who'd dressed in a green Santa sweater over corduroys, shrugged.

"Steve?" His mother eyed him.

"My boss revealed to the press that Hope turned down the trip to Disneyland, and because he was miffed, he must have also told them about her, um, living conditions. Some reporters tracked her to the café, and she . . ." He worked his tongue inside his cheek. "She panicked. She didn't want anyone to find out."

"There's no shame in how she lives," Ellery said. "Single mothers struggle sometimes."

"I don't think she liked the cameras," Lincoln said. "I wouldn't, either."

Steve gazed at his brother and suddenly realized how tone deaf he, Steve, and probably everyone else in the world, was. If newshounds were to highlight Lincoln's disability, Lincoln would have a tough time handling the questions and the harassment. Hope's concern was real and warranted. She didn't want her family predicament plastered all over the news.

"You owe her an apology, Son," Ellery said softly.

He nodded. "I'll do it. Promise." He kissed his mother's cheek and then began shadowing his brother, mimicking him, arms outstretched. "Who are you dancing with, dude?"

"Miss Mapleworth."

"Your teacher from third grade?"

Lincoln nodded. "She was so pretty."

Miss Mapleworth, a special education teacher, a wonderful woman who had enjoyed Lincoln's ability to rattle off numbers and statistics, had not been pretty. In fact, she'd had a bent nose and hooded brow, but her smile for Lincoln had been sincere.

Yep, a smile can melt a heart, Steve thought, and again flashed on Hope. She had that kind of smile.

The music ended. Lincoln stopped dancing and flopped onto the sofa. "I wish I had somebody to love."

Their mother nestled beside him and kissed him on the forehead. "You do, dear."

"Not like Steve does."

Chapter 33

Hope had stewed all day about how she was going to break the news to her kids regarding the prize, the cost to repair the van—all of it—so she'd waited until they'd hooked up at the trailer park and were eating a snack of cinnamon cream cheese on celery sticks before laying it out. She did it quickly. In two sentences. Short and not so sweet.

"That's not fair!" Melody shouted. "How could you? You said yes to Steve and took it back again? It's free!"

"Sweetheart, the van—"

"Works!" Melody shot out a hand. "It works."

"It wiped out our savings."

Melody blew out a dismissive breath.

"Also, think about it, sweetie. The reporters. They would tell our story."

"You said to be proud of our life." Melody pounded the air with her fist. "To hold our heads up no matter what."

"True." Hope had said that, and she'd meant it, but this was different.

"Well, I'm holding mine up now." Melody jutted her chin high into the air. "Change your mind."

Hope bit back a smile. Her daughter would make a good debater one day, but this battle Hope couldn't lose. "Stop, Melody. The discussion is over."

Melody wailed. "You're cruel, Mom. Mean and cruel, and it's so not fair."

Todd put an arm around his sister's shoulders and murmured, "Not fair."

"Life isn't fair," Hope said, a knee-jerk response, but she couldn't take the words back.

"Daddy would say yes," Melody said.

Before Hope could respond, Melody wrenched free of her brother and burst out of the van.

Todd slumped into his bean bag and opened one of his comic books. His lower lip was quivering, but he didn't cry.

An hour later, Melody slogged in and flopped into her corner. As clandestinely as possible, she wiped tears off her cheeks.

After the dinner dishes were cleared, Hope set out a plate of sugar-free cookies and two glasses of milk. "Doesn't our tree look nice? The little guy is quite merry, don't you think?" The tree lights' battery pack was doing its job.

Melody grunted.

"And I love the stocking we bought you at the bazaar, Melody," Hope added. "Santa will definitely be eager to put something in it. Yours, too, Todd."

"Mine's old." He scrunched his nose like Hope was wont to do.

"Santa doesn't judge a stocking by its age," she said. "Besides, your nana knitted it just for you. It's unique." Hope had hung them on the backs of the driver's and passenger's seats.

"What does it matter? Santa won't stop here," Melody groused.

"Sure he will," Hope said. In addition to the extra book for Melody and graphic novel for Todd that she'd already purchased, she had found each of them something special at a rummage sale and had decided that this season Santa would be a cash-and-carry guy. She would put ten dollars in each of their stockings and let the kids use the money any way they wanted, as long as it wasn't on candy. Not even sugar-free candy.

"I like the baseball card we bought at the bazaar," Todd exclaimed. "Thank you." He gave his mother a hug.

Hope tamped down the bittersweet sorrow welling within her. Who would have thought her littlest would be the bravest?

"Let's sing Christmas carols." She'd tabled the idea of breaking out the party poppers. Those would not be welcome at this point. She clicked the music app on her cell phone and pressed the icon for the holiday music list. She selected a rousing version of "Jingle Bell Rock" and clapped in rhythm.

Todd tried to be enthusiastic, but Melody had returned to her corner and was sulking.

When the song finished, Hope sat on the floor near Melody and stroked her shoulder. "Sweetheart, why don't we find a few things we can be thankful for?"

"Like my comic books," Todd said.

"And the Christmas play that you were brilliant in," Hope cooed to Melody.

"And Santa," Todd cried.

Melody whisked her hair off her face and stared daggers at her brother. "Santa isn't real."

"Melody!" Hope said. "Apologize to Todd."

"Santa is a figment of your imagination. He's—"

"Stop." Hope slapped the floor of the camper. Hard. "Todd, your sister is wrong."

"I want Daddy." Crocodile tears pooled in Melody's eyes. "I hate you. Hate you!"

Hope felt as if a knife had been plunged into her heart. She tried to kiss her daughter but Melody wanted none of it. Shakily, the girl tried to rise to her feet. She stumbled.

"Melody!" Hope clutched her. "Sit. I have to check your blood sugar."

A half hour later, when Melody was stable and calm, Hope tucked the children into their sleep sacks and read a story by flashlight.

When her children were gently snoring, Hope moved into the driver's seat, switched on the radio—Mr. Q was reading "The Night Before Christmas"—and she opened her ledger to review income and outgo. After a long moment, she sighed, relieved. Even after insurance payments and filling prescriptions and the impulse purchases at the bazaar and the small gift for Khloe at the Christmas Attic, because the sweet young woman had refused payment, she would have enough for two week's groceries.

Her cell phone *pinged*. She glanced at the incoming text message. From Steve Waldren. *Sorry. I was an idiot for putting you and your kids front and center.*

She smiled. At least she and he could finally agree on something.

And then she wept.

Chapter 34

Hope awoke Sunday with a major league headache. Going to sleep crying was never a good idea. A bell pealed in the distance. She scrambled out of her sleeping bag and tapped Melody's and Todd's shoulders. "Rise and shine," she said. "This is our day to help out at church."

Melody shrugged out of her sleep sack, her hair hanging on either side of her face like a curtain. Wordlessly, Todd slipped on his jeans and blue sweater.

Each day of the week, the food bank at Hope Valley Unitarian doled out hot meals in the morning to townsfolk struggling to make ends meet. One Sunday a month, Hope and the children made it a point to chip in. Her parents had done so, and Hope liked carrying on the tradition. Until a few years ago, little did she know that she would become one of them. She reminded the children that seeing others striving to make lemonade out of lemons kept things in perspective.

Hope tried to comb Melody's hair, but she wrenched away from her. Hope couldn't stand the silent treatment. She stifled a sob. "I love you both," she whispered. "So much."

Neither of them replied in kind.

A short while later, Hope pulled up in front of the church, a gray beauty with gothic-style stained glass windows featuring the apostles. A single spire rose into the sky. She paused at the crosswalk, allowing parishioners to cross, and spotted Gabe and Brie among them. They were holding hands and, for some reason, every protective instinct Hope felt as a mother came to the fore. She considered having a heart-to-heart with Gabe but decided against it. He was a grown man. He didn't need her input about whom he dated.

Pushing her thoughts aside, she veered around back and pulled into the parking lot near the church's kitchen. Over fifty people, simply dressed and thankful for those who offered to help, stood waiting to get their meals. She recognized a few from the trailer park and others from the low-rent district at the edge of town.

Addie Dixon, the gentle woman who ran the food bank, waved to Hope as she and the children approached. "Look at you two! How you've grown in a month!" she exclaimed, her eyes sparkling with love. She chucked Todd's chin and stroked Melody's hair. "My little elves, are you ready to assist me?"

Both children nodded.

"Put smiles on those faces, please," Addie chirped. "Nobody likes to get food from a glum chum." She tried to tickle them.

They reeled back, resisting yet giggling.

Addie said, "Melody, you take the syrup station with my granddaughter. Todd, you hand out the utensils with your buddy. Hope, if you would man the cocoa and coffee. Adults only with the hot stuff." She bussed Hope on the cheek and whispered, "Are you okay?"

"Long night. Didn't sleep."

"If you need a friendly ear, I'm always open, hon." Addie rubbed Hope's shoulder.

It was all Hope could do not to break into tears. "Cocoa." She pointed. "Think I'll pour myself a cup."

Two hours later, Hope gathered the children, bid good-bye to Addie and a few stragglers that she knew, and drove to the café. "We have the sugar cookie contest today, kids. Are you ready?"

"Who cares?" Melody said, her attitude surly again. "We can't win, and I can't even eat the cookies."

"I put aside sugar-free cookies for you. I even made sugar-free icing."

Melody grunted.

"I think I ate too much bacon at church," Todd said, rubbing his stomach.

"I'm sorry, sweetheart," Hope said. "You'll feel better soon."

When they arrived at Aroma Café, Hope gave the kids a nudge. "Both of you, please guide the other kids who are competing. They'll need your expertise."

In the kitchen, Zerena elbowed Hope as she was donning her apron. "Tonight's the night. Me. Roman. The Christmas tree-lighting ceremony. You're coming, right?"

"Yes, as long as my kids don't wage mutiny." Hope glanced through the arch at Melody and Todd, who had donned aprons and were ushering children to the rectangular tables that Gabe had set up at the far end of the café.

"What's going on?" Zerena asked.

"They hate me." Hope tied the apron's bow at the back and checked her face in the mirror on the wall. Gray skin, sad eyes. She pinched her cheeks.

"I'm sure it's a phase."

Hope wasn't so certain.

Zerena sighed, her gaze fixed on Roman, who was serving up a plate of ham and eggs. "Is it wrong for me to stare at him?"

Hope patted her friend on the shoulder. "Nope. You're in love."

"In lust."

"Same thing for now." She bussed Zerena on the cheek and got to work.

Chapter 35

Steve followed his brother into Good Sports and halted by the door. The place was packed with Sunday shoppers looking for last-minute Christmas presents. Large screen televisions hung on all the walls, each airing a different sport. Closed captions ran along the lower portion of the screens. The strains of "March of the Armchair Quarterbacks," a spoof Christmas song, was piping through the speakers. Their father, dressed in a red plaid shirt, jeans, and hiking boots, was standing with a customer alongside a line of colorful kayaks and gesturing like a display floor model. Steve had learned his salesmanship skills at his father's knee. If only his dad had taught him how to sell a free trip to Disneyland.

"What's that sound?" Lincoln asked.

Steve's cell phone was buzzing. He scanned the readout and saw a text from Gloria, of all people. She'd asked how he was doing. Honestly? After all this time? She wrote a follow-up text: *Miss you.* He grunted and swiped the screen to eliminate the message.

Seconds later, his phone buzzed again. This time his agent had sent him a text: *No offers yet.* Peeved, Steve wrote back: *Write when you have something. Not before.* He didn't want to hear the negative. Only the positive.

Then his phone rang. *Unknown caller.* Since Gloria's text had come directly from her, he knew she hadn't changed her phone number. It wasn't her.

He answered.

"Hi, Steve, it's me, Todd."

Steve grinned. "Hey, kid, what's up?"

"The sugar cookie contest is starting at Aroma Café. You should come."

Steve considered the idea. Maybe he'd see Hope and he could change her—

No. He wouldn't browbeat her. For whatever reason, she'd turned him down a third time. However, if he went, he could catch a glimpse of her, and that notion buoyed him.

"Good idea, squirt," he said.

Todd snorted.

"What's so funny?" Steve asked.

"My dad called me squirt, too."

Swell, Steve thought. He and the heel had something in common.

"See you soon, Steve," Todd said, and ended the call.

"Who was that?" Lincoln asked.

"Todd Lyons, Hope's son."

"He's nice. I liked looking at his baseball cards."

"I bet you did. So why are we here, bro?"

"I want a new lure," Lincoln replied.

More? Honestly? Steve sighed, knowing he was in for the long haul. Lincoln wouldn't be appeased until he'd found just the right one.

"Let's go fishing this summer," Lincoln said.

"You got it."

"I love to fish. I like trout, genus *Oncorhynchus*, species *clarki lewisi*, common name Westslope cutthroat trout. And I like salmon, genus—"

Steve flicked Lincoln's arm. "Cool it with the genus stuff. My head aches."

"Do you need aspirin? Mom gives me aspirin."

"No, it'll pass."

On one of the TV screens, an ESPN analyst was touting the NBA's superstar's latest stats. How Steve wished he could have landed a gig at ESPN in his twenties, but his parents had begged him not to move to Connecticut. Now Lincoln was older; he could cope, couldn't he?

Steve groaned. He was shallow. Heartless. He needed to rethink his priorities. It wasn't like he was ever going to have the career he'd dreamed of. Could he imagine something else he ought to be doing? Something noble?

"Bro?" Lincoln said. "Why is your forehead pinched?"

"I'm thinking."

"Does it hurt?"

"Yeah." Steve grinned. "A lot." He smacked himself on the side of his head and yelped on purpose.

Lincoln cackled and mimicked the move and response.

Steve chortled along with his brother. If he wasn't careful, he might lose his sense of humor. That would be dire.

In a short while, they found two lures that Lincoln didn't own. After paying for them—Steve wouldn't allow his father to give him the family discount—he and Lincoln exited the store and stood on the sidewalk. Snow was drifting down. Shoppers were out in droves. Everyone seemed content. Even Steve, in spite of himself, found himself whistling.

"Coming to the tree-lighting ceremony tonight?" one woman asked a friend as they breezed past Steve.

"Wouldn't miss it."

"See you there." The two women parted ways at the stoplight.

"Are we going to the tree-lighting ceremony?" Lincoln asked.

"You always do," Steve said.

"Yes, but are we going? You and me?" Lincoln wagged a finger between the two of them.

"Wouldn't miss it," Steve said, mimicking the cheery woman he'd overheard. He gazed up the street and saw a line of people entering Aroma Café. "Want to go to the sugar cookie decorating contest?"

"Sure. I love sugar." Lincoln *yukked* and offered a goofy grin.

Outside the café, Steve paused and looked in. The place was swarming with children and adults standing around tables covered with holiday tablecloths, each decorating Christmas tree-shaped sugar cookies. Hope and Zerena were moving between the groups, offering tips, guiding hands, showing how to swirl icing onto cookies.

Lincoln cupped his eyes to peer inside. "Are we going in? I'm hungry."

"You're always hungry."

Steve started to push the door open. At the same time, the Lyons children darted out, both bundled in jackets, snow hats, and scarves.

"I can catch more in a minute than you can," Todd exclaimed.

"No, you can't," Melody said.

They tilted their heads back and stuck their tongues out. Snowflakes landed on them.

Without closing his mouth, Todd said, "One, two . . ."

Melody cried, "Three, four, five. I'm winning. Six, seven, eight, nine."

"Hi, kids," Steve said. "How's it going?"

Todd said, "Hey, Steve! Look, Melody. It's Steve and Lincoln."

Melody said, "We can't talk to you."

"Why not?" Steve bent at the waist, bracing his hands on his knees, so she wasn't forced to look up at him.

"Because . . ." Melody licked her lips. "Because our mom wouldn't want us to."

"Why not? I don't bite."

She mulled that over.

"I bet I can catch more snowflakes than you." Steve tilted his head back and opened his mouth like the children.

"Uh-uh," Todd said, opening his.

Melody lost her attitude, and together she, Todd, and Steve searched for falling flakes. Lincoln joined in the fun.

Steve counted quickly. "One, two, three." Out of the corner of his eye, he spied Melody slyly gazing at him.

"I'm winning," she said.

"Yes, you are. Your brother is beating me, too. Guess I lose." Steve threw his arms wide.

"What about me?" Lincoln asked.

"You beat me, too, bro."

"I beat the Voice," Lincoln crowed.

"We all beat the Voice," Todd said. "Hey, Voice . . . I mean, Steve. Um, I've been thinking."

"About?"

"About the prize. Mom said she won't accept it, but . . ." Todd looked over his shoulder toward the café and back at Steve. Lowering his voice, he said, "What if our Dad said yes?"

Steve gawked. Their father. He'd never considered the notion. "Where is he?"

"He's—"

"Todd, stop." Melody gripped her brother's hand. "Mom will be mad."

Todd wriggled free. "He's on a trip. He's winning all sorts of money."

"Is he?" Steve said, not believing a word of it, but Todd was nodding, and Melody's eyes were bright. "What does he do?"

"He plays cards," Todd said. "He's very good. An ace."

So the guy was a gambler. That was how he'd run through their savings, by blowing it in poker games. What a cad.

"He's in Portland," Todd added.

Steve didn't know of any game parlors in Portland, but that didn't mean they didn't exist. Or perhaps Hope had told her children

Portland because that was a town they could wrap their heads around, seeing as they'd lived there. More likely, the ex-husband had migrated to Las Vegas to seek his fortune. However, if he was in Portland—

"I'm cold." Melody brushed snowflakes off her shoulders. "Todd, let's go back inside."

"Wait!" Steve said. "Todd's idea might have merit."

"Merit?" Todd cocked his head. "What does that mean?"

"It means you made a good point," Steve went on. "If your father accepts the prize and signs the contract, then you can still win."

"Really?" Todd smiled. "Except we don't have his—"

Melody thwacked her brother on the shoulder. "Great idea, Steve. We'll be in touch." She grabbed her brother's hand and dragged him into the café.

When the door swung closed, Lincoln stamped a foot and huffed. "Why did you do that, Steve?"

"Do what?"

"Lie."

"I didn't lie."

"Yes, you did." Lincoln folded his arms across his chest, making him look every bit as stern as their mother when lowering the boom. "You lied to Hope's children."

"Not really. If their dad comes through," Steve argued, "it's not a lie."

"Don't you get it? You're like Santa to them. If you lie, then Santa lies."

"But it's not a lie."

"Yes it is. Your boss fired you. You can't give Todd and Melody the prize if you don't work at KPRL." Lincoln didn't wait for Steve's rebuttal. He marched into the café.

Steve shoved his hands into his pockets, shocked by his brother's moment of clarity while at the same time ashamed by his own momentary lack of scruples. What the heck was wrong with him? Since when had he become a lying louse? Things had to change.

He had to change.

Chapter 36

Hope's stomach plummeted when she saw Melody and Todd reentering the café. Her daughter was gazing at her with such loathing. Hope wished the lyrics of "Angels We Have Heard on High" would lighten her daughter's mood, but no such luck. "I saw your cookie, sweetheart," she said. "It's amazing. The colors and balance and—"

"Give it a rest, Mom. I don't need compliments." Melody's chin trembled. She lowered her gaze. Her hair fell forward.

Hope caught sight of Steve and Lincoln strolling inside and wondered if Melody was troubled because she'd seen him. Had that made her realize the prize was truly gone? "Melody," Hope said, "the tree-lighting ceremony is in a few hours. Once we've finished here, why don't we get cleaned up and have a snack and then go to the Curious Reader and browse books before the ceremony. We can—"

"I don't like books," Melody snapped, and stomped into the café's kitchen.

"Me, either." Todd followed her, mirroring her attitude.

"Okay, no books," Hope muttered. "Message received loud and clear."

Putting on her best smile, she orbited the café, avoiding Steve and Lincoln. Zerena seemed to have them well in hand, although she did catch Steve glancing in her direction. Often. Did she look a mess? Or was he expecting her to explain why she'd said no to the prize a final time? Whatever the reason, she did her best to avoid his gaze, willing her cheeks not to turn crimson every time she noticed.

An hour later, Hope announced that Nathan Atkinson, Todd's arch enemy, was the winner. Todd, peering from the kitchen, wasn't happy.

AFTER THE COOKIE CONTEST ended and Gabe closed the café to give everyone the rest of Sunday off, Hope gathered the children and drove to the trailer park. She fed them take-home portions of stew from the café and then freshened up and changed into jeans, ankle boots, and her mother's sparkly green sweater. While donning a dab of lipstick, she saw Melody and Todd hunched over her phone pressing buttons. She wasn't sure what game they were playing, but neither seemed grouchy, so she let them have their moment.

"Find your hats and jackets and buckle up," she said when she was ready. "The tree-lighting ceremony starts at dusk."

On the way to the center of town, she rolled down the driver's window and listened to the strains of "Holly Jolly Christmas" being piped through speakers along Main Street.

"Ho, ho, the mistletoe," Todd crooned and sang *la-la-la* for the rest of the verse.

Hope glanced in the rearview mirror and studied her daughter, whose mouth was downturned, her gaze fixated on the street. How Hope wished she could devise something to perk her up, but knew it would be a losing battle. After parking behind the café, she walked with the children in hand toward the roundabout. Half of the street had been blocked off for the event. There was no traffic. A horde of people had turned out.

In a line down the middle of the street stood an array of food vendors' tents. One was selling hot cider. Another was offering iced donuts and cocoa. The hot dog hawker appeared to be doing a bang-up business. Same for the pretzel guy.

When Hope and her kids neared the roundabout, Todd shook free of Hope's hand and ran ahead to check out the nativity scene. Hope gazed at Melody. "Sweetheart—"

Melody wrenched away and chased after her brother.

Hope sighed. At least they were here. For now, that was enough. As her mother would say, *Where there is merriment, joy will follow.* She wrapped her arms around herself, drinking in the pretty strains of the next song in the queue, "O Christmas Tree," and scanned the crowd.

Zerena, looking radiant in a red coat over leggings and boots, was clinging to Roman's bent arm, the two of them talking nonstop. Their connection warmed Hope's heart. Not far from them, she spied Gabe holding Brie's hand. Like Zerena and Roman, the two looked utterly engaged. Brie pointed to the top of the tree. Gabe affectionately tapped her nose. Hope couldn't remember seeing him this happy since she'd started working at the café, and another pang of worry shot through her. Was Brie truly ready to give up her career? Would she seriously consider a move to Hope Valley?

Not my worry, Hope thought. She had way too many other things that she had to handle.

"Hope!" a man squawked. It was Lincoln, waving like a little kid. "Hey, Hope." He was dragging his mother toward her. "See, Mom, I told you it was her."

The pompom on Ellery's snow hat bounced as they drew near. "Frank!" She called over her shoulder. "Over here."

Frank and Steve strolled toward them. Like Lincoln, both were wearing peacoats, turtleneck sweaters, and jeans. Their strides matched. So did their smiles.

Lincoln was grinning from ear to ear. "Hope, did you see the tree? Of course you saw the tree. How could you miss it? Isn't it a beauty? I helped pick it out. The mayor let me go along. Isn't it a beauty?" he repeated. "I love hunting for trees. The smell is so good." He inhaled. "Right, Mom?"

Ellery patted his arm. "Yes, dear. Let's simmer down." She eyed Hope. "How are you?"

"Why do you ask?"

"I heard . . ." Ellery quickly peeked at Steve and back at Hope. "I heard my son showed up at your home. He . . ." She twirled a hand. "He shouldn't have intruded, though I was glad to hear you'd changed your mind about accepting the prize, but now he tells me—"

"I had an unavoidable issue. With my van. I had to say no. Don't worry about Steve." She touched Ellery's arm. "He'll find another winner. All will be right with the world."

"Not necessarily. When he couldn't seal the deal, he was fired."

"No."

Ellery put a finger to her lips. "I overheard him on his phone with his boss. He was yelling at him for sending those reporters after you."

Guilt gnawed at Hope. He'd lost his job because of her? That was wrong on so many levels. What kind of ogre did Steve—*had* Steve—worked for?

"Merry Christmas, Hope," Frank warbled as he and Steve drew near. "You look pretty in green."

"So much like her mother, don't you think, Frank?" Ellery asked merrily, clearly ready to change the subject.

Hope blushed. "I can't seem to get away from Christmas colors. Green was my mother's favorite, so it dominates my wardrobe unless I'm at the café."

"Uh-uh," Lincoln said. "You wear a green apron."

Steve stifled a chuckle.

"True." Hope studied Steve. She didn't think he looked worse for wear having lost his job. Maybe he didn't mind. Perhaps new doors would open for him. "How much longer will you be staying in town, Steve?" she asked.

"Mom talked me into sticking around a few more days. I'll be leaving right after Christmas."

"No." Lincoln pounded Steve on the arm. "No, no, no. You have to stay until New Year's."

"Not this year. I can't. I have to leave." Steve paused. "There are things I have to do."

Like find a new job because of me, Hope thought glumly.

"Frank, Lincoln, let's go check out the nativity scene." Ellery wrapped a hand around Lincoln's arm and gave a little tug.

Frank flanked him, and Lincoln went willingly, leaving Steve and Hope by themselves.

"My father was right," Steve said. "You do look nice."

"Thanks." Hope fingered her hair. She'd run a brush through it, but the curls, thanks to it being in a snood all day, were inevitable. "Did you have fun at the cookie decorating contest?"

"Lincoln was sorry he didn't win."

"I think the kid who won was a ringer. He'd probably practiced for months on his design."

"There's always one in the crowd," Steve joked.

"I guess he really wanted to win the prize. Free breakfast at the café for a month."

Steve looked impressed. "Given the way my brother downs pancakes that could have saved my folks a lot of money!"

Hope laughed, the sound burbling out of her. "So, what's next for you?"

"Back to work." His eyes flickered. "My boss is a slave driver."

Hope kept a straight face, loath to acknowledge that she knew what had happened. "Do you like being on the air?"

"I've done it ever since I graduated college."

Hope tilted her head. "That wasn't what I asked."

"I—"

Todd ran up. "Steve, Steve, did you see the nativity scene?"

"Sorry, squirt, I haven't had a chance to view it up close yet."

Todd snorted. "Mom, did you hear him call me squirt?"

"I did."

Melody skidded to a stop and gawked at Steve. "You."

"Yep, me." Steve grinned.

She looked nervously between him and her mother, and then waved awkwardly. "Hi."

Steve wiggled his fingers.

"Hey, Mom," Todd said, "I just heard a new joke. Want to hear?"

"You bet," she said.

"Why don't eggs tell jokes? Because they crack up." He slapped his thigh and roared. "Isn't that a good one?"

Hope giggled and rolled her eyes at Steve.

"I've got one," Steve said. "Why couldn't the bicycle stand up?"

"Why?" Todd asked.

"It was two-tired. Get it? *Two* tired." Steve held up a pair of fingers, his eyes gleaming with good humor.

"Bikes have two tires. Yeah, we get it," Melody said drolly.

"Two." Todd guffawed.

Steve let loose with a yuk-yuk laugh, similar to Lincoln's. The sound tickled Hope.

"I've got another." Todd gave Steve a thumbs up.

"Go for it." Steve spread his hands. "I'm all ears."

"What's green and red, and—"

"Ladies and gentlemen," the mayor said through a microphone. "We're just about ready to start the countdown. All the kids in the crowd, gather round. We need your voices."

Holding hands, Todd and Melody dashed off. They knew the drill. They'd attended the ceremony last year.

Steve bumped his shoulder against Hope's. "You're a great mom."

"Am I?"

A tender memory of her mother came to her. When Hope was lying in the hospital having just given birth to Melody, her mom kissed her cheek and whispered, *You'll be a terrific mother. And Zach will be a wonderful father. Just wait and see. Your hearts will be so filled with love, and that love will always carry you through. I promise.*

Promises, Hope thought sadly, *were meant to be broken.* She hated to admit that at times she missed Zach. He'd been like that girl with the curl on her forehead. When he was good, he was very, very good, but when he was bad—

"Did I say something wrong?" Steve asked

She swiped a tear from her eye. "I miss my mom and dad. Especially at the holidays. They owned the Curious Reader and would dress it to the nines for Christmas."

"It's a terrific shop. I went there a lot growing up." Steve cleared his throat. "How did the car accident happen, if you don't mind my asking?"

"There was a book festival in Arizona." Hope's voice cracked. "When the festival was over, Dad was tired, but he insisted on making the drive home in one leg. He—"

"Fell asleep at the wheel?"

Hope nodded.

"Gosh, I'm sorry." Steve clasped her elbow.

A frisson of desire ran through her. She gazed into his eyes, those incredibly warm eyes, and saw true concern and compassion. "Thank you."

"Twenty," the mayor yelled, and everyone echoed her. "Nineteen. Eighteen . . ."

Steve released Hope's arm and turned toward the tree. So did she.

When the mayor and children reached number one, a little girl in a white dress, coat, and stockings pressed a big red button, and the tree's lights illuminated. The crowd cheered.

Hope and Steve did, too. And then a star shot across the night sky.

Chapter 37

Hope awoke Monday morning with a start. All night long she'd dreamed of Steve. She remained snuggled in her sack as flashes of their brief connection cycled through her mind. She thought of the silly joke he'd told Todd about the bike. She recalled his comforting words about her parents. And the way he'd looked at her after the star had streaked the sky? Oh, wow. She was sure he'd wanted to kiss her. If he'd made a move, she would have let him.

Get the lead out, she told herself. She wriggled out of the sack and shivered. There was a bite in the temperature. The camper's front window was frosty with rime. She shrugged into a cardigan, and after waking the children, cleaned the VW's window. Her teeth were chattering by the time she climbed back into the driver's seat. "Dress in warm clothes," she called to the children as she made their breakfast. "And then come and eat."

Once they were on the road, Hope said, "Today will be a fun day with Khloe."

"Yeah!" Todd chirped.

"Don't you think so, Melody?" Hope asked.

Melody grunted while staring out the window, fingertips tapping the glass. She'd only eaten half of her breakfast even though it was her favorite—cream cheese and sugar-free jam on sourdough bread.

"Khloe has fun things planned." Hope turned in the direction of the community center. "I heard you're going to make papier-mâché ornaments."

"Big whoop," Melody groused.

Sunshine spilled into the camper as Hope drove, her thoughts still swirling of Steve. The way his hair swooped across his forehead. The desirable glint in his gaze. The compliment about her mothering skills. Given Melody's attitude, Hope was questioning his assessment.

"Here we are," she said, pulling into the lot by the community center.

Khloe, her orange hair in a knot and her burgundy parka zipped to the neck, greeted the children as Hope was sliding the VW's door closed. "Good morning! We're rocking and rolling today, kids. Twenty of you. Melody, your friend Josie is here. And Todd, I think you like Nathan, right?"

"No," Todd said, trying to close the zipper on his backpack.

Khloe knuckled his arm. "C'mon. It's the holidays. No grudges, okay?"

"He said Santa isn't real." Todd's mouth pulled down in a frown.

"Oho," Khloe said. "Well, we'll fix that right away. Do I have a whopper of a story to tell you about Santa. Why, just last year . . ." She slung an arm around him and steered him toward the front entrance.

"Kiss, Melody?" Hope asked.

Melody glowered at her mother and, with her backpack slung over one shoulder and basketball under one arm, raced into the center and didn't look back.

Battling the pain of rejection, Hope clambered into the driver's seat, jammed the VW into gear, and did her best not to stew. Melody's peeve would pass. Hope only wished it would pass sooner rather than later.

———⟨⟩———

AT THE END OF HOPE'S shift, an exhausting one in which she'd baked a dozen pies and served numerous pre-Christmas shoppers, she drove back to the community center. The temperature had dropped ten degrees, and snow had begun to fall in a steady drift. The windshield wipers were doing their best to flick off snow but failing. She hadn't replaced the blades in over a year, but now, having depleted her savings, she wouldn't be able to. After parking, she clapped her hands together to un-numb her fingers, exited the camper, and strode inside the building. The aroma of cinnamon wafted to her.

"I love Christmastime," a petite redheaded girl said to her mother as they were exiting.

"Me, too," her mother said, giving her daughter a warm hug.

Moving deeper inside, Hope searched for Melody but didn't see her. She spotted Todd standing at a table putting finishing touches on a papier-mâché ornament, a royal blue oval something. It looked like Todd had covered it with three times too many gooey strips.

Todd held it out to her. "It's sort of wet."

Hope grinned. "It'll dry." *Maybe in a week.* She turned in a circle, scanning the practically empty center but still didn't see Melody. Khloe was helping a boy about Todd's age into a jacket. A parent was kneeling in front of a young girl, straightening her snow hat. "Where's your sister, Todd?"

"She went outside to shoot hoops."

"In this weather?"

"She said she needed fresh air."

"How long's she been out there?"

"I dunno."

"Stay here," Hope said, and hurried to the playground. Melody wasn't there. No one was. Snow-filled footsteps marred the snow, but there were no ball marks. "Melody!" she yelled. Silence. Wind whistled through the trees.

Fear scudded through Hope. She raced into the center and cried, "Khloe, where's Melody?"

Khloe's face went white. "She's not outside?"

"No."

"But she said—" Khloe darted down the hall, opening one door after another.

Hope followed, adrenaline spiking. "Melody!"

Over her shoulder, Khloe said, "She went out about twenty minutes ago."

Hope breathed easier. Twenty minutes. She wouldn't freeze inside of twenty minutes.

"Maybe she came in to warm up," Khloe said, peering into each room.

Hope double-checked each after Khloe. "Melody!" she called. The word reverberated off the ceiling and walls.

Khloe opened the door to the girls' bathroom. "Melody?"

Crickets.

Suddenly, Hope couldn't breathe. Her lungs felt as if they'd been cinched with saran wrap.

"Mom, what's wrong?" Todd caught up to her, his young face pinched with concern. "Where's Melody?"

Hope grabbed his shoulders. "What was the last thing your sister said to you?"

"Nice ornament, dork." Todd's mouth drew thin. "I told her to—"

"About going outside," Hope said, trying to keep him on point.

"She didn't tell me. She told Khloe. Isn't she h-here?" His voice cracked with worry.

Hope clasped Todd's left hand and drew him into the main room to make one more sweep.

"Hey, there's her basketball." Todd pointed toward the Christmas tree decorated with paper ornaments and a paper chain. The ball was tucked beneath a low bough.

On tenterhooks, Hope rushed to inspect it, wondering whether Melody might have crawled beneath the tree and in her peevish state fallen asleep, but no such luck.

"Where's her stuffed elephant?" Hope asked. "And her backpack?"

"Follow me." Khloe ran to the front of the building. Hope and Todd hurried after her. "I asked her to leave the elephant with her coat. I didn't want it getting papier-mâché goop all over it." Khloe slipped into the coat room and turned in a circle. "Her jacket isn't here. Neither is the elephant or backpack."

"Mom, maybe she got bored and went to the Curious Reader," Todd suggested. "You know how much she likes to read."

Hope flashed on Melody shouting *I don't like books* the day before, but she adored books.

"Yes, my sweet son. For seven, you are wise beyond your years." Hope clung to the possibility that Melody had taken her elephant and backpack with her but had forgotten her basketball. "Let's go."

Khloe said, "Hope, I'm so sorry. I don't know what to say. I'll . . . I'll stay here"—she gulped in air—"and I won't leave. Promise. Just in case she comes back. I . . . " She raised a hand to her mouth. "I can't believe this."

Hope said, "It's not your fault. She's mad at me."

OVER TWO DOZEN PEOPLE were browsing the aisles at the Curious Reader when Hope and Todd arrived, many toting shopping bags from other stores.

They approached Isabel, who was busy tending to a wisp of a woman dressed in red and wearing bulky jewelry.

"Sorry to interrupt, Isabel," Hope said, "but have you seen Melody?"

"No. She's missing?" Isabel nudged her glasses higher on her nose. "Oh, my."

Todd said, "Mom, maybe she sneaked in when other people walked in. Let's search." He tugged on Hope's hand.

"Do you mind, Isabel?" Hope asked.

"Please do. You know how your daughter loves sports stories. I'd start there. I'll be over to help as soon as—"

Todd yanked hard. Hope gave Isabel a helpless look and went with her son. Together they peeked beneath the reading tables and behind reading chairs. No Melody. Hope checked the bathroom past the register. Empty.

Isabel caught up to them. "You haven't found her?"

Hope huffed. Did it look like she'd found her? She didn't lash out. Isabel wasn't the enemy. "Not yet," she said. "We're going to search all her favorite haunts."

"If she comes in, I'll call you." Isabel put a reassuring hand on Hope's shoulder.

"Thank you."

Hope left the shop with Todd in tow and headed down the street to the Christmas Attic. Whenever Melody visited the attic, she liked touching the vintage Shiny Brite glass ornaments.

As she entered, Ellery stepped from behind the register, brushing her hands on her sparkly red apron. "Hope, is everything all right? You look panicked."

Hope gasped, fear stifling her breath. "Melody is missing."

"Oh, heavens," Ellery said. "Should we call the police?"

"Not yet. She's upset with me. She's probably hiding."

The place was jammed with shoppers who were weaving through the myriad themed Christmas trees that included an all-red ornaments tree, a Santa and his reindeers tree, and a *Nutcracker Suite* tree. In addition to ornaments, the shop sold jewelry boxes, puzzle boxes, vintage dolls, trains, and stuffed animals.

Hope nudged Todd. They scooted around customers and, as they had at the bookshop, peered behind and beneath the displays. Todd tugged free and moved to a tree featuring comic book-style ornaments.

"Sweetheart," Hope said, "we can't shop. Let's finish searching."

Minutes later, without finding a hint of Melody, Hope said good-bye to Ellery.

"I'll keep an eye out," Ellery said.

"Thank you."

Hope and Todd continued on. To Good Sports. To Dreamery Creamery. To Sweet Place. No one had seen Melody.

Defeated, Hope went to Aroma Café. She didn't believe for a minute that her daughter would show up there and risk Gabe calling her mother, but she needed a shoulder to cry on. And she craved sober advice.

When she entered, Denny Benton saw her first. He was sitting at the counter nursing a cup of coffee, the remnants of pie crust on his plate. "Hope, are you okay? You look like—"

"My daughter. Melody. She's missing." She started to cry.

"Gabe!" Denny yelled.

Gabe bounded from the kitchen, wiping his hands on a towel. He tossed it in a bin. "What's wrong?"

"Melody is missing," Denny said.

"Either she ran away or—" Hope bit off the word. *No, no, no. No one has kidnapped my daughter.* "She ran away," she said matter-of-factly to convince herself. "From the community center. She's ticked off at me because . . ." She pressed a hand to her chest. "Because I turned down the KPRL prize." She almost started to explain why, but it didn't matter. What was done was done.

"Ah, honey." Gabe wrapped a comforting arm around her.

Hope wrested free.

"We should call the police," Denny said.

"Now, let's not go off half-cocked," Gabe said. "Where have you searched?"

Hope listed the shops.

"Mommy." Todd tugged on the hem of Hope's jacket.

"It's okay." She petted his head.

"Mommy," he said more insistently. "Maybe we should go to Steve Waldren's house."

Hope blinked. "Why?"

"Because . . ." Todd chewed his lower lip. "Because of the prize."

"Sweetheart, Steve doesn't have the prize, and now isn't the time to be thinking about it."

"No, Mom, you don't understand. Melody and I saw Steve yesterday at the cookie decorating contest, and I . . . I . . ." He pressed his lips together.

Hope's heart snagged. "What did you do?"

"I said what if we could get Daddy to say yes to the prize, and Steve said if he did, we could go to Disneyland."

"Oh, lord," Gabe said.

Hope groaned.

"What if Melody went to Steve's to call Daddy?" Todd mewled.

"How would he do that?" Hope asked.

"Melody found his number on your telephone." He turned up his palms. "We both wrote it on our hands."

Chapter 38

So that was what the two of them had been sneakily doing the other night. Hope's heart sank. She wasn't worried about Steve tracking down Zach. His number was defunct. He'd changed it the day he'd walked out. But she was worried that Melody, learning her father was nowhere to be found, might spiral.

Minutes later, Hope screeched the VW to a halt in front of the Waldrens' house, scrambled out, and, clinging to Todd's hand, raced up the path. The cheerful decorations that Frank and Ellery had so carefully put up did nothing to lighten Hope's mood. She was scared. To the core. A silver Lexus was parked in the driveway, so she presumed Steve was there. His parents each drove Ford SUVs and Lincoln didn't own a car.

"Mommy?" Todd whined. "You're squeezing my hand too hard."

She released it and kissed the top of his head. "I'm sorry. Mommy is worried."

Todd rang the doorbell. It chimed "Jingle Bells," which made Todd laugh.

"Don't," Hope warned. "This is not a laughing matter."

Lincoln answered the door, a goofy grin on his face. "Hey, Hope. Hey, Todd. Come in. Merry Christmas. Well, almost Merry Christmas. It's not quite Christmas."

"Lincoln, focus." Hope held up a hand. "Is your brother here? I need to see him."

"Yep. We're playing chess in the den. I'm beating him. He—"

Hope didn't wait for niceties. She pushed past Lincoln yelling, "Is my daughter here?"

"No," Lincoln said, following her.

Todd trailed him.

"Steve Waldren"—Hope stomped into the room—"is my daughter here?"

Steve bounded to his feet, rattling the chess board. Chessmen toppled. He hurried to reassemble them. "No. Why? What happened?"

"She's missing and Todd said . . . Todd said . . ." Hope placed a hand on her chest to steady herself, then yelled, "Melody!"

No answer.

"Melody!" she repeated.

"She's not here. I'm not lying." Steve caressed Hope's shoulder. "Breathe. C'mon. You're shaking."

"She's gone!" Hope cried.

"I'm sorry, Mom," Todd squeaked.

Hope aimed a finger at Steve. "You . . . You . . . You made my children a promise you couldn't keep. Not in a million years."

"What are you talking about?"

"I told my mom what I asked you," Todd said. "If maybe our dad could, you know, say yes to the prize, and you said we should call him, and Melody and me found his number, and—"

"Melody is missing, Steve, and she thinks—" Hope faltered. Lack of oxygen was making her dizzy. "She thinks—" The words wouldn't form.

Steve clasped her arm and guided her to the sofa. "Sit. Take a few deep breaths. Lincoln, get Hope some water."

"Sure thing, Steve." Lincoln saluted and ran out.

"Start at the beginning," Steve said, his gaze filled with concern.

Hope perched on the edge of the sofa and peered up at him. "Melody ran away. From the community center. She must have gone to find her father because she thinks if he says yes, then they . . ." She motioned to Todd. "She thinks the two of them can go to Disneyland. But she won't find him because Zach—" She inhaled sharply. "Because he went off the grid. No phone number. No address."

"Is it possible she managed to contact him anyway?" Steve asked. "You can track down people via the Internet. Not everyone can live under the radar."

"Believe me, I've tried. He's MIA."

A door slammed. Footsteps slapped the floor in the entry. Ellery and Frank bolted into the den, Ellery still in her red apron and Frank removing his cap and coat.

Ellery said, "Gabe called us and told us you'd come here." She leveled her son with a look. "Steven Richardson Waldren, what did you do?"

"I didn't, Mom." He threw his arms wide. "Not intentionally."

"Here's some water." Lincoln returned and handed a glass to Hope. "If you get the hiccups, I know how to fix them, okay?"

Steve said, "Drink slowly, Hope, then let's go through this step by step."

Hope took a few sips and felt the constriction of her lungs lessen. "I took the kids to daycare."

"Day *camp*," Todd revised.

"Day camp. Then I went to work. When I came back, Melody wasn't anywhere. She lied to the counselor, Khloe."

"I know Khloe," Ellery said. "Sweet girl. Diligent."

"Melody told Khloe she wanted to throw some hoops, but she took her backpack and ran. She . . ." Hope battled tears. "She thinks her father can agree to accept the Disneyland prize, but she won't find him. I've tried."

Todd sat beside his mother and took her hand in his. "There, there," he said the way Hope would if he was the one who was upset.

"There, there," Lincoln echoed, and perched beside Todd.

Steve hitched his trousers at the thighs and crouched in front of Hope. He put his hands on her knees.

The warmth soothed her yet unsettled her. "Steve—"

"*Shh*. Let me speak first. I know saying I'm sorry won't cut it," he began, "but let me help you. Let's go to the police. We'll file a report."

"What can they d-do?" Her voice hitched. "I've looked everywhere."

"Everywhere?"

"I've searched all the places my daughter likes to hang out." She ticked off the list as she had for Gabe, but paused as she realized Steve was right. She hadn't looked *everywhere*. She hadn't gone back to the trailer park. She hadn't gone to the school.

"We need manpower," Steve said, his voice warm and reassuring. "Bobby Capellini, the chief of police—"

"I know Bobby," Hope said. "Roman's brother."

"Right. He and I were buddies in high school. He's a great guy. He'll get everyone on board. Let's go. Mom?" Steve rose to a stand. "Can you watch Todd for us?"

"You bet I will."

Todd didn't budge. "I'm sorry, Mom."

Hope scrambled to her feet and clasped him in a bear hug. "It's going to be okay, sweetheart." Oh, how she wished that were true. But it had to be. Melody was fine, just stubborn. She wasn't lost forever.

"Hey"—Todd broke free—"what if Melody went to Portland to find Dad?"

"No, no, no. She wouldn't do that." Hope paused. "Would she?" She looked to Ellery for support. "She thinks she's older than she is, but she's only ten. *Ten!*"

Ellery said, "I'm sure she's close by." She reached for Todd. "Come with me, young man. I've got cookies."

Hope gave him a nudge. "Sweetheart, please stay with Mrs. Waldren."

"Which do you want?" Ellery asked. "Snickerdoodles or chocolate crinkles?"

"Both, please."

Lincoln said, "My mom makes the best snickerdoodles in Hope Valley. I should know. I helped make the batter. Didn't I, Mom? Didn't I?"

Ellery grinned. "Yes, dear, you did."

"They're almost as good as Steve's," Lincoln added.

"Almost. This way, boys." Ellery signaled to Frank to get more information.

Frank said, "What can I do to help, Hope?"

"I'm not sure."

Steve said, "Hope, do you have a picture of Melody?"

"On my phone."

Hope pulled her cell phone from her pocket and swiped through photos. She stopped on one of Melody on the first day of school. So pretty. So self-assured. She showed it to Steve. He took the phone and forwarded the picture to himself and his father.

"Dad, start a phone tree." Steve reached for Hope's hand. "Let's go. I'm driving."

Chapter 39

Hope pitched forward when Steve parked his SUV in front of Hope Valley Police Station, but she was too frazzled to care about her own discomfort. She unbuckled her seatbelt and, dodging melted snow puddles, raced up the path to the entrance. Twinkling lights surrounded the door's frame, but they didn't make her feel merry. She pushed inside, Steve at her heels.

The station was moderate in size and brightly lit, with all white walls and gray furniture. A fake Christmas tree with silver ornaments stood to one side of the foyer. Wrapped packages lay beneath it. A red-and-green wreath hung on the wall behind the clerk.

Bobby, aka Roberto, the eldest of the Capellini brothers, strode into the foyer. The creases of his brown uniform looked freshly pressed. He always dressed to impress. Like his younger brother, he was easy on the eyes. "Where's the fire?" he asked.

"Missing child," Steve said.

"My office. Now."

They crossed the squad room. He motioned them into his office. After they entered, he closed the door.

Hope was cold to the bone; her teeth were chattering. Steve slung an arm around her and helped her into a chair by the metal desk. He pulled another chair close, sat down, and showed Bobby the picture of Melody on his phone.

For ten minutes, Hope replayed the events, her voice cracking in the recounting. "She was wearing her pink puff jacket and jeans and snow boots. She's about fifty-two inches tall and weighs around sixty pounds."

Bobby listened and took notes. When he rose from his desk chair after saying he had all he needed, he added, "Don't worry. We've got this."

But Hope didn't believe him. What if Todd was right? What if Melody was determined to find her father? What if she went to the highway thinking she could hitch a ride to Portland? What if someone picked her up and . . .

The notion knifed through Hope. "My daughter is a diabetic," she exclaimed, praying Melody hadn't fallen into a coma.

"Hold on." Bobby made a quick call to the hospital. He inquired whether any children had been admitted recently. He described Melody and her clothing. He ended the call, his face grim. "No one fitting Melody's description has come in, but they've put the hospital staff on alert. The fire department, too. They'll check out the trailer park and school."

"The Unitarian Church," Hope said. "I didn't go there. Melody loves helping feed the less . . ." She sat taller and squared her shoulders, refusing to be ashamed of her circumstance. "The less fortunate of Hope Valley."

"Let's go there." Steve hustled Hope toward the door. Over his shoulder, he said, "Thanks, Bobby!"

Chapter 40

Addie Dixon was at the loading dock handing out the remaining rations. A line of at least twenty people were waiting patiently.

Steve eyed them and then Hope. "I had no idea there were this many needy people in town."

"And this is the tail end," she murmured.

Addie spotted Hope and beamed. "Hey, what brings you here, hon? We're almost done for the day." She tilted her head and eyed Steve. "My, my, Steve Waldren. Don't tell me you want to do a story on little old us?"

"You know me?"

"I know your mother and father. I haven't seen you since you were back in high school. You've had quite a run, haven't you? My husband is a big fan. He loves the Voice. He—"

"Addie," Hope cut in, "have you seen Melody?"

"She ran away from day camp," Steve said. "We thought she might have come here to help you."

Addie hopped off the dock and threw her arms around Hope. "Oh, lordy, no, she hasn't stopped by. You're as cold as ice, hon. Want some coffee?"

Hope shook her head. Her stomach was churning acid. "We can't hang around. If you do see her—" Her cell phone jangled. She scanned the readout. It was Khloe. Hope pressed Send and said, "Hi, Khloe. Did she come back? Can I speak to—"

"No, she didn't." Khloe's voice was brittle with fear. "But her friend Josie might know something." She rattled off the address.

JOSIE MOORE LIVED IN a pretty red house with white trim. It was decked out with nearly as much Christmas regalia as the Waldrens' home, except their Santa and reindeer were on the snowy front lawn, rocking back and forth to the tune of "Here Comes Santa Claus."

Hope pressed the doorbell. "If she's here—"

"You're not going to clock her." Steve offered a supportive smile. "You're going to hug her and hold her. Got it?"

"Got it." Hope shrugged, and her shoulder accidentally brushed Steve's arm, which sent a shiver down her spine. His tentative smile acknowledged their connection. Both of them startled when the door opened.

"Hi, Hope." Josie's mother, a petite brunette with wide-set brown eyes, hustled Hope and Steve inside. Wringing her hands, she said, "Khloe called us, and I'm so sorry. I can't get a word out of Josie. My husband is trying now but to no avail." She guided them into the bountifully decorated living room that included a giant tree, multiple candles, and an array of nutcrackers and elves. Stockings for each member of their expansive family hung from the mantel.

Ten-year-old Josie, her brown hair woven into braids, sat on the brick ledge in front of a crackling fire. Her legs were crossed at the ankles. Her head was lowered. Her father, a staunch jurist, stood nearby, hands behind his back. He was frowning, patently not pleased.

"Josie Claire Moore, it's now or never. Speak up," he ordered. "Your mother and I know you're not telling us everything."

Hope imagined the fear every witness who had to face him must feel. She hurried forward and squatted near Josie. "Hi, sweetheart, I know you want to be a friend to Melody, and you think by keeping quiet that you're helping her, but she's sick. If she misses her medicine, something horrible might happen to her."

Josie worked her lower lip between her teeth.

"Is she hiding somewhere?" Hope asked.

A shake of the head.

"In your room maybe?"

A violent shake of her head.

"Am I getting warm?" Hope did her best to keep her voice calm and steady.

"No," Josie whispered.

"Josie!" her father boomed. "For heaven's sake, spit it out!"

The girl jolted. Hope shot a frustrated look at the man. His wife curled her hand around his elbow and drew him away.

Steve crouched beside Hope. "Josie," he said, matching Hope's gentle tone, "did Melody tell you a secret?"

Josie murmured, "Mm-hm."

"A special secret she didn't want you to share?" Steve asked.

"Uh-huh."

Hope said, "About the prize and needing to find her father?"

Josie gasped. "Melody said you didn't know, Mrs. Lyons. She wouldn't tell you. Ever."

"Sweetheart—" Hope's voice snagged. "Melody won't be able to find her father."

"Yes, she will. She's going to go to—" Josie smashed her lips together.

"Where is she going to go?" Hope asked. *"Where?"*

"To . . . to . . ." The girl mewled and then whispered the rest.

"I didn't hear you. Please speak up, Josie," Hope cooed. "It's okay. She won't be in trouble, and you're not, either. I . . . We"—she motioned between her and Steve, the unlikeliest team she could have imagined—"just want to bring her home safely. Promise. I won't tell her you told me."

Josie licked her lips. "She's going to the bus station. She's going to sneak into the luggage bin on a bus and hop a ride to Portland."

"Hop a ride?" Hope squawked, panic racing through her because Josie's story had the ring of truth. Melody knew where the bus station was. Earlier in the year they'd taken a day trip via bus to Seattle so they could go to the top of the Space Needle.

Hope glanced at Steve, who swallowed so hard his Adam's apple moved up and down. Was he thinking what she was thinking? If Melody got on a bus, all bets of finding her were off.

Chapter 41

Hope Valley Bus Terminal boasted two stories of white cement blocks and a red marquee that reminded Hope of the overhang at the town's vintage theater. Facing the street was a small coffee shop with to-go foods. Located at the rear of the building were the boarding docks where buses pulled in to board or disembark, each protected by a wide red roof.

Before Steve had fully parked the SUV, Hope was leaping out. He cautioned her to wait, but she couldn't. She tore into the station. To the far left was a staircase. Straight ahead was an elevator as well as the stoned archway leading to the docks. A dozen people were passing through. Hope saw a tall woman holding the hand of a little girl—not Melody. Then she spotted an elderly gentleman with a child—not her daughter, either.

Steve caught up to her and put a hand on her shoulder. "Breathe," he said. "Let's do this methodically. We'll go room by room, including the upstairs."

"We should split apart."

"I think it's better if we stay together," he said.

Hope could tell by his gaze that he was concerned about her—worried she'd crack into bits. He wasn't far wrong. Every nerve fiber was quivering inside her. She nodded. "Okay." She inhaled deeply, the aroma of stale coffee making her nose twitch, and did her best to focus. She spotted the station's diner. "There." She pointed to the left.

"Good idea. She might be hungry." Steve clasped her hand and ushered her into the diner.

There were only two red booths and two silver Formica tables. The place was occupied by adult customers, but there were no children. Hope crouched to peek beneath the tables. She didn't spot Melody hiding or sleeping. She rose to a stand and crossed to the waitress in the boxy red dress who was ringing up an order. "Have you seen a little girl?" Hope flashed the cell phone image of Melody at the waitress. "Ten years old. About this tall." She held out a flat palm.

"No, ma'am. I'm sorry she's missing. If I do see her, I'll keep her here." The waitress added, "There's a restroom, not a lavatory, but a real rest room right next door. Sometimes people go in to lie down for a bit. Maybe she was feeling pookie."

Again, Steve led Hope by the hand, his fingers warm, the caress of his thumb soothing. But the restroom, a cubicle about ten feet wide with a cot and a chair and no door other than the one through which they'd entered was empty.

They returned to the center of the station's lobby, and Hope spotted a ticket taker hovering near the elevator. She broke free from Steve and approached the man. His blue suit sported shiny brass buttons. His mustache was tidily trimmed. "Have you seen my daughter?" She showed him Melody's picture. "Sixty pounds. Slim. Pink puff jacket."

"No, ma'am, sorry."

Hope persisted. "Have any buses left for Portland in the last two hours?" She heard the strain in her voice. Had they been searching for two hours already? Was her daughter halfway to nowhere by now?

"None lately," the man said, "but one's due to leave in about forty-five minutes. Feel free to take a look."

Hope thanked him, grabbed Steve's hand, and steered him through the archway. She spotted a bus with the destination sign *Portland* above the windshield and raced to it.

Steve said, "It's not leaving yet. Slow down."

"I can't."

Steve offered a wry smile. "Glad I wore my track shoes."

When they reached the bus, Hope leaned in and said to the silver-haired driver, "Little girl. Ten. Blonde hair. Name's Melody. Is she on the bus?"

"No, ma'am. No children allowed unaccompanied."

Recalling Josie's words, Hope said, "Can we inspect your luggage bin?"

"Have a go. It's wide open." He hooked his beefy thumb.

Steve led the way and peered in first. "There are a lot of suitcases. Let me pull a few out." He hefted one after another, setting each on the dock.

When he'd cleared enough for Hope to see beyond them into the bowels of the bin, she stifled a sob. Melody wasn't there.

"Let's check the other bus," Hope said.

"It's heading to Seattle."

"Please," she begged.

They reloaded the luggage of the first bus and then, repeating their actions, talked to the driver of the second and checked the bin. Nothing. Zilch. No Melody.

Hope sagged with grief. "Oh, Steve. She's gone."

He held her at arms' length. "Keep it together, kiddo. Let's check upstairs."

They took the elevator to the second floor, Hope stabbing the button repeatedly to make it perform faster. It didn't. When the elevator doors opened, Hope charged out, Steve at her heels. They hurried from one end to the other, inspecting room after room. One was an office. Two were lavatories. Melody was nowhere to be found.

Defeated, Hope slogged to the staircase. Steve gripped her elbow to steady her as they descended.

Near the bottom, Hope shouted, "Wait! Steve, look!"

To the right of the staircase on the floor lay a stuffed elephant. Not just any stuffed elephant. A pink one.

"She's here!" Hope exclaimed, wrenching free and dashing to the bottom of the staircase. "Or she's been here. That's hers." She scooped up the elephant and looked right and left. "Melody!" she yelled. "It's Mom. I'm not mad. I'm just worried. Melody, please come out and talk to me."

But Hope didn't hear anything. No sweet voice begging for mercy. No crying. Silence.

Finally giving into her sorrow, tears streamed down Hope's cheeks. "She's gone, Steve, and it's all my fault."

He drew her into his arms, his warm breath in her ear. With a single finger, he brushed hair off her cheek. The loving way he was looking at her should have calmed her, but it didn't.

"Hey," he said, "I just thought of something. When Lincoln was five, my mother put me in charge of him for a half hour so she could do an errand. He ran away. I was beside myself. I thought I'd lost him and I'd never see him again. But when Mom got home from the store, she held her finger to her lips and showed me where his favorite hiding place was. Tucked beneath the outside staircase of our house. It's not a solid staircase. It's the fire-escape type. He liked to hide there because he could see through the slats. It was his own personal duck blind."

Hope swung around and peered beneath the staircase, but Melody wasn't there.

"I noticed another possibility," Steve said. "Out on the dock. Maybe she's there, waiting until the bus is just about ready to leave." He clasped her hand and led the way.

Minutes later, Hope was staring at her beautiful girl, fast asleep beneath the metal staircase, curled into a ball with her head propped on her backpack, her arms crossed and hands tucked under her armpits.

Hope threw her arms around Steve. "Thank you. Thank you. You have no idea." She kissed him firmly on the lips. The connection she felt with him shocked her.

Steve noticed the electricity, too, if his "Whoa!" was any indication.

Quickly, she stepped backward, creating distance between them. "I'm sorry. I shouldn't have. I—"

He put a finger to her lips and gently kissed her forehead. "Go." He nudged her. "Wake her up, but don't be mad."

Hope handed Steve her purse, crawled to Melody, and touched her arm. "Sweetheart, it's Mom."

Melody didn't budge. Didn't open her eyes. Her chest was rising and falling, but her breathing was labored.

Dread churned inside Hope. "Steve, I need to give her juice. Fast. Would you—"

"On it." Steve raced into the building.

"Melody." Hope shook her again. "Mel—"

Melody's eyes blinked open. "Mommy? Oh, Mommy." She sat up and threw her arms around Hope's neck.

Hope's throat grew thick with emotion. She couldn't remember the last time her daughter had called her *Mommy*.

"I'm sorry," Melody went on. "I was mad at you, and I thought Daddy . . . I thought he could—"

"*Shh*. I know." Hope sniffed. Melody's breath smelled fruity, not a good sign. She hadn't eaten in such a long time, and the fact that she'd fallen asleep in such a noisy place spoke to her fatigue. "Steve!" she yelled as she lifted her daughter's chin with a fingertip and checked her eyes. Clear. No trauma. "Do you know I love you more than life itself?"

"I love you, too."

"Steve!"

From a distance she heard him shout, "I'm coming!"

Hope focused on Melody. "Speaking of love . . ." She shook the elephant. "I think this little guy has been missing you."

"Pinkie!" Melody clutched the elephant to her chest.

Steve swooped to a stop, knelt down, and handed Hope a small bottle of orange juice, the cap removed.

She held the bottle to Melody's lips. "Sweetheart, take a sip." Over her shoulder, she said, "She's fine, but we need to get her to the hospital."

Steve said, "Melody, hi. I'm going to pick you up."

"Okay."

Hope helped her daughter into Steve's arms. Darned if his eyes weren't misting over, too.

Chapter 42

On the drive to the hospital, Hope sat in the backseat of Steve's car with Melody nestled in her arms. The aroma of bus diesel lingered in her daughter's hair, but Hope didn't mind. For years, it would be a smell she'd treasure because it represented relief at finding her daughter alive.

Meanwhile, Steve auto-dialed the precinct and spoke to Bobby Capellini to say they'd found the girl and were on their way to the hospital to make sure she was stable. Bobby offered to contact the others, including Steve's parents, Gabe, and Khloe.

When Steve ended the call, he glanced at Hope in the rearview mirror.

She met his gaze and whispered, "Thank you."

"It was my fault. I should have—"

"No, it was mine," she cut in. "We'll accept the prize. You can get your job back."

"How did you know I lost it?" Realization dawned on his face. "Wait. Let me guess. My mom told you at the tree-lighting ceremony. Look, I don't want the job. I was ready to quit. I've been searching for something new. Don't worry about me."

"I can make it work. It was . . . my van . . . out of the blue . . . my savings . . ."

"Shh," he said. "It's okay."

"Your mother said your boss was venomous."

"Yeah, he's a snake alright. *Fuhgeddaboudit*," he said with a *Sopranos*-style accent.

"Do you want him to sleep with the fishes?"

"Sure, if I had my druthers." Steve chuckled and winked into the rearview mirror.

"For what it's worth, I believed you when you said you wouldn't have told my story."

Steve glanced over his shoulder. "Close your eyes. Take a breather. We're almost there."

Hope leaned her head back as thoughts swirled in her mind. Melody. Todd. Steve. The way his wink had sent a shimmy of desire through her. The memory of their kiss.

No. Uh-uh. What she was feeling was charged with emotions because of losing Melody. That was all it was. Steve would be heading out any day. They had no future.

WHEN THE HOSPITAL ER doctor released Melody saying she was fine but needed rest, Hope was euphoric. A short while later, Steve pulled his SUV into his parents' driveway.

At the same time, Ellery, Frank, Lincoln, and Todd raced out of the house. A light snow was falling. Nobody seemed to mind. Todd was wearing a string of Christmas lights around his neck.

"Oh, heavens, what does my son have on?" Hope was peering out the window.

"Don't blame him," Steve said. "That's Lincoln's doing. My brother loves when others *wear* the holidays." He opened her door and helped extricate her from her daughter's grasp without waking Melody.

Frank and Ellery gazed in through the opened door.

Ellery clapped a hand to her chest and whispered, "Aw, poor thing."

"Where is she?" Todd drew near.

"Back seat." Hope pointed. "Be quiet."

Lincoln said, "I want to see, too. Let me see."

Todd put a finger to his lips, "*Shh.*"

Mimicking his mother, Lincoln whispered, "Aw, poor thing."

"Let's go back inside, Son." Frank clutched Lincoln's elbow and guided him from the car. "Give them some space."

"Todd, climb into the camper," Hope said.

Todd removed his necklace of lights, handed it to Steve, and scrambled into the camper, leaving the door ajar.

Hope said to Melody, "Sweetheart, I need you to wake up. We're getting out of Steve's car, and I'm going to take you to ours."

Melody struggled to a sitting position. Hope took her hand and guided her out of the SUV. She situated Melody in the backseat of the VW, tucked a pillow between her head and the window, and secured her seatbelt. Todd, already buckled in, took hold of his sister's hand.

Hope closed the door and faced Steve's mother. Snow had dusted Ellery's hair and shoulders. "Thank you."

"We're so relieved." Ellery kissed her, adding that Hope should call if she needed *anything*, and then she caught up to Frank and Lincoln as they returned inside.

Steve flicked off the battery pack for the necklace of lights, but he didn't budge. He stared at Hope, his face suffused with something that didn't register as concern. It was more . . . intimate.

Shyness overtook Hope. She felt exposed. Was Steve interested in her? Was he remembering their kiss?

He said, "You were great today. Courageous and calm in the face of a storm."

"Liar. I was a blubbering mess."

"You held it together."

"Is that why your jacket is soaked with my tears?"

"Wait. What?" He glanced down. "You mean it wasn't raining inside the bus station?"

Hope grinned.

He brushed snow off her shoulders, tucked a loose hair behind one of her ears, and then drew her into his arms. He didn't kiss her, but he whispered, "You're something else, Hope Lyons. A real—"

A car screeched to a halt. A woman yelled, "Stevie!"

Steve broke free from Hope as the woman climbed out of a Honda Uber.

"Stevie, it's me!" Gloria Storm, rocking a holiday red sweater dress belted at the waist and stiletto heels, rushed to Steve and swooped him into a hug. "I've missed you so much." She planted a serious kiss on his mouth.

Loathe to interrupt, Hope slipped into the driver's seat of the camper and drove away.

Chapter 43

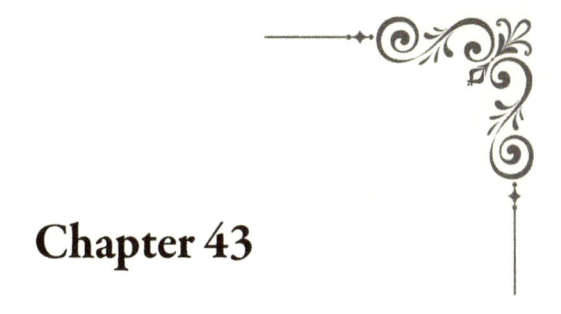

Steve shimmied free of Gloria. "What are you doing here?"
"I missed you."
Steve's mother appeared on the front porch. "Steve, do we have guests?"
Gloria said, "Hi, Ellery."
Steve gawked. Gloria had a lot of nerve to call his mother by her first name. They had only met once, briefly, when his parents had come to Portland to watch him tape a show. Despite that, Ellery, ever the hostess, invited Gloria inside. Gloria thanked her and ordered Steve to gather whatever luggage she had and to tip the driver.

Grumbling, staring after the camper's taillights as they disappeared from sight, Steve fetched Gloria's coat and overnight case, gave the Uber driver a ten, and carried Gloria's things to the foyer. His mother had already guided Gloria into the kitchen and was setting a cup of tea on the counter in front of her.

Steve joined them, conflicting thoughts ping-ponging in his brain. His father puttered in the refrigerator looking for something while offering sidelong glances at Gloria. Lincoln was sitting on a stool, kicking its rails. Steve knew what that meant. His brother was confused and vexed.

"You look good, Stevie," Gloria said.
"Steve," he muttered.
Gloria stirred honey noisily into her cup.

Lincoln hummed to calm himself but then blurted, "Why are you here?"

Gloria startled, dropping her spoon. "Um, because I missed your brother. A-a-and . . ." She dragged out the word. "I've got big news to share that involves him."

Steve bit back a retort. *Big news* as in she couldn't make it in Minneapolis and was hobbling back to Portland and wanted to strike up where they'd left off? Think again. He tapped her arm. "Let's walk to the café and we can talk."

"I want to go," Lincoln said, bounding off the stool.

"I was thinking just me and her, buddy."

"No. I'm going."

Steve threw his mother a baleful look.

"Let's all go," Ellery said. "Tonight's been quite stressful. I'm sure each of us could use a slice of pie. Lincoln, get your coat."

"Pie," Steve's father said, closing the refrigerator door. "Great idea."

"We're going to walk?" Gloria glanced out the window. Snow was still drifting softly outside. "Um, I'll need to change clothes," she said, pointing to her heels.

"Fine. Use the guest bath off the foyer." Steve aimed a finger. "I assume you packed boots."

"Of course. I'm not an idiot. I just thought you'd like to see me looking my best." Coyly, she clutched the seam of her dress and twirled half-heartedly. "Don't I look pretty?"

He didn't respond.

"Yes, you do," Ellery said.

Gloria blew her an air kiss and moved through the archway.

Steve called after her, "I'll book a room for you at the inn where Brie's staying."

"I thought I'd stay here," she said, poking her head back into the room.

Ellery and Frank exchanged a look.

"Not a good idea," Steve said. "My brother . . ." Steve tilted his head toward Lincoln. "It's complicated."

"Okay," she said meekly, and retreated to the foyer.

Moments later, she returned to the kitchen dressed in her wool coat over leggings tucked into fashionable Uggs and a heavy Irish sweater. She twirled a pompom ski hat on one finger. "I'm warm and cozy now."

Ten minutes later, Steve, his family, and Gloria were seated at Aroma Café. He scanned the place for Hope but knew she wouldn't be there. He pictured her happily hugging her kids and reading them stories.

After ordering beverages and pie for each of them, Steve unfurled his silverware from the napkin.

"Aren't you happy I came to town?" Gloria touched the back of his hand.

He flinched. His silverware clattered. He moved his hand to his lap. "Actually, I'm astonished." She'd never wanted to visit Hope Valley. She'd derisively called it a one-horse town.

"I wasn't kidding before. I missed you. Missed us." She twirled a finger in the hair at the nape of his neck.

He pulled away. "Stop."

"You always like when I do that."

"Not anymore."

"Not anymore," Lincoln echoed.

Zerena appeared with coffees for everyone except Lincoln, who'd ordered milk, and said she'd be right back with the pie.

"Gloria"—Ellery poured creamer into her coffee—"what's your big news?"

Gloria's eyes lit up with excitement. "The sports desk is opening up in Minneapolis, and Steve, thanks to me, is on the short list for the position." She *eeked* while air-clapping her hands. "Isn't that great? You get the job, and we're back together again. A team. A power couple. Won't that be fab?"

Steve's mouth dropped open. "Gloria, we were never a power couple. We were two people who dated."

"Lived together."

"Dated."

"Moved in together."

"For less than a month."

"We even got engaged."

"And you ended it," Steve said with a bite.

"Steve," his mother cautioned.

"Be gentle, Son," his father said.

"No, Mom, Dad. She broke it off with me and now she wants me back? And all I have to do is move to Minneapolis for the privilege? No." He tossed his napkin on the table.

Lincoln whimpered.

Ellery touched his shoulder and said, "*Shh*, Lincoln. It's okay."

Zerena brought slices of apple-cranberry pie for everyone, setting them on the table with a clatter.

Lincoln stared at his and pushed it away. "I want plain apple."

"Plain apple it is," Ellery said to Zerena.

"Leave his," Steve said. "I'll eat it."

He glanced sideways at Gloria. Her eyes had pooled with tears. Discreetly, she dabbed her napkin at the inside corners. His peeve irked him, but what had she expected him to do? Get down on his knees and thank her for condescending to love him again? Not a chance! He tucked into his pie, mulling over their fractured relationship. What had he ever found attractive about her other than her looks? Not her brain. Not the way she treated others. He downed a bigger than normal bite of pie, savoring the sweetness and the tang, and thought of Hope. Seeing her in action, holding herself together while struggling with deep-seated fear, had changed him in ways he couldn't have imagined. And he'd never forget the kiss they'd exchanged or the tender moment they'd shared at the end of the evening.

All of which blew up the moment Gloria appeared.

No. Uh-uh. He might not have a job in Portland any longer, but he sure as heck wasn't moving to Minneapolis to be a power couple with his self-centered ex.

THAT NIGHT, AFTER CATEGORICALLY ending things with Gloria at the airport—Steve had purchased a ticket for her on the midnight flight to Minneapolis—he felt better than he could imagine. Tuesday morning he awoke with a spring in his step and whistled—actually whistled—as he trotted downstairs.

While eating breakfast, a traditional Christmas Eve special his mother served every year—pancakes made with green and red M&Ms—and answering questions his mother and father asked about his future, an idea came to him. He let the plan brew as he washed dishes. By the time he'd dried them and stacked them in the cupboards, he was certain it was brilliant and fitting for the season.

When his parents announced they were heading to their respective businesses for the biggest shopping day of the year, they put Steve in charge of Lincoln. He didn't blink an eye. He knew his brother would spend most of the morning preoccupied with the wrapped presents beneath the tree that had magically appeared overnight, trying to guess, out loud, what was in each.

After pouring a second cup of coffee, Steve settled into the armchair in the living room, raised his cell phone, and tapped the number for the TV station with the broadest audience in Oregon. He asked to be put through to the person in charge of promotions. When a woman came on the line, Steve introduced himself.

Turning on the charm, he said he had a great idea for a human-interest story. Perfect for the holidays. It had Christmas spirit written all over it. All he needed was a small crew—

Before he could add more, the woman cut him off claiming she had no space on her agenda.

Not to be deterred, Steve bypassed KPRL and tried the next largest station, receiving the same kind of brush off.

When he called the station that was fourth in line, the promotions guy said, "Listen, Waldren, face facts. Dave Zamberzini has blackballed you. At the moment, you're persona non grata. You're toast to every station this side of the Rockies. Sorry, kid. Good luck."

Steve swore under his breath, shocked that Dave had that kind of power. How he'd underestimated him. He rested his cell phone on the arm of the chair and stood to stretch.

"What's wrong, Steve?" Lincoln asked, bolting to his feet, the bells on his ugly reindeer-themed Christmas sweater jingling. "Why are you toast?"

"I'm not toast."

"The last guy said you were toast."

"He didn't say—"

"I have ears." Lincoln tapped both of his. "I can hear."

"Fine, I'm toast."

"And you're mad."

"No, I'm not."

"Yes, you are. You made that sound Dad does." Lincoln growled.

Steve had to hand it to his brother. He was perceptive. "I'm striking out."

"Like Cavallo?" Lincoln popped to his feet and stood to face Steve. "He doesn't strike out a lot, but he does strike out. Batting average .3141. Or Vinton? He's not as good as Cavallo. Batting average .3059. Or—"

"Time out." Steve raised his hands in the universal *T* sign. "No stats." He needed to think. He had to formulate a new plan.

"Hey, bro," Lincoln said, "Dad always says to Mom to run something by him if she's mad. Want to run something by me? We can go out in the yard. I'll start running first."

"Wrong kind of run, buddy. To run something by someone—" Steve sagged. He didn't have it in him to explain. He gripped his brother's shoulder. "I've got to get my rear in gear."

"Rear in gear. Rear in gear." Lincoln wagged his butt and sang, "Shake your booty."

Steve chuckled.

Lincoln stopped moving and said, "What's a human-interest story?"

Steve cocked his head. "Um, it's about people sharing a story that might be of common interest to other people. It might show how other people's problems or accomplishments could motivate them and maybe even spur the TV viewer to help."

"Or the listener."

"Yes, or the listener."

Steve glanced at his watch. "Wow. Time flies. We've got to get to the Christmas Attic for the gingerbread house event. Mom will kill us if we aren't there. But first we need to freshen up. Brush your teeth, comb your hair, and grab a jacket."

Lincoln gave Steve a thumbs up.

Steve raced upstairs, shrugged out of his sweatshirt, threw on a button-down shirt and topped it with a sweater—his mother's favorite look on him—and hurried back downstairs. Lincoln was waiting by the door, bundled in his coat and wearing a red-plaid trapper hat with ear-flaps.

"Why the hat?" Steve asked. The snow had stopped falling. "We're only going from the car to the shop."

"I like to wear it."

Good enough. He wouldn't argue. Grabbing his keys, he jogged out the door to his Lexus.

"Shotgun," Lincoln cried as he climbed into the SUV's passenger seat.

"You always get shotgun," Steve joked. He switched on the car and kicked on the heat.

Lincoln buckled his seatbelt. "You didn't ask Mr. Q."

"What?"

"You didn't ask Mr. Q."

"What?"

"You didn't ask—"

"No, I heard you the first time." Steve flashed on the day when Lincoln and he had watched the classic *Who's On First* skit between Abbott and Costello. Lincoln couldn't stop interrupting, not understanding, just as Lou Costello hadn't, who *Who* was and who *What* was. In the end, Lincoln grew frustrated and in a typical meltdown ordered Steve to turn it off. "What didn't I ask Mr. Q?" Steve said, using a full sentence.

"About your human-interest story."

"Why would I ask him about it?"

"Because he has listeners. Radio listeners."

"This story isn't for his audience," Steve said.

Lincoln folded his arms. "I'm his audience. So are Mom and Dad. Isn't your story for us? We're humans."

Steve cocked his head, realizing his brother had a point. A really good point. On a whim, he made a U-turn.

Chapter 44

For the past twelve hours, Hope hadn't let either of her children out of her sight. Last night, she'd listened as Melody cried about missing her father. She'd been attentive as Todd told her how Khloe had proven Santa was real. She'd fed them a light meal and then, after reading them a story, had nestled between them, one hand on Melody's thigh and one on Todd's. She'd awakened every hour or so to make sure they were sleeping. Every half hour she'd thought of Steve and his tender kiss and the dogged way he'd helped her find her daughter . . . and then she would picture his ex-fiancée showing up and the tender memories would vanish. He was taken. End of story.

Now, given that she had to work on Christmas Eve as many in town did, she'd brought the kids to the café and had seated them at the counter, not in the back. So customers wouldn't be upset, she was using up all her employee food allowance to feed them nonstop. Gabe, bless his merry soul, was engaging Todd in conversation about basketball, and Melody was devouring her Lisa Leslie book, giving Hope way too much time to mindlessly replay that scene with Gloria. *Dang.*

"Hey, girlfriend." Zerena sidled to her after serving a table of four. She rolled her eyes. "Is it the merry tinkle of 'We Need a Little Christmas' that's irking you, or are you simply stressed beyond words?"

Hope grimaced. "I look that bad?"

"You're wearing your shoulders for earrings." Zerena hugged Hope with one arm. "Relax. Your babies are fine."

Hope gave her a thankful look.

"Melody knows she scared you," Zerena went on. "She scared herself. She won't take off again."

"Promise?"

"Been there, done that. I had Daddy issues, too." Zerena's parents had divorced when she was six. "By the way, Gabe told me how Steve Waldren helped you find Melody, and here I thought he was a selfish, albeit handsome man."

"He's not selfish."

"He's not?"

Hope shook her head. Over the course of the last twenty-four hours, she'd learned exactly how big Steve's heart really was. The way he'd stayed by her side. Supported her. She could still feel his arms around her and his warm, reassuring breath in her ear. And their kiss? Every fiber in her had tingled.

"He and his family came in last night by the way," Zerena said.

"Was Gloria Storm with them?"

"Yep. They looked pretty cozy."

Hope deflated. If Steve had included Gloria on a family outing, that sealed the deal. He was officially off the market. Whatever feelings had sparked between her and him were a thing of the past. "Speaking of cozy, you and Roman look pretty hot-cha-cha lately," she said, changing the subject. "I gather you had fun at the tree lighting."

Zerena's cheeks tinged pink. "Did I tell you he asked me to go on a picnic on our day off?"

"Does he know it's winter?"

Zerena giggled. "He said he'll bring an arctic oven tent."

"Ooh." Hope winked. "Sounds like something might be cooking."

"I think so." Zerena sashayed to her next table of customers.

Hope checked on her children and then followed up on an order at table ten. She offered more coffee and a free refill on the cocoa. The diners were ecstatic about their meals. They gushed about how adorable Hope Valley was. They'd never visited the town before, but having heard something about it while watching KPRL, they'd decided to drop in.

That something, Hope realized, must have been the mention of the family that had won the Disneyland vacation. Who would ultimately receive the prize? she wondered, and then realized she didn't care. Not a whit. Her prize was her family, pure and simple.

Gabe slipped up beside Hope. "It's almost time for you to end your shift. I smell gingerbread in your future."

"I almost forgot. Bless you." She blew him a kiss.

The gingerbread house event was just what the children needed. Something fun yet focused. Hope finalized all sales for her tables, cleared their dishes, and bid her customers and the staff good-bye. Then she gathered the kids and headed to the Christmas Attic.

An instrumental version of "Go Tell it on the Mountain" was playing as they entered, and the place was packed with people. In the center of the shop, there were two long tables covered with poinsettia tablecloths and topped with all the fixings to make gingerbread houses—precut sides of houses, roofs, chimneys and doors, as well as a wide variety of candies, candy canes, powdered sugar, piping tools, and the most important thing, royal icing, the mortar that would hold all the pieces in place. Smaller tables had been positioned at the outer perimeters of the store so if a group wanted to work in a less-crowded environment, they could pick up their tools and move away.

Ellery spotted Hope as she entered and rushed to her. "I'm so glad you made it." She petted Melody's and Todd's heads. "Hello, children. Are you ready to have a good time?"

They nodded.

Ellery put her hands on her thighs so she could meet them at eye level. "By the way, Melody, a little birdie told me you might want sugar-free candies in case you have the urge to splurge. Here you go." She pulled a sandwich-style bag from the pocket of her apron. "The sugar-free spice drops are my favorite. And that gingerbread house setup"—she pointed to an array of sides, roofs, and doors as well as a bowl of icing—"has a flag with your name on it because it's all sugar-free, too."

"Wow!" Melody's face lit up. "Thank you so much."

"Have fun today. May the best house win!"

Hope told the children to pick a spot but to stay where she could see them. She'd join them in a bit. They trotted away as if nothing untoward had happened the day before. Hope said, "Thank you, Ellery. That was so kind of you."

"It's the least I could do."

"Um, where's Steve?" Hope scanned the attendees.

"I've been wondering the same thing. He and Lincoln should have been here by now." Ellery pulled her cell phone from her pocket. "Aha. He sent me a text message. He has something very important to do. He'll be . . . Oh my." Her eyelids fluttered. "He'll be skipping the event."

Hope put a hand on Ellery's arm. "Are you okay?"

Ellery lifted her chin. "Of course. Right as rain. I'm sure there's a good explanation. It's just that this is one of Lincoln's favorite things to do. Steve was supposed to bring him."

"I could fetch him."

"No. That's not necessary. Steve says Lincoln is with him."

And Gloria, Hope imagined. What were they doing that warranted blowing off his mother's special event?

Something flickered in Ellery's eyes. Regret? Peeve? She forced a smile and adjusted the strap of her apron.

Hope said, "Maybe he'll surprise you and suddenly appear." She prayed he would.

Chapter 45

Steve followed his brother up the path to the one-story rustic building that housed KQHV and smiled as a memory flickered in his mind. For years, Lincoln had thought the Q in the station's letters had stood for Mr. Q until Steve had dissuaded him of the notion.

"I like the snowman," Lincoln said, noticing the one adornment in front of the building, a huge Frosty replica with blinking lights. A simple green wreath with bells hung on the door. It jingled as they entered.

A twenty-something office assistant with thick, straight hair was bent over the reception desk, slicing open envelopes with a letter opener. "Just a sec and I'll help you." After a moment, she raised her chin, brushed floppy bangs from her face, and smiled more broadly. "Oh, Lincoln, hi." Her warmth was real.

"Hi, Cici."

Steve noticed his brother seemed to be holding some kind of excitement in check. Was the assistant the real reason Lincoln liked visiting the station? Of course she was. He may be challenged, but he was still a guy.

Steve said, "Is Mr. Q available?"

"He's doing the news," Cici said. "Give him a few minutes. Have a seat."

"Can I . . . Can I help you open those, Cici?" Lincoln sputtered.

Yeah, he likes her. Steve stifled a chuckle. *Good for him.*

"Sure. Grab a letter opener." She pointed to a pencil container on her desk. "Christmas mail has been piling in. Mr. Q likes to read every single one." She flashed him a Mickey Mouse in Santa garb card. "Isn't this cute?"

"Uh-huh."

Ten minutes later, Mr. Q emerged from the sound booth. "Hey, Cici, any—" He gawped at Steve and Lincoln. "Well, greetings, boys. Merry Christmas Eve."

Mr. Q hadn't changed in all the years Steve had known him. He was a robust Indian man with a round face and the serenity of Gandhi. Even as a science teacher, he'd preferred Nehru-style shirts or jackets and black trousers. Never jeans. Never a lab coat. The man had a head for statistics and knew every chemical equation without having to look it up. Mr. Q attributed his expertise to a photographic memory. According to Steve's mother, the reason he'd bought the radio station was that after his wife passed, he'd become disheartened and withdrawn. Being around a classroom of students rattled him. However, he'd still wanted to impart information. The solace he found doing so at KQHV had been his saving grace.

"Shouldn't you fellas be at the Christmas Attic?" Mr. Q asked.

"Yes, we should, Mr. Q. We really should. We really, really should." Lincoln was vibrating with pent up energy. "But we're here. For a reason. A very good reason."

Mr. Q put a hand on Lincoln's shoulder. "Steady as she goes, Linc. Deep breaths. And full sentences. Remember how I've taught you?"

"Uh-huh." Lincoln drew in a yoga-style breath and let it out slowly.

"Okay, speak."

"Mr. Q, my brother has something he wants to ask you."

"Steve Waldren. It's been years, young man." Mr. Q's eyes narrowed as he sized up Steve. "Haven't seen you on TV this past week. Why is that?"

"I've been here," Steve said, not willing to say he'd been axed. "Helping out."

"So you're a helper now?" Mr. Q looked skeptical. "That's not your typical MO."

Steve winced. Exactly what kind of reputation had he earned during his teen years? He'd been ambitious, sure. Was that a crime? Big deal if he'd wanted a career away from Hope Valley. His parents had never guilted him about his choice. Even Lincoln had taken pride in the fact that his big brother had become a celebrity.

"I've changed," Steve said.

"Have you?" Mr. Q tapped his chin. "If I recall in your junior year—"

"I know, sir," Steve cut in. "I know." He and his buddies had an away game and, thanks to Steve's goading, stayed out of town rather than come back to Hope Valley to help the rest of the team with the drive Mr. Q had organized to collect canned goods. "I was pretty full of myself back then."

"I'm not full," Lincoln said. "I haven't eaten since breakfast."

Mr. Q offered Lincoln a wry look.

"Sir," Steve said, "I'd like to put together a human-interest story."

"Listen to this, Mr. Q," Lincoln said. "Listen, listen."

Steve had told his brother the idea in the car.

"Breathe, Lincoln," Mr. Q said. "Continue, Steve."

For the next few minutes, Steve outlined his plan. The photos. The interviews. How he planned to talk Ray Capellini, Bobby's father, into helping out. The angle being that the disenfranchised in Hope Valley needed to be seen, acknowledged, and appreciated in a big way.

Steve spread his hands at the end. "Of course, I think it would be best on TV because, well, it's easier to respond to visual stimuli, but Lincoln thought—"

"Stop, Steve." Mr. Q narrowed his gaze. "Don't kid a kidder. The TV stations turned you down, didn't they?"

Steve really disliked how intuitive his former teacher was. He squared his shoulders. "Yes, sir."

"Give him a chance," Lincoln said. "Please."

Mr. Q patted Lincoln on the shoulder. "Lincoln, you are one of my most devoted listeners, and I would do anything for you, but your brother is right. What he is proposing isn't for radio." He turned to Steve. "Why don't you do a live chat on the Internet? You have fans. They'll get the word out. I think that's your best bet. Sorry I can't help. And now"—he smoothed the front of his Nehru jacket—"I must get back on the air. Have a Merry Christmas, boys."

STEVE REFUSED TO BE deterred. He dragged Lincoln to the car and, without leaving the parking lot, called Brie. "Look, I know you're almost retired, but I need you to do me a favor. A photo spread. I'm paying." He explained the plan.

Brie sniffed. "Hope isn't going to like this. She doesn't want her story told."

"But this isn't her story. Not exactly."

"Gray area, Steve."

"Please, Brie. Get photos. Meet me at my parents' house in two hours. I'll explain more then."

Meanwhile, Steve went to Capellini Associates, a real estate firm in the center of town known for building extraordinary houses as well as state-of-the-art apartments and office buildings, in Hope Valley and beyond. Ray Capellini rarely took a day off. He lived and breathed real estate, one of the reasons neither of his boys had followed in his footsteps. Steve had warned Lincoln not to say a word when they entered the chic offices. Lincoln had nodded his assent and had mimed locking his lips.

"Mr. Capellini." Steve extended his hand as he was escorted by the man's executive assistant into his office. "Thank you for seeing us."

Ray was sitting at his large oak desk. He nodded to his assistant, who exited, closing the door behind her.

"Call me Ray, Steve. What an unexpected surprise." He was as handsome as his boys, but his eyes lacked mirth. "What's the reason for your visit?" He rested his arms on the edges and tented his fingers. "Thinking of moving back? Ready to invest in a beautiful home?" He gestured to the wall to his right, which was filled with framed pictures of available houses.

"Actually, sir, my request is for others. I think your wife will be on board with this idea."

Mentioning his wife seemed to soften Ray. She was light to his dark and loved donating to good causes.

"Sit. Proceed."

Steve settled into one of the office chairs, and Lincoln took the other, working hard to steady his restless legs. Quickly, Steve laid out his plan. Ray Capellini nodded throughout.

When Steve finished, Ray said, "Yes, you're right. The wife is going to love this. Tis the season, boys. Count us in."

Chapter 46

Steve swung the SUV into his parents' driveway and stopped short of running over Brie, who was arriving on foot. In her hand was an envelope. Steve clambered out of the car. So did Lincoln.

"Mission accomplished." Brie pulled a number of processed photos from the envelope. "Now what?"

"Steve is brilliant," Lincoln said to Brie. "Brilliant."

"Don't go overboard, bro."

Brie whispered, "Steve, I still say Hope—"

"Hush. Don't jinx this. I haven't told you everything."

Steve led Brie and Lincoln into his father's office and scanned the photos into the desktop computer. Working on the project with the same diligence he'd given in college to every project that would lead to the career he'd craved, he created a flyer by collaging the photo images and adding the call to action words in the center to draw focus. He used bold green-and-red borders to drive home the Christmas theme.

As the art came together, Lincoln chanted, "Steve, Steve, Steve."

"Okay, that's enough adulation," Steve said. "Give me a minute. I'll be right back. Lincoln, get Brie some milk and cookies."

"Sure thing. You 'da man!"

Steve retreated to his bedroom, removed the Santa costume from his suitcase, and slipped into it while humming "Jolly Old St. Nick." He shoved his feet into the big black boots, unable to remember feeling more in tune with himself.

Brie's eyes widened when he trotted down the stairs. "No, Steve. Don't. Listen to me, Santa . . . it's a bad idea. Bad. Idea."

"You don't know what I've got in store."

"I'm not blind. You want to get Hope to accept the Disneyland trip again. Don't. If Dave finds out—"

"Wrong." Steve made a game-show buzzing sound. "I'm not going to beg her to take the prize. That ship has sailed. And if you'll recall, Dave is no longer my boss, so I don't give a flying—" he glanced at his brother—"*truck* what Dave thinks."

"Ouch," Lincoln said. "A flying truck. That could hurt."

"Then what is your plan?" Brie folded her arms and lasered him with a look, waiting.

"You'll see. Hop in the car," Steve said.

"Shotgun," Lincoln called.

"I can't go with you." Brie shook her head. "I offered to help Gabe out at the café. He was slammed when I left."

"Okay, well, before you leave . . ." Quickly, Steve outlined how the rest of his plan would unfold.

When he finished, Brie released a sigh of relief and finally smiled. "Wow. I love it. Your brother was right. It's brilliant."

"Told you." Lincoln radiated confidence.

Steve drove to KQHV humming. Literally humming. "Ho, ho, ho, Merry Christmas," he crooned as he entered the building.

Cici was still opening envelopes. Many of the cards that she'd removed earlier were now push-pinned to a corkboard. Mr. Q was one popular guy, Steve noted, realizing he'd never received that much correspondence and certainly no cards that required postage.

Mr. Q emerged from the sound booth. He must have seen Santa enter. "What's going on?"

"Ho, ho, ho, Mr. Q!" Steve bellowed.

Like a little kid, Lincoln popped from behind Steve and jutted his hands in Steve's direction. "It's my brother Steve."

Mr. Q stifled a grin. "I didn't have a clue." He regarded Steve somberly. "Care to tell me what's going on, young man?"

Steve produced a packet of flyers and thrust one at Mr. Q. "We need to secure a team of students to post these all over town."

Mr. Q read the flyer and clicked his tongue. "Not bad. Not bad. So, that's where I come in? Getting students on board?"

"They listen to you," Lincoln said.

"Plus . . ." Steve hesitated.

Mr. Q rotated a hand for him to continue.

"Plus I'd like to chat up the plan on the radio. This is a local call to action. I'd like to urge Hope Valley's fifteen thousand residents to show their true Christmas spirit and give, give, give."

Mr. Q clapped Steve on the shoulder and said, "My boy, I didn't know you had it in you. Your parents should be proud." He eyed Lincoln, "And you, young man, are a great Santa's helper." He drew Lincoln into a bear hug.

To Steve's amazement, Lincoln hugged back. The way his brother was beaming sent chills through Steve. Good chills. He'd never seen him so happy. Obviously, Mr. Q's praise was akin to magic.

In the studio, Mr. Q relayed a message to the teens of Hope Valley to come to the station and help with a worthy cause by posting flyers. Streets had been cleared of snow, he said. They had a window of opportunity before the next snowfall. Within a half hour, the Hope Valley High School cycling team plus a number of recreational cyclists were lined up and ready to help out. When they all departed, Steve's admiration for Mr. Q grew tenfold as well as his realization that radio wasn't dead after all.

Next, Mr. Q situated Steve at the microphone and said, "Ever done this before?"

"Not since high school, sir," Steve replied. Back when he'd thought radio was dorky, he'd been the voice of Hope Valley High. He recited morning news. Led the pledge of allegiance. Dumb stuff.

"A few tips," Mr. Q said. "Don't yell. Don't get too close or too far away. Speak slowly and distinctly. There's a knack." He tapped the script Steve had placed on the desk. "When you're ready, go for it. And smile."

"I'm off camera."

"Believe me, young man, a smile transmits through the airwaves."

Chapter 47

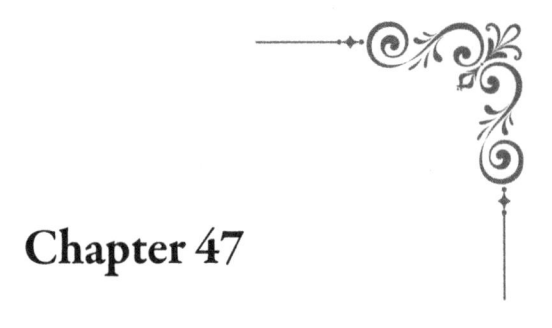

Hope stood near the front door of the Christmas Attic holding her children's darling—okay, overly-decorated—gingerbread house. They hadn't won the contest. Nathan and his sister had, which had irked Todd no end, but Hope suggested he congratulate his friend. "One day, you two won't be enemies. Do your best to forgive and forget," she said, thinking of Steve and how she wished he'd shown up to the event so she could have at least said good-bye to him before he left Hope Valley. And if she was honest, so she could've given him a piece of her mind about disappointing his brother and mother. A tear leaked down her cheek. She swiped it away.

"But, Mom, Nathan's wasn't that good," Todd said.

"It wasn't that bad, either," she kidded. "You got a little . . ." She twirled a finger.

"Heavy handed with the royal icing?"

"Heavy handed is an understatement."

Todd guffawed.

Melody hadn't restrained herself in the candy department, either. Hope had never seen so many candy canes on one house.

Ellery sauntered to Hope and held the gingerbread house until Hope had donned her parka. "I'm so glad you came. Did you have fun?"

"You bet." Hope kissed Ellery's cheek. "Thank you for everything, and . . ." She hesitated, battling the emotions swirling inside her as she compared the two versions of Steve. One, giving of himself to help her find Melody, versus the other, who hadn't had the grace to put in an appearance at his mother's big event. "Have you heard from either of your sons?"

"No." A worried expression crossed her face.

Hope hadn't considered that something might have happened to them. Had they been in a car accident? Had Lincoln had a meltdown? Or had Gloria convinced Steve to return to Portland and he'd dumped his brother at home?

Ellery fanned the air. "I'm sure they're fine, dear. Just preoccupied. Steve will be sorry he missed you before heading back to Portland," she said, as if reading Hope's mind.

"Please tell him good-bye for me."

"THAT'S RIGHT, HOPE Valley," Steve said in his best announcer's voice. He was sitting in the KQHV sound booth, noise-canceling headphones over his ears, elbows propped on the desk, the microphone inches from his mouth. "Project Christmas Hope Valley is real. Capellini Associates has promised to build a co-op that will house sixty of our disenfranchised families. What's that? You didn't know we had struggling families? Yeah, I've been blind, too, friends. I needed a special someone to open my eyes and make me realize that in order to be the best community in America, everyone in Hope Valley needs to pitch in and help. We are a family."

Through the sound booth window, he saw Lincoln shaking something. He gestured and mouthed: *In, in, in.*

Steve motioned for Lincoln to enter, but he held a finger to his lips as he continued his spiel. "Folks, we all need to pitch in to make this town the best place on earth. Are you with me?" He held a hand to his ear. "I can't hear you."

Lincoln rushed to Steve. "Look, look, look."

Steve covered the microphone. *"Shh."*

"Look what Mr. Q gave me." Lincoln showed him a teeny silver bell. He rang it. Repeatedly.

"Linc, I'm on the air. You—"

"I'm Clarence in *It's a Wonderful Life*," Lincoln continued undeterred. "Every time I ring a bell, an angel gets its wings, and we need more angels, right? They help humans. Mom said so."

Steve felt a lump catch in his throat. Angels. Of course. That's what this project needed. Lots of angels. He held out his hand. "Got another one, bro?"

Lincoln did. A gold one. He plopped it into Steve's hand.

Steve rang it three times. "Ho, ho, ho, Hope Valley. Me, again. Steve Waldren. Where was I? Oh, right. Project Christmas Hope Valley. Why are we doing this on Christmas Eve? Because it's a magical night." He shook the bell again. "Do you hear that sound? Everyone knows that whenever a bell rings, an angel gets its wings, right?"

Lincoln pumped his fist. "Yeah!"

"So come on, Hope Valley, are you going to be one of those angels and chip in for Project Christmas Hope Valley? We need angels."

Within an hour, there were over a thousand pledges to help fund the co-op. Within two hours, that number had tripled. Mr. Q and Cici were manning the phones. A couple of the teenagers who had posted flyers were standing inside the door accepting cash donations. Cars filled with donors were lined up around the block.

Steve looked on, emotions swirling through him. Never in his life had he felt this kind of satisfaction. He glanced at Lincoln, who was grinning at him. "Bro, we're doing it," he said.

"Yeah, we are." Lincoln threw his arms around Steve and crushed him with a hug.

Steve could barely breathe. "Hey, whoa. Need air." He broke free. "You nearly choked me."

Lincoln laughed. "Because I love you."

Steve stopped in his tracks. Lincoln had never said those words. "Did you say you love me?"

"Yep."

"Up high!" Steve raised his hand. "Give me some skin. I love you, too."

They slapped hands and a feeling of sheer joy coursed through Steve.

Chapter 48

After dinner Tuesday night, Hope accompanied the children to the facilities at the trailer park. They brushed their teeth and washed their faces, and then she took a comb to their hair to remove remnants of royal icing. When they returned to the camper, she said, "Do you want a Christmas Eve present?"

Their eyes lit up.

She handed each of them their rummage sale gifts. She'd wrapped them in wrapping paper purchased at the dollar store and had taken extra care to craft a pretty tag. "For you, Melody, and for you, Todd."

"You go first," Melody said to her brother.

Todd ripped open his package and found a binder filled with baseball trading cards. Hope knew that none were valuable, but Todd wouldn't care. He would memorize every statistic and rearrange them for months. "I love it!" he cried, and hugged his mother. Then he looked expectantly at Melody. "Your turn."

Slowly, carefully, she pulled the tape off the corners of her gift, the same way Hope's mother had. She hated tearing into a present.

"Hurry," Todd cried.

"No. I want to take my time." When she finally got the package unwrapped, she gasped. "Oh, Mommy, she's perfect."

Hope hadn't believed her luck when she'd found the blond, basketball-playing bobblehead with the red-and-white jersey.

Melody tapped the doll's head and giggled as it wobbled to and fro. "She looks like me."

"Yes, she does. I thought she could inspire you to greatness."

"Like that'll happen," Melody sassed.

"You never know."

Melody hugged Hope with the same fierceness she'd displayed at the bus station, further reassuring Hope that her daughter wouldn't be running away again any time soon.

"Okay, time for bed." She tucked them into their sleep sacks.

"Mom," Melody whispered. "Someday will you tell us the truth about Daddy and show us pictures?"

A pang shot through Hope. She swallowed hard. It had been selfish of her to keep him from them. Her bitterness didn't need to seep into their memories. "Yes, sweetheart. How about on New Year's Day?"

"Do you mean it?"

Hope nodded. It would also be her new year's resolution to track him down, somehow, some way.

"Can we listen to the radio tonight?" Melody asked.

"No, it's too late. It's been a very long day. Besides—"

"Santa won't come if we're awake," Todd said.

Melody gave her mother a sidelong look.

Hope waved her off. "That's right, sweet boy." She kissed them both and said, "Sleep tight and dream with the angels."

AT SIX A.M. WEDNESDAY, Hope awoke with a start. Quietly, she slipped out of her sleeping bag and inserted a ten-dollar bill into each of her children's stockings. Then she dressed in a red sweater and corduroys, hurried to the facilities to do her ablutions, and returned to wait and watch as her children awoke.

Todd was first. His eyes opened wide with wonder when he saw money poking from his stocking. "Wow! How did Santa know I needed this?" He flapped the bill in the air. "I knew he wouldn't be able to bring me what I wanted because he didn't make it. It's at the Toy Palace. Can we go there? Please, Mom?"

"In the next few days."

Todd hooted. "Melody, what did you get?"

Hope elbowed her daughter.

"The same thing!" Melody said with exaggerated animation. "That Santa is so smart."

Hope blew her daughter a kiss and mouthed: *I love you.*

Melody returned the sentiment.

Hope clapped. "Okay, open up your presents."

"Wait!" Todd reached into his backpack and pulled out a handmade envelope. "For you, Mom."

Hope opened it and withdrew a small booklet held together with staples. On the cover were three stick figures holding hands. They were flanked by a boxy VW camper and the Hope Valley Christmas tree.

"Read it," Todd said. "It's our story. I drew the pictures. Melody wrote the words."

Her heart swelled with joy as she read the book from front to cover. Melody's beautiful cursive writing told the story of a mother who showered her children with love and boosted their confidence, which meant they were the luckiest children on earth.

"I love you both so much," she gushed, and gathered them in her arms. "Best Christmas present ever."

After the children opened their other gifts—Melody loved her book and Todd was super excited about his graphic novel—Hope announced it was time to make breakfast.

"Can we listen to Christmas music?" Melody asked.

"Sure." Hope turned on the radio, certain one of the stations would be airing nonstop tunes throughout the morning.

As it turned out, KQHV was doing just that. "The Happiest Season of All" was in the queue.

Using the microwave, Hope put together three bowls of oatmeal with sliced bananas and a dash of sugar-free brown sugar, then she propped up the dining table with its single leg, and said, "Sit."

They all tucked into breakfast.

When the song ended, and Mr. Q said, "Hey, Hope Valley-ites, if you're just tuning in, then you're late. Where have you been all night?" He clucked his tongue. "You've missed all the excitement. We have raised hundreds of thousands of dollars for Project Christmas Hope Valley. Take it away, Santa." Mr. Q made a funny whooshing sound followed by the tinkling of bells.

"Ho, ho, ho. Merry Christmas, Hope Valley," a familiar voice said.

"That's Steve!" Todd pointed at the dashboard. "Mom, that's him."

"As I've been saying for the past twenty-four hours, Project Christmas Hope Valley," Steve continued, "is all about our residents stepping up and helping our disenfranchised neighbors. Don't we have enough for everyone? Isn't it time we shared? C'mon, you must have seen the posters around town. Donate. With your help, Capellini Associates will build, at cost..."

As Steve continued his pitch, it dawned on Hope that his charitable project must have been the reason why he'd missed the gingerbread house event. He hadn't been selfishly pursuing his own happiness; he'd been helping Hope Valley. She felt a tug on her heartstrings and tears pooled in her eyes as she realized that this was exactly who she'd dreamed he would be. How she wished she could start over with him, but she knew that was an impossibility. He wouldn't be able to make room in his life for her, not even as a friend now that Gloria was back in the picture, and her chest heaved with an ache she couldn't shake.

Melody said, "Steve is really nice, isn't he?"

Hope nodded. "Yes." Her throat clogged with emotion. "Yes, he is."

Someone knocked on the camper's door.

Hope juddered. Was a trailer park resident going to complain that she was playing the radio too loudly? Sighing, she said, "Stay seated," and moved to the door.

"Hope!" a man called.

Hope paused as she grasped the door handle. It wasn't a resident. It was Gabe. Until Saturday, he'd had no idea how she and the children lived. She prayed he hadn't come to take pity on them.

Shimmying away embarrassment, she finger-combed her hair and opened the door. "Merry Christmas," she said with forced cheeriness.

Gabe, bundled in his black overcoat and wool cap, stood with his arm around Brie, who was wearing the winter jumpsuit Hope had seen the owner of Cathy's Closet tweaking in the window. Zerena was with them, looking blissful in a red parka over white jeans, candy-cane striped scarf tied artfully around her neck, and red gloves. Hope regarded Brie for a second time and, realizing she wasn't aiming a camera at her, breathed easier.

"Merry Christmas," the trio sang.

"What brings you to my neck of the woods?" Hope asked. "It's not the typical spot for caroling."

"Mom, who is it?" Melody called.

"Gabe, Brie, and Zerena." She eyed her boss. "I'd invite you in, but it could get a bit crowded."

Gabe grinned, clearly doing his best not to feel sorry for Hope. "No worries. This isn't a social visit. It's business. I've decided to retire."

"I heard a rumor."

"This time I mean it."

Hope's insides wrenched. Had he stopped by to say he was going to sell the place? On Christmas? Did he lack all sensitivity as to how she'd take the news? She glanced worriedly at Zerena and back at Gabe.

After a long moment, she accepted her fate. "Why tell me today?"

"Because, darling Hope"—he gave Brie a quick squeeze—"my beloved and I want to travel the US of A while we have time so . . ." He let the word hang in the air.

Brie prodded him.

"So I was wondering if you would like to manage the café with Zerena?"

Zerena let out an *eek* of excitement. "Say yes! Say yes!"

"Wh-what?" Hope sputtered.

"You two manage it, and along the way, maybe we could work out a plan where you two buy me out."

"Please say yes, Hope." Zerena aimed a finger at Hope and back at herself. "You. Me. Partners. I'll be great at promotion and balancing books and bossing people around. You'll manage the kitchen and baking, and, well, what could be better?"

Hope's mouth fell open. "But, Gabe, what about your daughter?"

Gabe snorted. "She's never moving back to Hope Valley, and she's set for money with that fancy career of hers. Being mayor of Hope Valley established her course in politics years ago. Who knows? Maybe she'll run for president."

Hope bit back a laugh, recalling how Steve had asked her if she'd wanted to become president, and she'd said not on a bet.

"So . . . will you?" Gabe flourished a hand. "There will be an insurance package and four-oh-one-K included for all employees. Did I mention that?"

"Please say yes. Please, please." Zerena pressed her hands together in prayer. "Just think. You can bake all the pies you want!"

"Yes!" Hope cried. "Yes, of course." She leaped from the camper and threw her arms around Gabe. And then Zerena. And before she knew it, it became a group hug with Brie getting in on the action.

Chapter 49

Steve followed Lincoln into their house, exhausted from pulling an all-nighter but feeling more alive than he had felt in years, as if, for once in his life, he'd done something good for all the right reasons.

"Mom!" Lincoln called.

"In the kitchen, dear."

Lincoln raced ahead.

The aroma of fresh coffee made Steve's mouth water. The coffee at the station had turned putrid around one a.m. He walked through the arch and halted.

Lincoln was hugging their mother full bore. Sheer joy was flooding her face. Was it a Christmas miracle? Or was Lincoln actually getting comfortable in his own skin? Comfortable enough to say the words *I love you* to his brother and to demonstrate this kind of love for his mother?

Amen, Steve thought.

"Merry Christmas, boys. We heard you on the radio," Frank said, pokerfaced to the displays of emotion. He unbuttoned the buttons of his cardigan before perching on a stool. "Wish you'd looped us in."

"It was spur-of-the-moment." Steve sauntered into the room while removing the Santa beard.

"Spur-of-the-moment," Lincoln said, breaking free. "On impulse. Spontaneous." He drummed the counter with his fingertips. "We rang bells."

"We heard," Ellery said, adjusting the front of her robe and pulling the belt tighter.

"Bells bring angels," Lincoln went on. "Right, Steve?"

"Right-o."

"They do, indeed." Ellery patted Lincoln's cheek. "Do you want some cocoa?"

"Yes!" He bounced on his toes. "Cocoa. With marshmallows. Lots of—"

"Sit," Ellery ordered. "Can't have you sloshing chocolate all over the place."

Lincoln obeyed but his toes continued to tap the floor.

"How much did you raise?" Frank asked Steve.

"As of six a.m., five hundred thousand."

Frank whistled. "I knew we had deep pockets in Hope Valley, but that's a miracle."

"Too bad you won't be able to oversee the project, Steve," Ellery said, filling a snowman mug of cocoa. "Want some?" She held up the matching pitcher.

"Coffee, please." Steve tilted head. "What do you mean I won't be able to oversee it?"

"Your agent called the landline when you weren't returning his calls."

Steve checked his cell phone. Five missed messages.

"He got you a job in Chicago," his mother said.

"Chicago!" Steve whooped, and then drew up short. Wait. Hold on. Was this some new ploy Gloria had figured out on her flight back to Minneapolis? Did she think scoring him a job in a big-ticket market like Chicago would win him back? If it was, she had another *think* coming.

Lincoln frowned. His feet stopped tapping. "Chicago is far away."

"Yes, it is." Ellery glanced at Steve's father.

"Why?" Lincoln whined.

"Why what, buddy?" Steve placed a reassuring hand on his shoulder.

"Why do you need to take a job so far away? Why can't you stay here? Hope is here."

Hope. Steve heaved a sigh and settled on the stool next to his brother. "Linc, we've been through this. I'm a sports announcer. I need to go where the jobs are. There's no job for me here."

"Yes, there is." Lincoln put his mug down and bounded off his perch. "Mom. Dad. I have an idea. A good one. A really good one. It's really, really good."

Ellery put her hands on his shoulders. "Calm down, Son. Tell us your idea."

"You and Dad should buy KQHV."

Frank's mouth fell open. "Buy the radio station?"

"You said you wanted another business, Dad."

"I never said that." Frank exchanged a look with Ellery.

"Yes you did. You said you should buy all the businesses in town." Lincoln flailed his arms. "I heard you. You said, 'Ellery, if I bought all the shops in this town'"—he brandished a finger the way his father would—"'Hope Valley would run like clockwork.'"

Ellery snickered. "You have said that, Frank."

"I was joking, Son." Frank smirked.

"You have two businesses. Why not three?" Lincoln jutted a hand at him.

"Because there's only your mother and me. Two adults. Two businesses."

"If you buy the radio station, Steve can run it for you."

Steve had sensed where this was heading and swallowed hard.

"He's the Voice. He can do whatever programs he wants. He can do sports statistics and sports history, and every Christmas he could run Project Christmas Hope Valley, just like he and I did last night and this morning, and . . . and . . ." Lincoln whirled around and faced Steve. "You could stay here with me and Mom and Dad and, and, and . . ." He took a deep breath. "And Hope."

Steve straightened. The possibility of seeing more of Hope sent a thrill through him, and to be honest, the notion of staying in town with his family and touching people personally, as Mr. Q had all these years, was growing on him. Maybe that was what he'd been missing at KPRL. The human connection. Was it time for him to abandon the idea of a big—bigger than big—career and come home to roost? His cell phone rang. He answered.

"Steve, it's Ray Capellini. I can't believe it, boy. You did it. You really did it. I know it's Christmas day, but if you have time, stop by the office. I have a business opportunity I think you might like."

Chapter 50

Snow fell throughout the early morning hours, but Hope didn't mind. Each snowflake felt like a tiny miracle. Every few minutes, she'd wanted to pinch herself to make sure Gabe's offer was real. Around eleven, she talked the children into taking a walk into the forest beyond the trailer park. She needed to drink in the fresh air and sing at the top of her lungs.

Holding each of their hands, she encouraged them to sing "Joy to the World" with her. They did. Moments later, she heard others in the forest join in, and her heart filled with delight.

At noon, she hustled the children into the camper, asked them to change into their Christmas best. Melody's year-old dress was a tad snug, but she didn't complain. Cheerfully, she slipped on her wool stockings, tucked her feet into boots, and clicked her heels to signify to her mother that she was ready to go.

Todd struggled with his hair. "Mom, it's sticking out everywhere."

Since when did he care? Hope wondered.

Melody whispered, "I think he has a crush on someone."

"Really? Who?"

"Addie's granddaughter Polly."

"*Hmm*," Hope said. "And here I thought he had a crush on Khloe." She helped Todd manage his unruly hair, kissed his cheeks, and said, "Let's get a move on. We don't want to keep everyone waiting."

HOPE FOR THE HOLIDAYS

STEVE PULLED INTO HOPE Valley Trailer Park and followed the road to Hope's site, but the camper wasn't there. "Drat," he muttered.

"Don't swear." Lincoln was pulsating with so much excitement in the passenger seat, the bells on his sweater were tinkling.

"Drat isn't swearing."

"Mom won't let me say it."

"I'm not you."

A white-haired woman in a blue warmup suit tapped on the driver's window with her cane. Steve rolled down the window.

"Looking for the Lyons family?" she asked.

Steve nodded and opened the door. Lincoln reached to open his. Steve said, "Stay in the car."

Lincoln saluted.

Steve switched off the car and stepped out of the Lexus. When he straightened, he was a good head taller than the woman. "Merry Christmas, ma'am."

She tilted her head back, assessing him. "I know you."

"I don't believe we've met."

She waggled her cane. "Yes, indeed, I'd know that voice anywhere. You're Steve Waldren. I'm Grace Holmes. My late husband listened to you every night, rest his soul. He couldn't get through dinner without hearing everything there was to know about sports. When he wasn't listening to you, he was over at Good Sports talking to your dad about you." The woman cocked her head. "I think he had a bit of a crush on you."

"I'm sure he only had eyes for you, Grace," he said.

Her eyes twinkled. "Oho. You have a silver tongue, young man."

"His tongue isn't silver," Lincoln said through the opened window.

Steve smiled. "Grace, do you happen to know where the Lyons might be?"

"Heavens yes. It's Christmas. Everyone from the trailer park plus all the others are at the Unitarian Church for Christmas dinner."

"The others?"

"You'll see."

Steve cocked his head. "Why aren't you there?"

"Being social isn't my forte."

"You seem pretty social to me," Steve teased.

"One on one, I'm fine, but in a crowd, without my sweet Henry, I falter. Hope promised to bring me back a slice of pie." She aimed her cane at Steve. "Go on, now. Go to church."

"I shouldn't intrude."

"It's a party. A celebration. Everyone is welcome. Go. I know you want to. I can see the gleam in your eyes." Grace twirled a finger. "Don't talk yourself out of it. You'll regret it if you do." She tapped Steve's arm. "If you're feeling a bit shy, go incognito. That's what Henry did when he asked me out on our first date." She placed a hand over her heart. "He wore a porkpie hat and a mustache, and he pretended to be from Italy and sang 'O Sole Mio.' What a card he was."

"I'll bet."

"Go on now." She shooed him away.

Steve tipped his head in thanks and flung open the car door. He slipped into the driver's seat and ground the Lexus into reverse, but he pressed on the brake as an idea formed. He yelled out the window. "Grace, how many children will be there?" he shouted.

"Forty. Maybe fifty."

Steve cranked the car into forward.

"Where are we going?" Lincoln asked.

"The Christmas Attic and then Good Sports."

"For lures?"

"Not for lures."

HOPE STOOD JUST INSIDE the church's gathering room and said, "Melody and Todd, do exactly as Addie asks tonight. If she says set the table, you set the table."

"Yes, Mom," they said in unison.

"But for now, go play. I see Polly and the other kids making paper chains to string on the Christmas tree. Join them."

Melody grabbed Todd's hand and led him to the art table.

At the piano, a white-haired woman was playing "It Came Upon a Midnight Clear." A few aging attendees were crooning along. One was horribly off key. No one seemed to mind.

"Hi, Mom!" Todd waved to her from where he stood next to Polly.

Hope waved back, her mind buzzing with excitement about Gabe's offer. Insurance? A 401K? Would he let Zerena and her make a few subtle changes to the menu and to the display case? Aroma Café didn't lack for clientele, but the café could do an even better business with a tasty takeout menu and, of course, more to-go desserts.

Addie sidled up to Hope. "I'm so glad Melody is safe."

"Me, too."

"She doesn't look the worse for wear."

"Luckily."

"How are you?" Addie asked.

Hope shared the good news.

Addie gave her a supportive hug. "That's wonderful, hon. Just what you've been praying for."

"*Mm-hmm*," Hope murmured. "I'll save a bit more money and, in a year, we'll be able to move into an apartment."

Addie caressed her shoulder. "You make those plans. You deserve the very best."

Hope kissed Addie on the cheek. "Thank you for doing . . . all you do."

"It's my calling."

Hope joined the children and helped make paper chains.

An hour later, when the tree was overloaded with decorations, Addie announced that dinner was about to be served. Eight extra-long tables had been covered with red tablecloths. More than sixty adults and forty children had come to celebrate.

Just as the attendees were bowing their heads to give thanks for the beautiful bounty, the door opened and Santa strutted inside with a big red sack slung over his shoulder.

"Ho, ho, ho!" he bellowed. "Merry Christmas."

Children swiveled in their chairs, eager to get a look. A chorus of *It's Santa* rang out.

Hope leaned toward Addie. "This is new. You've never invited a Santa."

"I didn't this year, either."

"You didn't?"

"Nope."

Hope's heart leaped into her throat when she realized Santa was Steve. The beard couldn't hide his sculpted cheekbones or his gorgeous eyes. Why was he here? His brother was standing just inside the door, batting an envelope he was holding against his leg. Where was Gloria?

Addie started to rise.

Hope put a hand on her friend's shoulder. "Sit. I've got this." She placed her napkin on her chair, smoothed her hair, and strode to Steve. "Hello, Mr. Claus. Looking good. Your mustache is a little loose." She pressed it in place for him. With the nearness, she inhaled his woodsy scent and desire rushed through her. "Where'd you get the red bag?"

"From the décor on my parents' roof."

"Why are you here?" she whispered.

"What does it look like?" He patted his bag. "Bringing toys for all the good girls and boys."

"Why?"

"Because it's Christmas."

"That's so sweet of you."

"I'm also here because you're here," he said.

"Where's your fiancée?" Hope asked, expecting Gloria to materialize in a sexy elf costume.

"Back in Minneapolis. Where she belongs. For good."

"I thought you and she—"

"Were hooking up again? Nope. I didn't re-invite her into my life. And I won't. Her appearance was a surprise." He paused. "An unwanted surprise."

A delicious swizzle of desire ran down Hope's spine. "How did you know I'd be here?"

"Your neighbor Grace clued me in. So Lincoln and I—"

Steve glanced over his shoulder. Hope beckoned Lincoln. He shook his head.

"Is he okay?" she asked.

"He's not comfortable with the unfamiliar," Steve said. "I've got this." He strode to Lincoln, took the envelope, pocketed it, and whispered to him. Whatever he'd said made Lincoln perk up. "Ho, ho, ho, children!" Steve bellowed again, a cheer that filled the meeting room. "My assistant is going to help me hand out toys. Who wants one?"

All the children's hands shot into the air. Over the course of the next few minutes, Steve and Lincoln delivered the gifts—dolls, baseballs, puzzle boxes, trains, and more.

Hope watched in amusement, realizing that in addition to raiding their parents' rooftop, Steve and his brother must have ransacked their parents' stores. She was pretty sure that hadn't been Lincoln's idea. *Steve Waldren*, she thought to herself, *you're surprising me at every turn.*

When Steve and Lincoln completed their task and children were showing off their toys to one another, they approached Hope.

Chapter 51

"Tell her," Steve said to Lincoln.

"You tell her."

"No, you wanted to do it," Steve countered.

"I can't."

"Sure you can." Steve pulled the envelope from his pocket and handed it to Lincoln. "Go on."

Lincoln turned it over and over.

"What do you have?" Hope coaxed, hand extended. "May I see?"

"It's for you." He thrust the envelope at her.

"Is it from you?" she asked.

"No. It's from Ray."

Hope cocked her head, confused. "Ray?"

"Ray Capellini," Lincoln said, exasperated, as if there was only one man named Ray in town. "He's—"

Steve covered his brother's mouth with a gloved hand and said to Hope, "Open it."

She lifted the flap and pulled out what appeared to be a document. Not an official document. It looked more like an award. She read it out loud. "One free unit in Capellini Towers." She glanced at Steve. His eyes were glistening with anticipation. "What is this?"

"Ray Capellini will be building Capellini Towers, a sixty-unit housing project."

"I heard on the radio."

"He's putting it on the fast track, and it'll be completed by June. And you, Hope Lyons, after suffering the humiliation of being chased by reporters, thanks to me, and after enduring the heartache of looking for your missing child, also thanks to me, have been awarded the first unit. All of them will be two bedrooms."

"Steve, I can't afford—"

"*Shh,* there's more." He held up a finger. "For my part in conceiving the project, Ray granted me the opportunity to dole out the first unit, rent free for two years, to whomever I pleased. I chose you for your indomitable spirit and your giving heart. He will be covering the expense for all of the other units for one year, and—"

Hope yelped with joy and threw her arms around Lincoln. He ducked out of her embrace and backed up two steps. "Sorry, Lincoln," she said. "I didn't mean to invade your space, but you did this. You made this happen."

Lincoln shook his head and pointed at Steve. "Not me. Him."

Steve slung an arm around Lincoln. "Both of us, bro. You were the inspiration. Without you, I never would have come up with the idea." He knuckled his brother in the belly. "You, you, you."

Hope laughed, loving their camaraderie.

Lincoln scuffed his shoe. "Can I look at the tree, Steve?"

"Sure." Steve gave him a nudge. "I'm going to talk to Hope outside. Okay?"

"Yep."

"Grab your coat, ma'am." Steve removed his gloves and stuffed them in his pocket. "The sky is clear, but it's cold."

Hope fetched her parka and exited the building first. Dusk had settled in and the crisp air stung her cheeks but she didn't mind. Delight was effervescing inside her, keeping her warmer than she could ever remember. "I don't know what to say," she turned to face Steve. "I can't believe it." She eyed the envelope in her hand. "I . . ."

Steve put a finger to her lips. "My turn." He clasped her arms gently. "Hope, you opened my eyes. Because of you, my belief in humanity and the spirit of Christmas is renewed. Because of you, I have gotten back my self-respect and, even more, my desire for a better life and brighter future. Because of you, I realize that family matters. Not me by myself. Family. As a thank you, I wanted to do something to pay you back and lift you up."

Hope glanced at the envelope and back at Steve.

Softly, he said, "By the way, I'm staying in town."

"Until New Year's?"

"For good. My folks are buying the radio station. I'm going to become the voice of KQHV."

Hope's eyes widened. "You're giving up your sports anchor career?"

"No. I'm giving up TV."

A star shot across the sky. Hope trembled.

Steve stroked her hair and gazed into her eyes. "So I was wondering, um, may I take you to dinner soon?"

"Are you asking me on a date?"

"Yes. I have a few questions I need answered."

"Like what?"

"The secret to your pie crust."

"Why?"

"I told you I'm an occasional baker. My specialties are chocolate chip cookies and snickerdoodles, but I'd love to learn to make a killer pie. Also"—he ran a finger along the line of her jaw—"I want to know why your nose twitches."

Hope covered her nose with her hand. "It does not."

"It does. Like a bunny's. I figure it's because you're sensitive to aromas, the sign of a good cook."

Hope chuckled. "I suppose I am always trying to pick up what might work in a new recipe, and now I'll get the chance."

"What do you mean?"

She told him about Gabe's offer.

"You said yes, right?"

Hope rolled her eyes. "Do I look stupid?"

"No one will ever call you stupid, Hope Lyons, ever." Steve lifted her chin with his index finger. "May I kiss you?"

"Um, the beard, Santa." She wrinkled her nose on purpose. "Who knows where that bad boy has been?"

Steve removed the beard, mustache, and hat, and then he kissed her tenderly and, for the first time in a long time, Hope felt wonderfully and merrily at peace.

Also by Daryl Wood Gerber

Hope for the Holidays

Watch for more at https://darylwoodgerber.com.

About the Author

Agatha Award-winning author Daryl Wood Gerber is best known for her nationally bestselling mysteries, including the *Fairy Garden Mysteries, Cookbook Nook Mysteries,* and *French Bistro Mysteries.* As Avery Aames, she penned the popular *Cheese Shop Mysteries.* In addition, Daryl writes suspense novels and short stories. Fun Tidbit: as an actress, Daryl appeared in "Murder, She Wrote." She loves to cook, fairy garden, and read. She has a frisky Goldendoodle who keeps her in line. And she has been known to jump out of a perfectly good airplane.

Read more at https://darylwoodgerber.com.

Printed in the USA
CPSIA information can be obtained
at www.ICGtesting.com
LVHW041927061024
793066LV00001B/189